HOW TO READ A KILLER'S MIND

TAM BARNETT

Boldwood

First published in Great Britain in 2025 by Boldwood Books Ltd.

Copyright © Tam Barnett, 2025

Cover Design by Head Design Ltd

Cover Images: Shutterstock

The moral right of Tam Barnett to be identified as the author of this work has been asserted in accordance with the Copyright, Designs and Patents Act 1988.

All rights reserved. No part of this book may be reproduced in any form or by any electronic or mechanical means, including information storage and retrieval systems, without written permission from the author, except for the use of brief quotations in a book review. This book is a work of fiction and, except in the case of historical fact, any resemblance to actual persons, living or dead, is purely coincidental.

Every effort has been made to obtain the necessary permissions with reference to copyright material, both illustrative and quoted. We apologise for any omissions in this respect and will be pleased to make the appropriate acknowledgements in any future edition.

A CIP catalogue record for this book is available from the British Library.

Paperback ISBN 978-1-83633-062-2

Large Print ISBN 978-1-83633-063-9

Hardback ISBN 978-1-83633-061-5

Ebook ISBN 978-1-83633-064-6

Kindle ISBN 978-1-83633-065-3

Audio CD ISBN 978-1-83633-056-1

MP3 CD ISBN 978-1-83633-057-8

Digital audio download ISBN 978-1-83633-059-2

This book is printed on certified sustainable paper. Boldwood Books is dedicated to putting sustainability at the heart of our business. For more information please visit https://www.boldwoodbooks.com/about-us/sustainability/

Boldwood Books Ltd, 23 Bowerdean Street, London, SW6 3TN

www.boldwoodbooks.com

For our beautiful daughter, Harlowe

1

Is there anything more crass than popping open a bottle of champagne to celebrate the discovery of five dead bodies?

Such vulgarity fails to trouble our host, however, as he pours three generous flutes of ice-cold Armand de Brignac.

'Ladies,' he says, passing Chi and myself a glass each and raising his own to the chandelier above. 'Here's to making the birdies sing.'

We sit in a mould-scented snug in the Palace of Westminster. The secretary of state for justice – one Barnaby C. Harrington MP – is our toaster-in-chief.

His first sip alone probably costs the taxpayer £70.

I look at Chi and clench my jaw. Not that she notices.

'Thank you so much, Mr Harrington,' she gushes, eyelashes aflutter. 'This last week has been such a vindication of all Emy's work.'

I take a large gulp. The faster we drink, the sooner we leave.

The shabby tan-orange sofa we've been plonked on is set against tall oak-panelled walls. A grand portrait stares down at us; the austere military man in the frame looks like he was painted midway through colonic irrigation.

Harrington stays standing – classic power play – in a dark grey pin-striped suit, complete with bulging waistcoat. 'This is seriously good news for all of us,' he states. 'Just think of the headlines.'

Barnaby Harrington is the kind of man who gets an erection looking in the mirror. He swindled his way into government with the stellar contacts and blind self-assurance that can only be acquired from public schooling. To him, 'international affairs' are simply a pursuit one keeps from one's wife.

'We've leaked the story out this afternoon, naturally,' he drawls. 'Young Chi here made clear you're still not media trained, Dr Rose. No matter, I can do the TV and radio rounds in my sleep. But we do need some kind of appearance. Play you off as a stuttering brainiac, not a hermit.'

'Chi warned me,' I say.

'Good. *The Times*' editor's a golf pal. He's lined up one of their bods. Chi has the details, don't you my dear?' He makes no effort to disguise his thorough inspection of her low-cut blouse.

She nods at him so hard I fear she may get whiplash.

'Splendid!' He roars. 'Goes without saying, you need to *sell* this whole project. "Pioneering", "world-leading"... terms like that are best.' He takes a second to mull over his own unique magnificence. He's the only man I've ever met whose accent alone basically confirms his forefathers traded in slaves.

'I wouldn't mention this little soirée though,' he instructs, wagging a sausage finger. 'Could be misconstrued. Just call it a conclave. Yes, an official conclave.'

'Can't we just say it's a meeting?' I ask, frowning.

'People don't get invited in here for *meetings*,' he scoffs. 'I just thought you'd both get a kick out of supping champers in the corridors of power. One to tell the grandkiddies.'

Chi giggles in agreement.

This isn't even Harrington's office, it's basically a broom closet he's nabbed for ten minutes. I wish it was an office, then he might stand a little further away and I wouldn't have to breathe in his onion breath. His office is at the Ministry of Justice: the place he deemed it suitable to meet us when we were plain old Emy Rose and Chi Aoki – before we became *world-leading pioneers*. I finish my drink and thud it down on the mahogany side table.

'One other thing, Dr Rose. You're a player down now George Petty's off the books.'

'We're still discussing whether it's better to introduce another inmate or stay with the remaining two for—'

'You can't have only two prisoners!' He scoffs harder. 'The treasury won't abide it. The cost is astronomical as it is, even before you take away a third of the attractions.'

'The cost is justified by the fact we got Petty to give up the bodies,' I fire back.

'That's not how it works. But you should be thanking me. I've saved you time picking the fresh meat.'

I give Chi daggers but she returns my look with a nonplussed shrug.

'Oh no, this will be news to Miss Aoki too,' the gammon goblin says, spotting our silent exchange.

I feel something real for the first time since sitting down in this room – dread. 'Don't meddle with this. Please. It's working. The project's working.'

Harrington lets out a little half-laugh and sighs. 'You know what your problem is? You don't understand the true potential of what you've created. You've found a way to make murderers give up their secrets.'

'One murderer,' I correct him. 'Selected under strict conditions and on specific scientific parameters. With two other men still in a very delicate phase of the study.'

'But Petty changes everything,' Harrington states, pouring himself another hearty glass without sharing. 'You said it yourself straight after he confessed, you'd manipulated the environment around him to such an extent that he *wanted* to give it all up. "Clandestine consent", that was your phrase.'

I very much regret the loose-lipped conversation I had with the secretary of state in the jubilant minutes after George Petty revealed where he'd buried that mother, father and their three beautiful children.

'Leave us to select the next inmate, at the very least.' I hate how quickly he's got me begging.

The sweaty oaf plasters his wispy dyed-brown hair back over his sweaty oafish head and takes another sweaty oafish look down Chi's top. 'It's time for something bigger, girls. Tim Shenton is the new man, and as I hold the purse strings, you can either take it or we mothball the whole thing.'

He's frowning as he hulks over me now, a headmaster out of patience with his lippy pupil.

'Tim Shenton,' I repeat.

'The man accused of—'

'I know who he is,' I snap. 'He hasn't even gone to trial.'

'Precisely. That's the new reality of all this. Never mind getting long-forgotten murderers to admit where they hid the bodies of their victims. What if this project starts convincing criminals to admit to *crimes*, gets them to change their plea? We could wipe millions... billions... off the legal aid bill if we start coaxing confessions out of inmates *before* they get to trial. We could have the most efficient court system in the Western world.'

'The whole point of the experiment is that the participants pleaded guilty. It's fundamental to the study that the haves have accepted the crimes they committed. This is about finding answers for families, not short-circuiting justice.'

I slam a sharp elbow into Chi's ribs.

'Err, I must say Mr Harrington, I agree with Emy. She's created this project with scientific rules and boundaries. It would undermine the process to suddenly introduce a subject quite so different from the others.'

The MP shakes his head, a patronising glower smeared across his haughty mug. 'Maybe I didn't explain myself. This is happening. The money this thing is costing, it's not good enough to just get one win every six months. Either we dream bigger or we get cut before the Spring Budget.'

'In March?' I gasp.

'Exactly, which is why it works well with Mr Shenton. H trial is slated to start in the new year. I've spoken to the attor general. She's happy for you to take him for three mo which will then leave them about six weeks for both si finalise the case with any extra evidence that arises fr time with you. But if you do get a confession out o Harrington mimes washing his hands.

'And what if he's innocent?'

'Prosecution assures me he's guilty. But just betwe case they've been passed by plod is a bit thin. It's a cal; over your heads. But that's why a confession i the game. You've had your little experiment. V victory, at last. But to survive from here, we r crumbs.'

'Crumbs!'

I feel sick. He's always been a fetid arsehole, but until now I'd truly been stupid enough to believe he at least bought into what we were trying to achieve.

'Oh, and *The Times* have got the tip about new recruit, ton,' he blusters on. 'So no letting the side down in the interv with any of this Negative Nancy routine.'

We're on our feet and being ushered to the door. I follow Chi in a daze.

'Here're some docs on Shenton,' he states, passing me a brown A4 envelope – it feels heavy. 'Sets out the three-month timeline in more detail; agreement in there signed off by the AG, overview of the case... some choice images from the crime scene , so watch out for them. But I'm serious, you've got three hs to come up with the goods on this chap, or it's *sayonara*

no words. Lost between panic and fury.

C. Harrington. One can only speculate as to what ial stands for.

could have the most efficient court system in the Western world.'

'The whole point of the experiment is that the participants *have* pleaded guilty. It's fundamental to the study that the inmates have accepted the crimes they committed. This is about getting answers for families, not short-circuiting justice.'

I slam a sharp elbow into Chi's ribs.

'Err, I must say Mr Harrington, I agree with Emy. She's created this project with scientific rules and boundaries. It would undermine the process to suddenly introduce a subject quite so different from the others.'

The MP shakes his head, a patronising glower smeared across his haughty mug. 'Maybe I didn't explain myself. This is happening. The money this thing is costing, it's not good enough to just get one win every six months. Either we dream bigger or we get cut before the Spring Budget.'

'In March?' I gasp.

'Exactly, which is why it works well with Mr Shenton. His trial is slated to start in the new year. I've spoken to the attorney general. She's happy for you to take him for three months, which will then leave them about six weeks for both sides to finalise the case with any extra evidence that arises from his time with you. But if you do get a confession out of him...' Harrington mimes washing his hands.

'And what if he's innocent?'

'Prosecution assures me he's guilty. But just between us... the case they've been passed by plod is a bit thin. It's all very political; over your heads. But that's why a confession is the name of the game. You've had your little experiment. We've got a PR victory, at last. But to survive from here, we need more than crumbs.'

'Crumbs!'

I feel sick. He's always been a fetid arsehole, but until now I'd truly been stupid enough to believe he at least bought into what we were trying to achieve.

'Oh, and *The Times* have got the tip about new recruit, Shenton,' he blusters on. 'So no letting the side down in the interview with any of this Negative Nancy routine.'

We're on our feet and being ushered to the door. I follow Chi in a daze.

'Here're some docs on Shenton,' he states, passing me a brown A4 envelope – it feels heavy. 'Sets out the three-month timeline in more detail; agreement in there signed off by the AG, overview of the case... some choice images from the crime scene too, so watch out for them. But I'm serious, you've got three months to come up with the goods on this chap, or it's *sayonara* to it all.'

I have no words. Lost between panic and fury.

Barnaby C. Harrington. One can only speculate as to what the middle initial stands for.

2

'I'm trapped and he knows it,' I fume at Chi in the glitzy hotel bar. 'He's going to ruin everything.'

She stays mute, the straw of her cocktail ever-present between her lips.

'I know a bit about Tim Shenton; he doesn't fit our profile at all. He's a lot younger too. With Petty gone it was full steam ahead on Elkins. But now... what if I've missed my chance? What if it never happens? What will I tell Mum? I want to kill him!'

Chi puts her empty glass down and waits for my eyes to meet hers. She's all the kinds of calm I usually pretend to be. 'You're spiralling Em. Tomorrow will be better. Just treat the newbie like the others. New man, same approach. Tim Shenton is just the new George Petty.'

'Yeah, but if Shenton doesn't confess, we get shut down. That's not like Petty. What if he's innocent? The case would collapse if it ever gets out that the MOJ *wants* him found guilty. Harrington's gambling on me keeping schtum. And he knows I will... Prick!'

'*Wait and see* is my advice. You knew they wouldn't fund this forever. And who knows, if you do get a confession, maybe you'll get months... *years* longer to work on Elkins, if you even need it,' she says, flagging down the bow tie-clad waiter at the bar and ordering herself another Amaretto Sour.

The barman looks at me.

'Malbec please,' I knock back the remainder of my last one and embrace the rich, moreish tang as it slips down. 'Maybe I just basically ignore Shenton. Put everything into Elkins.'

'That's what you've been doing the whole time anyway,' Chi observes, mischief in her eyes.

'Shut up,' I reply, smiling. 'And can you stop grinning and laughing whenever we're with Harrington?'

'If I'm nice to him, it makes him nicer to me.'

Our fresh drinks are pushed across the bar towards our high stools. We chink glasses.

'I've got a new nickname for him, y'know. Thought of it earlier while he was staring at my chest,' Chi says.

'Yeah?'

'King Leer.'

My big, booming laugh shatters the ambience of the art deco bar.

Chi is the funniest, biggest-hearted and unashamedly honest confidante one could ever hope to have. My best friend for almost 16 years. An exceptional listener with an incorrigible zest for adventure. She's an impeccable dresser too, outfits always striking, yet effortless; tonight's black Zara blouse, white AllSaints jeans and Saint Laurent mules prove no exception. We're very different though. I once told her she'd been too coquettish with a teenage male barista at our local Caffè Nero and she just replied: 'Thank you.'

We met at uni. Both doing English Lit, neither having a clue what to do afterwards. I stumbled towards publishing for a while, my heart not really in it. By the time I went back to study psychology, she was travelling the world, teaching English as a foreign language, always struggling to justify to her parents why she hadn't found a husband, settled down and started popping out mini Chiyokos.

Don't ever call her by that full first name though; she'll stab you in the eyes.

Then, about three years ago, I asked her to proofread a paper I'd written evaluating the potential of intensive, prolonged surveillance with murderers who refuse to divulge where they've hidden victims' bodies. The concept was all hypothetical, based on scientifically reviewed studies, but realistically beyond the remit of any normal firm or research institute's budget. And that's when Chi caught fire. She dragged me, kicking and nay-saying, through several months of building up a pitch for the Ministry of Justice, the actual parliamentary Ministry of Justice. I humoured her, flattered by the attention for my pipedream. And then, miraculously, laughably, impossibly we found ourselves in front of Harrington, about this time last year, being offered the Earth. It seems a long time ago now.

'I might head back to the room, start forming my own opinion on whether Tim Shenton's a child-killer,' I say, slugging half my fresh red wine in one go and motioning to the thick envelope Harrington gave me.

'Not yet! We need to prep for the journalist in the morning. His name's Leon Courtney-Peltz,' Chi explains. 'He'll be...'

'Excuse me, girls,' a cockney voice interrupts. We both turn to see a couple of men in spray-on jeans and Ralph Lauren T-shirts eyeing us up. Cheap, synthetic aftershave hangs like a fart around them. 'Mind if we join you?'

'Yeah, sorry. Not tonight, lads,' I profess far too politely.

Mr Chatty's not so easily perturbed. 'Nah. We'll get ya next round in.'

I don't need to look at Chi to know she's keen.

'I only drink bubbly,' she flirts.

Chatty looks at his mate, Mr Fake Tan. The diamond in Chatty's left ear twinkles against the soft lights of the bar as he whispers something to his terracotta friend then looks back at us. 'Cheeky! Go on then.'

They turn to pull up two extra stools and I use the moment's privacy to shake my head vigorously at Chi. I raise my voice so Tweedledum and Tweedledumber can still hear me. 'Sorry guys, it's been a long day.'

'Ah, go on!' whines Chatty. 'We ain't poofters, we'll show you a proper night.'

'How ironic...' I start. 'Predictably homophobic and yet I bet you watch a tragic amount of lesbian pornography.'

Both men stand in silence, stumped by the observation. Poor Chatty; he couldn't blow his own head off if it was made of dynamite.

'I'm going,' I finally announce. 'Chi, you coming?'

I get up and a soul-destroying silence follows as I realise my best friend has no intention of ending her night with me.

'Come on, babe!' the diamond geezer pleads. 'We ain't dodgy or nothing.'

'Good to know,' I bat him off, packing my handbag and whispering to Chi about leaving her Find My Friends app on.

'It'll be fun. Stay!' He badgers. 'We can all have a laugh.'

'If promising us a laugh is your way of admitting we're going to see your penis, then I think I'll pass.'

I float up to my hotel room on a cloud of Chatty's tears.

* * *

'So, what am I supposed to tell this guy from *The Times*?' Chi asks over the phone. From the croak in her voice, last night's impromptu jolly must have been a real blowout.

'I dunno. Say something came up. Say I got no notice about Shenton and need to study his case.'

'Harrington's going to go mental when he finds out.'

'Even better,' I reply.

'I can't believe you paid extra for an earlier ticket.'

'Maybe if you'd slept in our hotel room you'd have been there to change my mind.'

'Oh, so we're plain slut shaming now, are we?' There's enough mock-resignation in her tone to indicate she isn't actually offended.

'What can I say?' I crow. 'Early bird catches the train.' I certainly was up early, I barely slept after leaving Chi, worried out of my mind that she might not be safe, imagining the worst, pillorying myself for not going with her. But since she's clearly made it through the night, it's her turn to squirm for a hot minute. Anyway, the idea of an interview with a national newspaper hack sounds about as appealing as Tabasco eyedrops.

'The PR stuff's your domain, babes,' I tell her.

'That's not the point. We need good press.'

'I'll see you back in Newcastle. If it helps, get yourself an 'I heart London' T-shirt before you leave. We'll stick it on expenses.'

The call ends with Chi muttering expletives.

My government-paid taxi from Newcastle Central back to Mum's house in Gateshead this sunny late-August afternoon is very handy. The smell of shepherd's pie as I open the front door suggests I've timed the country-long commute well.

'Hey!' I call out.

Mum – complete in her cupcake-patterned apron – inches into the hall and wraps her arms around me.

'It's been full on,' I say, giving her a gentle but prolonged hug.

She passes me a Post-it note:

I'm really proud of you!

I can't hide the truth from her. This was not a triumphant trip to the capital. 'Harrington's giving us three months to get something on a new inmate or he's shutting us down.'

The news is too much for Mum, as I knew it would be. She shuffles back into the lounge and sits down.

'Obviously I'm going to keep the focus on Elkins,' I reassure, following her. 'I'll get him back in first thing tomorrow. See if all this change has dislodged anything.'

Mum motions to a whiteboard she keeps on the coffee table; I pick it up and pass it over.

Her small, fragile hand keeps a shaky grip on the felt-tip as she scrawls in her usual spidery script. She gives the whiteboard back and stares at me, her wide eyes laden with worry. I read the message out loud: 'Three months? You've already had six. What if it's not enough time? There wasn't supposed to be a deadline.'

'It's bloody Harrington,' I reply. 'The only positive is that if we do get this new guy to confess, we can use it to justify keeping the project open. Or maybe it won't take three months to get Elkins,' I say, trotting out the same prosaic claims Chi used last night.

Mum nods and returns to the kitchen to plate up dinner. The home-cooking is as delicious as it smells: luscious, buttery mash on top of rich, earthy lamb mince, crunchy carrots and a hint of mint – just the way I like it. We listen to the news on the radio as we eat, then I do the washing up. It's always been the same routine.

Ditching my original degree and career in my mid-twenties in favour of pursuing a doctorate in psychology was about as financially savvy as buying shares in the Titanic – hence why I've never properly been able to move out. It's been a godsend in recent months though. Her osteoporosis is worse than she'd been letting on. She needs someone here every day. On her GP's advice, all potential tripping hazards – door stops, stray plug cords, her floor lamp – have been removed or hidden around the home and we've installed disability rails in every room.

Each night, she runs a bath. That would be on the 'too risky' list if she lived alone, but the hot water helps with her back pain and I can make sure she doesn't slip.

What is different tonight is that she hasn't passed me any notes since serving dinner. There are whiteboards, notepads, Post-its and pens all over the house. We've both learned some sign language too over the years. But tonight – nothing.

I'm kneeling next to the bath, stroking a steaming, soapy flannel down her back when her tiny bird-like frame begins to jitter. I lean forward hoping it's a cough, but her gaze-less eyes instead give way to tears.

'Oh, Mum!'

I want to pull her towards me and squeeze all the pain away, but her condition forces me to settle for a pathetic arm around one shoulder, nestling my chin on her damp head. 'Mum, we'll keep going. I promise. I promise!'

Her delicate sobs nudge her up and down. I caress the snowy hair back from her face and move forwards so she can see me. 'We will do it, yeah? Better to have three months than nothing.'

She raises her head a little, forces a stoic smile out and nods.

Thank you. I love you. She signs with her hands.

I love you too. I sign back.

Dried off and pyjamas on, we watch EastEnders until Mum nods off. She looks peaceful when she sleeps. I know everyone does, but with Mum it's the only time the tension truly melts away, her features softening, only to freeze solid again the moment she comes to and remembers where she is – who she is.

I'm lost looking at her when she wakes herself up with a snore.

Helping her upstairs, she takes her medication then I ease her under the duvet. She leans over and scribbles in her bedside notepad:

Tomorrow could be the day!

Gazing at me, her childlike eyes yearn for reassurance. It's the same message she's repeated to me every night since the project started. It's the maxim she's lived by most of my adult life.

'Tomorrow could be the day,' I echo.

Mum hasn't spoken a word out loud since Friday 24 April, just over ten years ago.

Why do I know the date? Because it's the date mass murderer Frank Elkins abducted my darling brother Sam, aged twenty-one.

This is the best chance we'll ever have to find Sam's body. But if my hyper-intensive project can't uncover where Frank Elkins buried his victims, no one ever will, and Mum's broken heart won't survive the disappointment that comes with such brutal defeat. I know that for a fact.

That man has already robbed me of my brother. I will not let him take my mum too.

3

When the Ministry of Justice was looking for somewhere to host this project, I'd stipulated it must be within commuting distance of Mum. The only state-owned location nearby deemed secure enough was Beeswell Barracks.

A dilapidated officers' quarters was transformed into a surveillance-heavy micro-prison. 1,200 square feet dedicated to unpicking the darkest minds in British criminal history.

Frank Elkins. Joe Okorie. And, until last week, George Petty. All mass killers who – crucially – have confessed to their murders but are withholding where they've hidden the bodies. Harrington's shat all over that essential characteristic, of course, by foisting Tim Shenton on us.

Barnaby C. Harrington. Let me count the excruciating ways in which I've dreamed of chopping off your Member of Parliament.

Once up and running, Chi and I christened Beeswell Barracks 'The Hive'. The puns flowed far too freely at first: the prisoners were the bees, their secrets were the honey, Chi even started calling me the Queen. Too much – but the Hive nickname stuck.

Three cells and a common room for the inmates, an office for myself, Chi and our research assistant Robbie, a security suite manned around the clock. And the main theatre of combat – my interview room – where Elkins eternally crushes me.

He sits in there this Friday morning. As ever, his arms are cuffed to the sides of his chair and, as ever, he doesn't acknowledge my entrance.

Thin straggly grey hair weeps down the sides of his puce face, falling towards his eyes as he hunches forward, staring at the floor beneath the table. His medical records state he's 6 ft 2 in tall, but you wouldn't guess it. His proportions don't match up. Withered legs and arms under his dark blue tracksuit are little more than scaffolding. A wilted nose and shrivelled lips seem overwhelmed in his broad, gaunt face. But a protruding pot belly appears to be the main foundation stopping his head and shoulders tumbling forwards onto the table.

Don't be fooled by the feeble physique, however. This man was capable of unimaginable cruelty.

He's known as 'The Dentist'. That's his serial killer moniker. He pulled out three incisors – two top, one bottom – from each of his five victims. That's fifteen teeth – all found in a bag when he was arrested. Our working hypothesis is he did it to stop these young men gnawing at the metal frame of the dog cage he kept them in. That insight alone haunts me every single day.

Sam's innocent, full smile flashes across my mind and my stomach lurches. I repeat Mum's notepad mantra. *Tomorrow could be the day.*

It's a hard truth to keep telling myself, though.

With the other two inmates – George Petty and Joe Okorie –

progress has been palpable. Trust has grown, details have emerged and, in Petty's case, we cracked the code.

Not Elkins. He devours countless books on nihilist philosophy. He never causes any trouble with his fellow prisoners. Observing him via the camera in his cell, we've even ascertained a complete lack of libido.

But in here, with me – nada. In the office we keep chalking up new ways to outsmart him; not one has worked. We can't even claim we're back to square one because we've never left it.

The only chink in the armour we've ever glimpsed is a bizarre tendency to snap into his late mother's voice, mimicking her, reliving childhood conversations.

'*Don't do that Frankie, please don't do that darling,*' he squawked once, suddenly high-pitched and desperate.

'*I love you Frankie, you know that don't you?*' That was another one.

A haunted skull could fall on me in the middle of the night and start gnawing at my face and it would still be less creepy than that time-travelling voice he does. It sends sickly shivers down my back every time. His mother died when he was still a teenager, leaving him in the hands of his violent father. Who knows what trauma and lost innocence he's resurrecting as he breaks into character?

But today, even that level of detached interaction seems beyond him.

'You'll be getting a new housemate tomorrow,' I tell him.

Elkins shrugs – his absolute favourite hobby.

Today's line of attack: make him feel cleverer than his fellow inmates. See if stroking his ego encourages him to boast about his crimes. It's the exact opposite of the minimisation techniques I've used in the past to chip away at so many inmates' belief in their own legend. Usually that would undermine men's self-assuredness, challenge their dominance, make them more susceptible to giving in, confessing. But I've tried that with Elkins. I've tried most things.

'Tim Shenton's his name,' I elaborate. 'Accused of raping and murdering a young boy.'

Unmoved, he sighs. His irises are light blue, but not in a charming, twinkly way. They're rheumy, soulless.

'I get the feeling he might not have too many opinions about Schopenhauer though, if you see what I mean.'

'I hope he doesn't,' he states.

'He might click with Joe more – less of a deep thinker.'

Those corpse-like eyes roll on to me. I've only said four sentences and yet he knows I'm buttering him up – sees me coming. He always sees me coming. Never have the words *bang head* and *brick wall* been more aptly applied.

My Sam. Utterly beautiful both inside and out; funny, warm, a whirlwind of energy. But no one remembers that. Websites never reported that he'd started up his own driving school business. TV reports never mentioned that his heart would melt every time he saw a dog in the park. Newspapers didn't explain the way he could make me laugh until drinks came out of my nose and my sides ached for relief. All the things that made him an individual were forgotten. He was just Sam Whirberth, the fifth and final victim of Frank Elkins. The most thorough descriptions might give his age and where he was from, but that was it. A gorgeous, generous, patient young man, distilled down to the footnote on another man's charge sheet. It's an injustice so heinous I will never get over it. And the architect of this reality, who still lives and breathes and has the callous cognitive freedom to conceal details of his killings, sits in front of me.

421 days between Sam going missing and Elkins being caught. How many of those days did my brother last? A week? A

month? Was he still alive when we held the candle-lit vigil a year to the day after he was taken? And what must he have gone through? Elkins liked to kill, but he also liked to hold hostage, to torture.

That's the other horror. It's not just that Sam was murdered – a ray of light snuffed out. It's how much he must have suffered. Of the five, just one Elkins victim has been found. The teeth had been pulled out while the poor man was still alive. Pathologists believe he eventually starved to death.

It's too harrowing to dwell on. And yet dwell on it I must. Confronting every fact while still retaining hope, burying feelings, continuing to prod and pry for an opening: all in Elkins' hideous presence. The most cathartic thing I could do would be to claw the skin off his miserable, self-serving face. But I put that aside, every single day, and observe him, engage with him, share air with him – for the shadow of my brother's smile and the echo of my mother's voice.

I could win the EuroMillions and it wouldn't pay for half the therapy I need.

Elkins isn't buying today's schmoozing. I switch tack. 'Why did you admit to the murders if you didn't want to talk about them? Why not plead not guilty and claim you were innocent forever?' I ask, as if I've not put a variation of this question to him dozens of times over the past six months.

His response is as predictable as my line of enquiry: 'Don't know.'

There's a lot Frank Elkins *doesn't know*. First among them is that I'm his last victim's sister – that, he must never know. I don't use my surname 'Whirberth' in my work, I use my middle name 'Rose', to go undetected.

In psychologist circles, it's called Goal Theory. If you create a specific target for someone to focus on, they're more likely to achieve it. If you tell Elkins his psychologist is one of the relatives he's purposefully withholding information from, it further motivates him to keep the bodies hidden. I need all the help I can get.

So I conceal my true identity from this man, week after week, month after month.

Today he's giving nothing. Who cares? I'll still be back tomorrow to go through another forty minutes of meaningless interrogation that only serves to undermine any confidence I have in my ability to get answers out of him.

But it will take more than professional humiliation and emotional obliteration to stop me, because stopping would be admitting to Mum we've lost – she's lost.

Never.

Tomorrow could be the day.

4

Joe Okorie sits at his digital chessboard in the Beeswell prison common room. He'd dearly love to play with proper, wooden, 3D pieces. But that request was denied. While his eyes stay on the flat touchscreen, his ears are glued to the exit door. He needs to be in position as soon as the keycard clicks.

The game in front of him is all but over anyway: knight takes knight; pawn takes knight; rook slides along the back rank; check; king moves; queen takes queen; computer resigns. Maybe he should just restart and try—

Bleep. Click.

On his feet and at the door to George Petty's cell in a split-second, he stands ramrod-straight, hands behind his back. The zap of excitement is short-lived, however, as Frank Elkins tramps back into the common room and lowers himself into his usual seat at another table, where his big boring book has been sitting waiting for him.

Joe lets out a groan, his shoulders slumping forwards as he pads back to his own seat. Why does Frank get so many meetings? He's so dull and rude. When *Joe* is in with Emy their conversation is electric. There's sparring, flirting, a frisson of forbidden desire. No way Frank Elkins is bringing that to the party. Silly idiot.

It's just typical though, always has been. Treat a girl right and you get punished, they play with you, ignore you, take you for granted, don't know what they've got. But a boy that treats her like rubbish... she can't get enough, has to have him, has to change him. Most girls are psychopaths, for sure.

'How's Emy this morning?' Joe asks, hating himself for still caring, but also aware the CCTV cameras pick up audio that Emy listens to.

Frank doesn't look up from his big book.

Joe is still shaking his head at the affront when...

Bleep. Click.

Gazelle-like, he's out of his chair again and back at Petty's old cell in one fluid skip. This will be fine, they'll let him move, no reason why they shouldn't.

The main door to the inmates' quarters clangs open and a young man is led in by two of the warders. They are heading towards George Petty's old cell just as Joe anticipated.

'Oh sorry,' he splutters. 'I've moved in to this one, fancied a change, thought the new man could have my old room. Nice to meet you, by the way.'

'Okorie, you know that's not up to you.' The gruffer of the two guards wanders into the in-demand cell to see Joe's toothbrush and spare tracksuit in there. 'Put your stuff back or I'll chuck it...'

'But why can't I switch? It makes no—'

'Okorie!'

'Ask Emy, she'll be OK with it!'

The guard retrieves Joe's possessions and chucks them onto

the floor of the common room. The new recruit observes from behind, apparently amused.

Of course, the black guy gets last pick again. Joe huffs, gathering everything up and stomping back to his original cell. 'Can you *please* sort out my bed then? I keep telling you that leg's dodgy but *nothing* happens.'

He throws his tracksuit on to the floor of the cell he hates so well, sitting on the old mattress – the squeak of the loose bed leg taunting him.

The guards bang the main door shut again as they leave and the new-found silence transforms Joe. An icy blast of reality grips him. It happens like that sometimes. Silly things froth and fester in his head, become life-defining in their intensity, and then just sort of go; rain giving way to brilliant sunshine.

He handled that terribly. He's probably made a woeful first impression on the new inmate. What an idiot! Joe is desperate for a friend in here. And he's just acted like a petulant child.

Be cool, Joe! Why weren't you cool?

He needs to go back out: welcome the poor man.

He creeps over to the doorway of the new arrival.

'Hello?'

The young man is sitting on his bed with his feet up; eyes closed. He must be half Joe's age at least. Curling soft fingers along his forehead and down the sides of his face to move greasy brown hair, the stranger gives a vacant half smile. 'Joseph Okorie? Yes?'

'That's right!' Joe can't believe his luck. The man's not annoyed! 'I'm Joe, and we've also got Frank out in the pen.'

'You're the Ghost Killer...'

'Erm, well yes but please call me—'

'Do you know who I am?' the man interrupts, speaking slowly, eyes still closed as if he's about to drift off to sleep.

'I... don't, sorry.'

'Tim Shenton,' the man replies.

Joe repeats the name in his head then looks back at the spindly twenty-something. 'I reckon I know that name.'

'Do you know *why* you know it?' Tim returns.

'That dead child.'

Tim tilts his chin forwards and then back again but stays immersed in his own thoughts.

'Nice to meet you, Tim.'

'Did you try to nick this cell because your bed's broken?' Tim breathes.

'Oh, erm, sorry, sorry. Just a misunderstanding,' Joe gabbles. 'No harm done; it was just...'

'Shut my door,' Tim demands, bored yet emphatic.

'I'm really sorry, I'm actually here to welcome you to Beeswell Barracks as—'

'*Shut my door!*' The instruction is more assertive now, Tim's black eyes flashing open, dripping with disdain as they glare at the intruder at the end of the bed.

Joe offers a garbled apology as he back pedals, stumbling and falling over in his haste to leave. He hauls himself back up on the handle of the door and yanks it shut.

Retaking his perch in the pen, Joe looks over at Frank, who in turn slams his book shut and wanders back to his own cell. Noise, drama, interaction – it's everything Frank Elkins stands against.

Joe tiptoes across the newly vacated common room, fills two paper cups from the water cooler, then goes back to his usual table and waits.

What have you done Joe? What a mess!

He's been desperate for a friend and he might have ruined

his chance with the new man straight away. All over a stupid bed leg.

He sips at his chilled water and nudges the cup he's got for Tim around the table with his index finger. *Just wait out here for him. Apologise when he emerges. Reset.* Joe just needs to show Tim how warm and friendly he is.

He shouldn't start a new game on his chessboard; Tim might see him playing and assume he's busy.

Minutes become an hour.

Tim will come out soon. Joe is positioned facing the cell door, ready to make amends.

A second hour goes by.

He still sits alone. What an idiot he was to try to change rooms. What a wretched idiot! That's not how you make friends.

Tomorrow. Tim will feel more settled tomorrow. Joe stays sitting, thinking about topics the two of them will be able to discuss. He'll start with a massive apology for trying to swap rooms, that's for sure.

Be cool, Joe. Be cool.

5

Traumatic mutism – that's Mum. Total loss of speech due to a catastrophic breakdown after losing her son.

She saw a speech therapist, then a psychologist, then a psychiatrist. None got even a syllable out of her.

But their assessments were all the same. Her mind had locked a door. Grief was the only key to unlocking it, but she couldn't grieve until she had a body to bury.

Some incredibly insensitive arseholes down the years have questioned this. 'If you know he's dead, you can grieve, why do you need a body?' Not one person who says that has ever lost a loved one and had no body to bury. It's a basic truth: until you have the body, you can't prove to your deepest, most fundamental self that they are definitely dead. Another much crueller instinct takes hold instead: you do not grieve – you search. Because part of you will never accept they are gone until you see it with your own eyes. You can tell people you know Sam is dead, you can believe that you know it yourself, but that last atom of hope at your core won't accept it. So grief never comes. Only searching.

Searching, emptiness, disappointment. Then more searching.

I didn't switch from English and publishing to psychology to break Elkins. I did it to help Mum. I thought I could research cutting-edge, mind-altering techniques to help her grieve, help her talk again. But the more I learned about trauma, the deeper I understood how critical finding Sam's body was to any hope of progress. Ultimately, I abandoned all attempts to get her to 'move on' from her son. She may be mute, but the one thing she needs screams from everything she does.

No yummy smells hit me from the kitchen as I open the front door. No din of the radio either.

'Mum?'

No sound of slippers padding over the shag carpet in the lounge.

I live in fear of this scenario: she's fallen somewhere, brittle bones snapped like twigs.

'MUM! Where are you?'

A strong foot thumps down through the ceiling. My heartrate halves.

Charging upstairs, I find her in the spare room, scrutinising the huge ordnance survey map pinned to a cork board on the wall. A red cross near the middle marks Frank Elkins' old home. A black cross near it marks the place the one discovered victim's body was found. Apart from that the map is bare. No string connecting disparate points, no photographs or writing covering half the roads and place names. This isn't a Hollywood prop, this is what's left of my mum's life.

Thousands, and I mean thousands, of paper cuttings lie in piles, in ring binders, in disarray, forming mini skyscrapers of bad news leaning against the walls. There's barely room to move between these paper pillars and the boxes crammed with videos of old TV reports of the case and notepads of thoughts she's scribbled to herself or me or Dad over the years and albums of photos she's taken of different potential burial sites. The room is a hectic, macabre museum of Elkins' murders.

Mum's 'patch' is a fifteen-mile area around Elkins' old property near the market town of Bedale, about an hour south of here. Rain or shine, Christmas or birthdays, she's there every Saturday. She knows that land better than the local farmers themselves. Genuinely!

It's an eye-watering, soul-sapping, hope-crushing expanse to cover with so few clues to go on. But Mum has covered every blade of grass of it. She and Dad used to go several days a week. But it takes so much out of her now, and I am her only chauffeur since Dad died, so Saturdays have to suffice. The fact she has never uncovered anything would floor most, but not Mum. As I say, until you lose a central foundation of your life, you have no idea the punishment you'll put yourself through to bring them home, give them closure, create one last tiny, dignified memory with them.

'Where are you thinking for tomorrow?' Better to be keen about her weekly expeditions, the day she wants to stay home will be the end of her.

She draws a circle with her tiny index finger at an area about a mile wide. She'll have been there a dozen times over the years, but it'll be our first time together.

'Great!' I rub her back and lean forward to nuzzle into the crook of her neck.

She's warm and smells of... well, she smells of Mum. She kisses me gently on the cheek.

She also has out the infamous CCTV grab from the day itself, on a camera located about three-quarters of a mile away from where Sam vanished: it's grainy but you can make out

Elkins driving and his van's number plate. It wasn't enough evidence alone of course. But slowly – far too slowly – police put this together with some other sightings of that van and Elkins at suspicious times relating to several of the disappearances. By the time officers had put enough pieces together and gained a warrant, Sam had been gone over a year. The only traces of him left were his teeth in the front of the van and his blood in the back of it. Detectives just seemed relieved to have caught Elkins before he struck again, which was about as comforting to us as a sledgehammer to the temple.

I slip the CCTV picture back into a binder, out of sight, and give the top of Mum's head a small tickle. Her hair used to be blonde like mine, but jumped to bright white within a year of the disappearance. 'Come on. I'll run you a bath.'

Tomorrow could be the day, she signs, looking up at me.

'Yeah,' I whisper.

Grief never comes. Only searching.

* * *

We're in Bedale before 9 a.m. The rain isn't heavy but it exists and the end-of-summer air cloys, sweat clinging to the inside of my khaki-green waterproof. Mucky walking boots laced up tight, Mum walks slowly, but with purpose. I insist on holding her hand throughout; one fall when you've got osteoporosis and you might never get up again.

It's heartbreaking if I dwell on it too long. What is she hoping has changed? Some bones have miraculously bubbled to the surface of the earth over the last decade? An underground bunker-cum-tomb has somehow emerged that she didn't see the first ten times round?

It doesn't serve anyone to think like that though.

Her hunting ground is not totally random, it must be said. While I may not have managed to extract any extra clues as to where the bodies are, we do have one or two slivers of evidence to go on. Elkins lived in the same house near Bedale his whole life, he worked as a farmhand from the age of 16, he had a van that he used for this work, but never had a licence, with farmers who worked with him regularly noting how poor he was at driving. This all heavily suggests he will have hidden the bodies in the local vicinity – he didn't have the wherewithal to plot anything more elaborate. Law enforcement and fellow psychologists agree that almost every killer will hide bodies in an area they feel comfortable and familiar with. This is the only place Elkins has ever known.

If he had wanted to throw detectives off his scent, he should have at least abducted from further afield, but the victims all vanished less than six miles from Elkins' home.

And there is the biggest clue of all: one of the bodies was found – buried in a shallow grave in the far corner of a field on one of the farms where Elkins did harvest work. Ollie Vaughn: discovered about two months after he went missing.

This was actually the second murder Elkins admitted to once caught. He'd killed his own brother, Vinny, first. Then Ollie Vaughn. Third was Damian McAree. Fourth was Nathan Brockhurst. Fifth was Sam. All young men between the ages of fourteen and twenty. He's never given us a sniff of motive but our working theory is that he maybe killed his brother, in a fight, and then mentally collapsed, flitting between wanting replacement brother-clones, then growing guilty or bored of them but knowing he couldn't let them go, leaving them to die in the cage in the back of his van.

The discovery of Ollie Vaughn was barely three miles from Elkins' front door. Exactly as all statistical models would suggest. It would be astonishing for a killer such as Elkins to change his MO very much, even in relation to body-disposal. Mum's cast-iron conviction is that Elkins didn't start dropping his victims into the sea or dissolving them in acid after Ollie Vaughn was found. What serial murderers often do is hone their techniques, develop their skills, learn from their mistakes. And that is what Elkins has done. He got complacent with the second body, so resolved never to make the same mistake again. He still buried his victims, he still used the fields he knew well. But, my word, did he make sure he did a better job in future.

Other families who go on weekend strolls must find the trips so tedious, without the eternally silent walking partner and lack of dead brother to search for. I pity the sods, I really do.

Speaking of sods, we trudge on, the squelch of loosening mud under our boots as the mizzle encroaches. But all Mum's reasoning is important. This isn't pointless plodding. This is the psychologically logical, evidential route any sane person would take if they had studied every aspect of body discovery half as long as she has.

Put another way, if Elkins had abducted Mycroft Holmes, Sherlock would be looking in the exact same places Mum is.

She's shared everything she's learned with the relatives of the other victims too. Occasionally we'll bump into a fellow parent or sibling from the Brockhurst or McAree families out on their own endless search. What jolly reunions they aren't.

Mum and I play a game sometimes, while we walk. Test how well she knows the terrain.

'Tell me something unique about the next meadow, through that gate.'

That's an easy one by Mum's standards, she could probably name and describe every tree, shrub and hillock in North Yorkshire at this point.

Big bog on the left... on the right, she signs.

'What on the right?' I check, not recognising the signage, a failure of mine all too often.

She gives up on sign language and mimes blowing a kiss, charades-style.

'Kissing gate!'

Mum nods.

We reach the next field – both her predictions are on the money.

She grins, rightly proud of her photographic memory for the land.

Thickening rain seeps through my mac as I smile back at my beautiful mum. We used to be about the same height but she's a couple of inches shorter these days. She pulls her hood forward to keep out the moody sky.

'Let's go back,' I suggest, nodding upwards.

She doesn't dignify me with a response, turning forwards again and marching on into the new field.

6

Monday morning always means a fresh go at Elkins. Two days alone with Mum fills the tank up afresh with desperation for cracking him.

This interview room is so bleak. No character, no colour, just a white box containing a grey table, a CCTV camera, an odd whiff of sawdust and fresh paint and the mild thrum of halogen lights. That's on purpose, of course. No distractions, no bells and whistles. But I have taken to hanging mental pictures on the walls, ones of Sam. I've got four along the back wall, and three along the two sides. Photographs of him growing up, based on ones from the family album. There's one of him wearing Dad's cricket whites as a boy at primary school, complete with leg pads and a bat that's almost as tall as he is. The pride in his grin could melt ice caps.

Another photograph I've hung invisibly on the right-hand side is of the four of us away in Cornwall, sitting in a row on the beach. Mum roars with laughter about something as Sam flicks my leg and Dad tries to keep us apart. I can't remember who took that photo but I remember it beginning to rain soon after.

Dad whisked me up and we all ran towards the ice cream hut for shelter. All except Sam, who ran the opposite way into the sea. We watched as the downpour peppered the sand, and Sam splashed and screamed in delight, waving over, beckoning us to join him. We all stayed under the hut's shelter. I wish so badly that I had gone and joined him. Every memory's a regret when you're mourning.

Elkins sits, usual blank expression, head lolling, hands locked in place.

The chair he's in had to be custom-made with metal arm clamps. Interviewees default to biting their nails or clicking their knuckles if their hands are cuffed together. Not on my watch. Habitual behaviour is a micro-comfort. Or put the other way, denying habitual behaviour is a micro-discomfort. My first peer-reviewed journal article demonstrated how subjects are more likely to show candour if their environment is disrupted. The mind has to work that little bit harder to settle, leaving a nanogram less headspace for constructing a convincing lie or hiding deceitful body language. It was a damn good study, even if I do say so myself.

Not that it helps with this vampire, endlessly sucking on my self-esteem.

Bib on, knife and fork in hand, time for me to chow down on another day of inevitable disappointment. 'What d'you think of the newbie?'

'Not spoken to him,' Elkins grunts without looking up.

What even is my plan today? What's my new strategy? What's the point in coming up with clever schemes if they consistently fail and leave me feeling more useless than if I hadn't come up with them in the first place?

Urgh, I make Eeyore sound like a Samaritan counsellor.

We talk about Elkins' childhood for a while. Well, I talk as he shrugs. Maybe if I coax him, he'll fall into his mum's voice again, the way he has a few times previously, that uber creepy parrot-like imitation of his past: a memory, an absent-minded line of conversation that gives a clue we didn't have before.

But no. It's like an incel's brain scan in here – no signs of activity whatsoever.

How do I break the cycle? I'm so predictable, so vanilla. Be creative, catch him off guard! But what does that even mean? Erupt into song? Flash him my tits? If someone's resolved not to answer, it's impossible.

'You know my inability to get anything out of you is professionally devastating,' I admit, in a defeated tone that *will* be new to Elkins. 'I leave our interviews feeling like a complete fraud. I don't know why I'm telling you, but I have not left one single chat with you thinking I have a foundation on which to build future interviews. No sense of why. No sense of how. No sense of who you are.'

He gives a twitchy glance up, then the eyes roll back to the floor.

'Do you ever think about them?'

Elkins blinks, but nothing more.

'You know who I mean? Your brother and the other four. How do you remember them? As men? Pets? Toys?'

He lets out a deep, weary sigh but doesn't attempt to reply. He looks bored. How dare he? My mum wasn't bored when she half shivered to death out looking for Sam on Saturday. She wasn't bored when police showed up with a death certificate, telling her they'd matched teeth in Elkins' van to her son. She isn't bored every time she's forced to use a notepad to communicate with me because this man's actions have literally stolen her voice. His apathy is abhorrent.

Months of Elkins' refusal to engage suddenly feel like a trail of gunpowder I'm racing along. 'OK, how about this? Every time you don't respond I'll assume the answer's "yes" but you're just too chickenshit to admit it.'

Silence, but the cadaverous eyes are back on me.

'Do you think about them?'

Silence.

'OK. So that's a "yes". Progress. Have you thought about saying more to me at any point since you've been here?'

Silence.

'Interesting. Do you feel guilt for what you did?'

'I'm not playing this game,' he growls, jolting his wrists in their metal constraints.

'Ah-ha. So you *don't* feel guilty. Because you think they deserved it?'

'Let me go back to my cell.'

This is gladiatorial; my spear to his neck. 'OK, so they didn't deserve it. What, then? Did *you* deserve it? That power, that control – it was all about you and they were just...'

'STOP!' His jaw is jutting forward, baring his yellow teeth. 'You want to get to me? No chance. I will never say a word about them. Nothing. Get that into your thick skull and put me back in my FUCKING CELL.'

Making sure he's the one to break eye contact, I leave my hands flat on the table, heavy as lead. No nerves here. In fact, it's harder trying to hide a smirk. I don't know what just happened, but it's the most blood I've got out of this dry, old stone since he arrived at the Hive.

And despite his protestations, I'm sure Sam's name has never felt closer to his lips.

7

I whizz back into the office. Neither Chi nor our research assistant Robbie look up.

Chi sits, calm and serene, patting away at her computer keyboard, an enormous Starbucks cup by her side.

Robbie stares at one of the screens from the mosaic of CCTV streams we've got set up on the back wall, scribbling down notes as inmate Joe Okorie plays on a computerised chessboard in the common room.

'Did you just see my interview with Elkins?' I demand, enough buzz for the three of us combined.

They did not.

'Robbie, go back through it and type up the transcript. We need to discuss.'

He nods and slips on a pair of headphones, turning back to his own screen and plucking a pack of wine gums out of his bag as he gets down to work.

Robbie is a twenty-three-year-old PhD student. His diet might be the worst I've ever encountered. At home he subsists on potato products alone: crisps, chips, roasties, mash. Irish tapas, he calls it.

In the office he does at least add variety with an endless supply of sweet snacks too. He could collapse with scurvy at any moment. Weekends are spent playing online chess tournaments and 'watching grandmasters stream on Twitch' – whatever that means. Oh, and he doesn't drink. Honestly what is wrong with GenZ?

'Harrington's already called again about *The Times* interview you ditched. He's pissed, Em,' Chi says, anxious and unimpressed as she finally deigns to acknowledge my existence. 'And he's ordered a weekly progress report on Tim Shenton.'

'Ordered?' I cry. 'What does he think we are, a chip shop? We don't take orders.'

She tuts and tells me it's important to keep him sweet.

I tell her Harrington's not a meringue, he's a moron.

Chi's always so pristine, whether it's out for drinks, meeting the secretary of state for justice, or just turning up for work on a Monday morning. Full make-up, knee-high black leather boots and matching miniskirt, nude tights and a cream-coloured cotton T-shirt with puff sleeves.

Transcript transcribed, Robbie prints out three copies.

'Wow, that's a pump of the tyres, isn't it?' He chirps as he passes copies to Chi and me. Robbie has a nauseatingly bright view of life, always loaded, ready to fire trite optimistic quotes when my guard's down. I could chop off one of his legs and he'd simply thank me for the opportunity to practise his hopping.

But since I, too, am most enthused by this morning's developments, I'll allow the rose-coloured specs on this rare occasion.

We run through the interview, watching the footage back, playing the sound through the office speakers and following the words on paper.

Getting to the shouty crescendo, Chi's eyes bulge. 'He's rattled.'

I nod. 'OK, how do we build on it?'

'You've got under his skin. But why?' she begins.

I encourage her to go on.

'Could be he didn't like the conversation being out of his control?'

I tap my pen against my cheek and scrunch up my face. 'But then he'd just let me rabbit on. I've tried to jump to conclusions before and he just ignores me, or shakes his head. Water off a duck's crack.'

'He first started getting agitated when you brought up guilt,' Robbie tries, cradling his bag of sweets, launching a few into his mouth and chomping. 'Could be burying the shame of what he's done and you got too close for comfort?'

'Mmm, but I don't think he does feel guilty. He's shown no remorse under all types of questioning,' I say. A disheartening silence stretches out. 'Oi, are you two buffering? More ideas, more theories! We've struck a nerve – we need to work out which one and how we exploit it.'

Robbie can't find any words but flicks a wine gum along his knuckles like a rockstar playing with their guitar pick. If he ever works out how to use those mesmeric fingers on a date, he'll have a woman for life.

'It's the first time he's actually acknowledged the murders,' Chi spots, scanning the transcript. 'He says, "I will never say a word about *them*." That's something, isn't it!' Her odd tone takes a moment to place. But then I realise – it's pitying encouragement. She doesn't see this as a breakthrough at all. She just doesn't want to hurt my feelings. Robbie isn't making eye contact with me either. They both think it's a fun little interview where the inmate got hot, but of no further merit.

They're wrong! I just can't work out why yet.

Chi's computer makes a noise as an email pops up on her screen. 'Harrington. Wants a video call.'

'It's not even Monday lunchtime, don't ruin my week already.'

'He's obsessed with *The Times* guy and getting going with Tim Shenton,' she explains. 'He's not going to stop pestering until you—'

'Oh, screw Harrington!' I say, throwing my hand up in contempt. 'I'll email him later.'

'Can you do it now? He gives me grief when I don't reply to his messages quickly.'

'Messages?' I check. 'He's messaging you?'

'Not messages. Emails. Whatever.'

'I was going to say... If it's *messages* now, what's next? Cat memes... dick pics?' I look over to Robbie for a cheap chuckle but he's already back at his desk, copying out moves into a notepad from Joe Okorie's latest chess game while also attacking a fresh packet of crisps. 'Twas ever thus.

* * *

I do send Harrington an email. Brevity is the soul of it:

No Shenton recording today, first later this week. E.

This, apparently, is not deemed sufficient, however. Which leaves me in the disastrous position I am now: waiting for the secretary of state for justice to work out how to unmute himself so we can chat about what he termed my 'belligerent streak' in his email of reply.

Still, we should be grateful it's only a Zoom meeting given that he sees halitosis as a superpower.

I've sent Robbie out on a break so we can speak frankly; Chi pulled her chair up next to mine for the video call on my laptop. There are no pleasantries when Harrington does finally come off mute.

'I don't think you appreciate how important it is that you make immediate progress with Shenton,' he informs in that ridiculous aristocratic accent. Has he ever been north of Cambridgeshire? Certainly not for something as lowly as visiting this micro-prison he professes to care so much about. And why's he wearing a waistcoat with a pocket watch? Just check the time on your phone like a normal person, you preposterous toff.

He's still droning on in the background. 'Not having an initial recording or video clip is lamentable.'

'You won't be listening to it anyway, it'll be one of your flunkies,' I remonstrate. 'And anyway, you've said we've got three months, so we've got three months. If anything, you're distracting us from cracking on right now.'

'You're a feisty young filly, I'll give you that,' he says, smirking and taking a sip from a cut crystal tumbler. The amber liquid suggests he's either been stealing apple juice from children or he's day-drinking whiskey. It could so easily be either.

There's a huge bookshelf of leather-bound volumes behind him. Is this his country pile we've got a window into? He's so posh, he's probably got acres of manicured gardens watered solely with champagne.

I'm still waiting for him to make a half-intelligent argument.

He clears his throat. 'Look, I know you just see me as a glorified paymaster...'

I let out a tiny chuckle. 'I never said "glorified".'

He adopts a deeper tone: '...but let me reiterate, Tim Shenton *is* the priority and it's critical you—'

'We're not a kangaroo court,' I burst. 'He's innocent until proven—'

Louder, he jumps back in: 'It's critical... that you know you'll lose *all* inmates if you don't get answers out of Shenton.' He knows exactly what he's saying, the lowlife. We contemplated not letting on who I'm related to when we pitched the Hive to Harrington, aware it was a conflict of interest. But, ultimately, we were honest, rightly anticipating the MOJ background checks would flag the link either way. He's used that link against me ever since.

'What if Shenton's not guilty?' I shout louder still, desperate to smash my hand through the screen and squeeze Harrington's neck until it pops. 'That's an impossible challenge and you know it!'

Chi's apparently taken a vow of silence next to me. Where's the moral support? Where's the vomitous indignation at the plain blackmail being crushed upon us?

I'm too angry to speak. I could threaten to go public – out this man as the vile swine he is. But his threat is always the same: Piss him off, lose Elkins.

I'm here for Mum, not my ego.

Harrington swills his drink and decides to fill the void with some more wisdom. 'Do you know what I'm addicted to?'

'Breathing, sadly,' I mutter.

'Perpetual improvement.' He takes another sip from his glass, allowing all three of us a moment to marvel. 'We must all constantly upgrade and modernise. As a state-backed enterprise, it's incumbent on you to approach this little project with the same zest I approach everything I'm involved in.'

'Right,' I mumble with resignation.

'But I'm telling you straight, ladies. Either play ball, or lose it.

And you can't get out of the interview with *The Times* either. So next time they call, pick up the blasted phone, will you?'

More silence is my answer to that.

'I really think you need to look at the bigger picture, Dr Rose. You could be *finding* killers, not just digging up bones, if you just...' he tilts his head back and points at the ceiling to mime *aiming higher*. 'You know? All I'm saying is, don't let family stuff get in the way of that perpetual improvement.'

Looking back, I'm sure the fact I'm Sam's sister was key in pushing Harrington towards saying 'yes' – solely because now he gets to own me, forever. Or at least until Elkins confesses. Which could be longer than forever.

I slam the laptop shut.

8

Almost three decades *inside* has conditioned Joe Okorie very precisely. He awakes at eight o'clock every morning. On the odd occasion he does rise too early, he has the ability to guess with pinpoint accuracy how many minutes early he is.

Today he is right on cue. He can tell because about 30 seconds later the red light above his door turns green and electric locks clank open, echoing between all three cells.

Stretching out, the grating squeak of his metal bedframe and its wobbly leg are infernal early irritants.

He takes a sip from the paper cup on the small table next to him – the water's too cold, having sucked in the night's chill the same way the concrete floor of his room has. A pair of slippers would make things so much nicer. And a dressing gown. But he doesn't deserve such comforts. Not any more. Instead he takes two pairs of socks strategically left under his pillow overnight, and stuffs them down the front of his pyjama bottoms.

The newspapers will be in the common room already, but they can wait. The idea of placing his lovely warm feet on the glacial ground is still out of the question. He'll get up when breakfast arrives.

Sitting up straighter and adjusting his pillows, he thinks about Emy. Hopefully she finally calls him back in this morning. It's been nine days since they last connected. He knows George Petty going and Tim Shenton arriving will have caused her lots of extra work, poor thing, but she's seen Elkins numerous times. It must be Joe's turn today.

He nudges his hips back and forth on the mattress quietly, arms behind his head, letting his weight sway in a small, soothing way – despite the dodgy bed leg. The calm motion helps him think, lets his mind wander from time to time.

Things still haven't clicked with Tim Shenton; the man seems quite distrustful. Joe's fault of course for his idiocy on the man's first night. Joe really would like to befriend him though. The days can be so, so lonely when he doesn't see lovely Emy. Sometimes he hopes she's watching the CCTV in his room and thinking of him too. But in weaker moments he just pleads for God to take him, so he can be back with all his beautiful girlfriends, sharing with them, basking in them, loving them unconditionally. What is joy if it cannot be shared?

'Grub's up!' a security guard hollers from the main room a few minutes later.

'Thank you, Nigel,' Joe calls back from his room. Neither of the others show any gratitude, which is rude.

He plucks the two pairs of socks out from their nook between his legs and pulls the warm cotton over his feet. Such a smart innovation in the mornings.

Good job, Joe!

Stepping on to the icy floor, he glides to the door and pulls it open. Tim is already up reading one of the papers. An opportunity!

You can do this, Joe. Be cool, be cool.

'Morning, Tim,' he says, extra chirpy.

The other man looks up, sweeps his unwashed hair back behind his ear and grunts.

'Oh, I wouldn't sit there,' Joe warns, ignoring the bowl of cereal left out for him and padding towards his cellmate. 'It's just... that's, erm, that's Frank's seat. Usually.'

Tim dismisses him. 'They're all the same.'

'No, no...' Joe forces out a chuckle to show he means no judgment – he's more than happy to show Tim the ropes, so to speak. 'Look,' he says, standing behind his new pal and tapping the leg of the chair in question. There's a small loop of string round it. 'Frank's, you see.'

Tim peers at it but doesn't move.

Uncomfortable in the silence, Joe leans forward to see what Tim's been reading. 'Oh, *The Guardian* puzzle pages! Brilliant,' he beams. 'I love the... Oh you're doing it, the Sudoku.'

'I saw you'd been doing them. I've done *The Times* already.'

'All of it?' Joe questions. It usually takes him until well gone 11am to complete the full set. Whipping out the T2 supplement from *The Times*, he flicks through to the brain teaser page. All of the number games have been filled in: the Sudokus, the Futoshiki, the arithmetic chains, the Kenken. 'These are all wrong!'

'No they aren't,' Tim responds, continuing to scribble digits in, box after box. 'And why don't we get any of the fun papers? These are shit.'

'I like *The Guardian* and *The Times*.'

'You don't know anything,' he says, his pen pushing down hard against the table as he scrawls at pace.

'We could ask Emy to get another paper, maybe,' Joe suggests.

Tim doesn't respond.

The endless scrape of ballpoint on thin newspaper punishes Joe like a fox's scream in a baby's ear.

'Let me do one with you,' he says, unable to take the sight of his puzzles being violated any longer. 'I always do the Sudokus in the—'

A conspicuous snatch at the paper is anticipated by Tim, who yanks it out of Joe's reach.

'I'm doing them,' Tim says, menacing and certain.

'Sorry... sorry,' Joe replies with a deep breath.

Be cool Joe, be cool.

BUT HE'S RUINING ALL OF THEM.

'Erm, it's just... Maybe we could... You aren't doing it right. Stop just writing numbers. Tim. Stop for a sec. Tim. Tim!' Another lurch towards the pen sees its holder stand up, bundle both newspapers into his arms and stalk back towards his room.

'Tim! I just meant... we could go through them together. Yeah?' Joe pleads. 'That would be good, wouldn't it? Something to do. Maybe you were doing them right. You could show me.'

At the threshold to his cell, Tim turns back to his fellow inmate. 'Freak.'

Joe's heartfelt apology is interrupted by the banging shut of the steel cell door. He cowers, bewildered, but very familiar with the agonising, self-devouring shame of rejection. All Joe wants is a friend – someone who genuinely likes him. Does no one else feel like that?

No they don't, Joe. Tim's right. You're a stupid, worthless freak.

9

I get in early and spread the photos over the main table in the office before Chi and Robbie arrive. Then I wait at the door and warn each of them before they enter that the crime scene images we are about to study are at the very darkest end of anything they will ever be expected to endure.

They both nod and still choose to enter.

'Can we put them away now?' Chi asks about five seconds later. 'We get it.'

'No, let's do this properly,' I lead. 'I don't want Tim Shenton here any more than you two, but Adolf Harrington wants updates. So let's get a basic understanding of the case.'

We all return to our computers and turn our chairs inward to face each other with the table between us. Robbie can't help glancing back at the CCTV screen homed in on Joe's chessboard. I get up and switch that single screen off. He clenches his jaw, sighs, then pulls a bag of Walkers Salt and Vinegar out of his bag. Getting that boy to sit still without fidgeting is like asking Gordon Ramsay to stop swearing – impossible.

Chi has the opposite problem: stuck, staring down at one

image. The victim's pale bony arms are stretched taut by handcuffs chaining him to the bed. Lying on his stomach, his face is tilted to the side. The bag over his head is misted with condensation but, looking closely, it's possible to see that his mouth and eyes are both wide open, immortally locked in terror.

'Screw Harrington,' I correct myself, taking a sip of water. 'We're here for the kid's family. To get answers for them.'

Chi inhales deeply before meeting my eye and giving a little nod.

Robbie leans over the A4 glossy pictures on the table, getting crisp crumbs on the until-then spotless copies. 'What's the boy's name, again?'

'Andrew Stride. Aged eight. Tim Shenton was babysitting him. Claims an attacker came in, tasered him, knocked him out with a baseball bat, and when he came to, this was the scene he found.'

'What's the CPS case?' Robbie fires more morsels onto the photos before apologising and half brushing them onto the floor.

'Prosecution says Shenton killed Andrew, inflicted the injuries on himself, hid the taser and baseball bat, then called the police.'

Neither speaks.

'We need to build a profile of the *killer*, whoever that is. Not make everything fit Tim Shenton. Then, once we've done that, we can start analysing *him*, see what fits and what doesn't. And only after that can we start trying to get a confession, if we do even come to the conclusion he did it. Have you both read the backgrounder I forwarded on the case?'

They have. Good. I comb the crime scene out loud: 'The first thing that strikes me is the level of planning. Handcuffs, heavy duty bags, cable ties.'

'The report said the victim had a sock put in his mouth too, which would both stifle screams, but also stop him biting through the bag for air,' Robbie spots.

'Exactly. Planning was meticulous. Whoever did this had been plotting and fantasising about this for a long, long time, had maybe carried out similar attacks before,' I reply.

Chi hugs her knees up to her chest. She's barely audible. 'Andrew was an only child. That implies the victim was premeditated to simplify things at the scene.'

'So, an organised killer. Ultra organised. Suggests intelligent, no?' I stir.

'And that's before we get to the lack of DNA on the body or in the bedroom,' Robbie adds.

'Unless it *was* Shenton. His DNA was found on Andrew Stride and the duvet,' I remind.

'Yeah, but it would be, wouldn't it? What babysitter doesn't put a child to bed? And they didn't find *that kind* of DNA,' he points out, not-so-subtly.

I nod as he rewards himself with a fresh mouthful of crisps.

'OK, next step then... the act itself. Did you both see the footnote about the video?'

'I'm not watching that,' Chi shoots.

'No, I know. We won't... we don't have to. At all. The pictures say enough. But the existence of a video tells us a lot.'

'Like what?' Robbie asks.

'There are stills of it I haven't put on the table. Wanted to see how you'd cope with the pathologist's stuff first. But it'd be good if we could at least study one of the stills from the recorded footage.'

'Make it the tamest one,' Chi instructs, turning her head away from us and the table to look into the empty corner of the room, as if it is the only pocket of space from which to draw clean air.

I pull out a single image of Andrew Stride's bedroom. Huge Buzz Lightyear painted on the wall above the bed; blue duvet dotted with footballs; two old, well-loved cuddly toy dogs sitting patiently at the foot of the mattress. An innocent, happy background to the photograph.

No one is looking at the background.

On the bed, the cuffs are already on little Andrew, who is on his stomach. His face is much clearer than in the forensic photos, with condensation yet to build on the inside of the bag over his head – clear enough to see the dark brown of his wide, crazed eyes. Kneeling over him is a grown man in a full-body pea-green morph suit with a hole cut out around the crotch.

I give my colleagues time to absorb the depravity.

'So?' I eventually push.

Chi hugs her knees tighter. Rocking forward and back, she lasts about ten seconds before shutting her eyes.

Robbie might never have observed anything quite this graphic before but at least he's a psychology graduate, trained to see past the gratuitous crime, to peel back the horror and analyse the clues underneath. For Chi, this must be a whole other level of ordeal – no precedent, no practice to prepare her. It's unfair to think she'll process the scene enough to observe *anything* useful right now. She'll need days, maybe weeks to come to terms with it.

Robbie clears his throat more confidently. 'The very act of filming it suggests a narcissist, doesn't it? Not just to carry out the act, but to want to watch yourself back.'

'But this wasn't found on Tim's laptop…'

'He's not going to be stupid enough to have it on his laptop,'

Robbie scoffs. 'But there's got to be some element of exhibitionism about whoever did this, otherwise why do it?'

'Money? Kudos? Arrogance? Normal couples film sex without it making them narcissists,' I scoff back.

'What's your theory then?'

He's got me there. What is my theory? 'The video was sent to the mum on disc afterwards. That shows ridiculous levels of cruelty.'

'Suggests the killer knew her, to care enough to put her through that,' Robbie adds.

I take another sip of water and agree. 'That would lean towards it being Shenton.'

'It's his stepsister's kid, right?' Robbie checks, scrunching up his now-empty pack of Walkers. 'His own nephew.'

'Don't jump straight to disgust. We don't know he did this.'

'Ahh,' he groans, frustrated at falling into the trap. 'Socrates said, "The only true wisdom is in knowing we know nothing."'

'Right,' I mutter. Is that a compliment? A tip? Is he agreeing? Who knows with Robbie. 'Post-mortem didn't find haemorrhaging behind the eyes, which suggests the boy wasn't smothered at any point, just left to suffocate. Even crueller, don't you think?'

They sit like statues – I've lost them. That was too dark even for Robbie; they've both already had to digest enough brutality. So have I. This is objectively hideous. A nightmare brought to life. But what's the point of abusing our senses with such horror? We've been wrestling with three appalling killers, and our reward for outfoxing one of them is a fresh atrocity to sear into our minds forever. All these distractions, all these harrowing extras, all they make me do is resent the world I've been left in. The more cases pushed our way, the less likely I am to unravel the one I do care about. Yet I *will* wade through this

Shenton shitshow, just to keep Harrington onside. That's no comfort to Chi and Robbie, however. They don't get their brother back if Elkins coughs. They don't get anything. How do I motivate them to keep caring as the Hive's novelty gives way to bleak, relentless grind? It's not fair on anyone, let alone the two angels who believed in the project enough to join me here.

'The killer isn't an exhibitionist,' Chi murmurs; I'd almost forgotten we were still mid-huddle.

'Why?' I return.

'They've cuffed the boy's arms at the top end of the bed. If the killer was bothered about watching their own performance, they'd have Andrew's head at the other end so they were both facing the mirror.' She stands up and picks out a picture off the table, taken inside the bedroom but looking back out to the landing. A floor-to-ceiling wardrobe stands next to the doorway, the front of which is all mirrored. 'If you wanted to see yourself doing it, you'd want to watch yourself *during*. This person didn't.'

Robbie and I look at each other, both outsmarted by an amateur.

'Chi, that's brilliant.'

She doesn't respond and goes back to cradling her knees on the chair.

'Where does that leave us?'

'The killer wants to inflict cruelty, but maybe it's more about torturing the mum than the boy?' Robbie offers. 'Is there any evidence of anyone having a grudge against her?'

I shrug. 'Good question.'

'And there's the child porn charge on Shenton's file too,' the increasingly confident man of the room reminds us.

'Definitely bad for his case.' I pick up my notes and tap them on the table. 'OK, not a bad morning's work gang.' I'm looking at Chi but she's still in the mire.

'Teamwork makes the dream work!' Robbie announces, moving back to the CCTV screens to turn Joe's Chess Cam back on.

I let out a cry of laughter that ricochets off the walls like a bouncy ball. 'Even by your standards that's an abysmal cliché.'

'Clichés are nothing less than perfect phrases that captured too many imaginations,' he proclaims, playing up to it now.

A tiny giggle escapes Chi, colour returning to her cheeks.

'Don't encourage him!'

'It's worth it to watch you squirm,' she smirks.

'Well, fuck you very much.'

'Do another one,' she grins at him.

Robbie's eyes light up, the human Gatling gun ready to fire more benign BS. 'Yesterday's the past, tomorrow's the future, but today's a gift. That's why they call it the present.'

I put a very definite end to the nonsense, promising to sack him if he opens his mouth again. It's nice to hear them both laughing though.

'I'm still getting grief from *The Times* by the way, insisting on an interview,' Chi spills as we remain facing each other. She's no novice: spying my levity as a chance to needle me without getting an earful back. If she gets any more calculating we'll have to build her an extra cell with the other inmates. 'You aren't going to outrun him,' she adds.

'We'll see,' I respond.

'Why are you so desperate to avoid the media?' Robbie enquires.

'Because they're going to want to ask how we got Petty to confess, and as soon as we give away our tactics the inmates will turn on us. If they get even a sniff of how broad and varied our strategies are, they'll lose all faith and trust and refuse to come into the interview room. We need to operate quietly, discreetly, under the radar.'

It's half true. The inmates realising quite how radical we are being in outfoxing them would be detrimental, for sure. But I can't admit my bigger reason, not in front of Robbie – that the more spotlight we have on us, the more likely it is the press will work out I'm Sam's sister and that'll leak back to Elkins. That cannot happen.

Robbie accepts my original defence, however. He and Chi turn back to their desks, leaving me to shuffle the photographs of Andrew Stride's murder into a single pile. The additional one, mid-attack, ends up on top. Despite my composure in front of the others, these pictures do more than disturb me – they panic me, make my head swim. Because the perpetrator of this evil may be feet away; and unlike Chi and Robbie, I must now meet him.

10

I peer through the interview room door porthole. Tim Shenton is slumped in his regulation blue tracksuit looking into space, apparently bored.

Dark brown hair flops either side of a skinny face, a greasy sheen on it reflecting the ultra-white glare of the lights.

Is he a child murderer? Impossible to say yet. Has he got a personality disorder? I've not even spoken to him. Should he be at the Hive? Definitely not.

Enough seething.

I push open the door and introduce myself.

Shoulders back now, his eyes reach me. 'So, you're the woman who's going to get me freed.' The words ease out at a deep, unhurried pace.

'We'll be having regular meetings and I'll be sending the recordings to the Ministry of Justice, your defence team and the CPS.'

Longer armed than Elkins and Okorie, Shenton sits back in his chair, despite his wrists being clamped down. His skin is ghostly pale, a husk drained of all blood and heat.

'You've met your two neighbours,' I go on.

He doesn't reply straight away. He wants me hanging on his every word; he's the megastar, I'm the autograph hunter.

No dice, hun. I make a big gesture of leaning back too and looking around the room – more than happy to distract myself with my beautifully hung, ornately framed invisible photographs of Sam. If this bloke is as taciturn as Elkins at least it'll make for short interview transcripts.

Shenton does eventually give up on his little game and speaks again, soft and sedate: 'I hope you'll give me a fair hearing, Dr Rose.' His head's tilted down now, his eyes landing on me out of the top of their sockets. He's twenty-six years old but his long, unwashed hair and emaciated cheeks could be borrowed from a sixth former.

'It's Miss Rose. Or Emy,' I tell him.

'But you're a doctor... in forensic psychology,' he states, intrigued.

'Touching that you've stalked me in advance, but "Miss Rose" is fine.'

'As you wish, Miss Rose, so sorry.' He shakes his head. 'You mentioned two other men. Who are they?' His eyes roll in the direction of the inmates' quarters, then dart back.

'You're already bullying Okorie. Don't play dumb.'

'Bullying? No. He tried to lump me with his inferior room. He has not earned my respect. Anyway, I've been here four days, you've been watching them for *months*. Catch me up.' He produces a small, unconvincing smile.

I stare at him. Did he do it? How could *anyone* do that to an eight-year-old? But if he did, what does it say about him that he can sit here, so serenely, concealing such a barbarous mind? Antisocial personality disorder at the very least. But that's me breaking my own rules. Don't make this man fit the crimes, let the evidence present itself – for or against. Or, better yet... find Sam's body so I never have to speak to Tim Shenton, or Joe Okorie, or Barnaby C. Harrington ever again.

Tall order, I know, but hey... dreams can come true! Gabrielle said so.

I take a deep breath and decide to humour Shenton's vapid request. 'We've got Joe Okorie, the "Ghost Killer". He abducted eight women in three years. We're working with him to establish how he did it and where the victims' bodies are. And Frank Elkins, who killed five men including his own brother.'

His eyes scan me but he chooses not to reveal what's on his mind. I press on, the volume and pace of my voice exquisitely constant: 'But there's only one person we're in this room to talk about, Tim. And it's not Okorie or Elkins.'

'OK, let me guess...' He flicks his chin up as he repositions in his seat, ten times more comfortable already than I've ever seen anyone else in this interview room, myself included. 'You go back to my start, lack of parents, brought up by Barnardo's, the charge at nineteen, the fact I was in the house at the time, tie it all together and make a neat little bow around the prosecution case.'

'It wasn't a charge, it was a conviction for possessing child pornography,' I correct him.

'I'm innocent of killing Andy, Miss Rose.'

'Can I be honest, Tim?'

He raises his eyebrows in accord.

'I don't want you here. You don't fit the study. We want murderers who have confessed. But here you are... so I'm going to spend the next three months working it out – are you a convicted paedophile caught in the wrong place at the wrong time, or are you a child-killer who lacks the spine to admit what he's done?'

A light wheeze comes from his skeletal chest as it rises and falls. 'You're different, aren't you?'

I laugh out loud. 'And you're more diplomatic than I'll ever be.'

A glimmer of fascination slips across his face.

'Why are you here, Miss Rose?' The stare morphs into something closer to single-minded concentration, glued to me, frightening and quizzical. *What's he getting at? He doesn't know about Sam. He's grasping.*

'OK, if you want to talk about the other two. What are your first thoughts of Frank Elkins?' I enquire.

Tim Shenton doesn't miss a beat. 'Scar on his head looks like it was made when he wasn't fully grown. Given what he went on to do, I'd guess his father beat him. He marks items that are his, classic older sibling habit. Maybe he hated his younger brother – how dare someone else come along and take everything that had once been his. So he marks things to say, "This is the property of Frank Elkins". And maybe that's what he was doing with the victims too – take out the teeth, mark them as his. He reads nihilistic literature because it's the only framework that affords space for the dark world of beatings, hatred, abduction and murder that his whole life became. He's still trying to make sense of it all, seek solace or comfort, or worse justification. He wants absolution for a crime he was willing to commit over and over again – an impossible contradiction. How am I doing?'

I sit dumb. What was that? It's not that most of it is new, but it's new to Tim Shenton. 'So you've stalked Elkins' credentials as well as mine...' I test.

A shake of the head. 'We both know that's a whole lot more than you'll get from Wikipedia.'

'You say he marks things as his? What do you mean?'

'You're the one watching him 24/7.'

'Indulge me,' I tell him.

'There's string tied round the leg of his favourite seat. And he's wrapped a strand of thread from the spine of a book around one of the pens.'

Is he bluffing? I haven't spotted either of those.

'Why are you here, Miss Rose?' he repeats, even more absorbed.

'Elkins got angry with me for the first time yesterday. I was throwing wild accusations at him and he snapped in a way he doesn't usually. Why do you think that is?' I ask, unsure what I'm doing but unable to stop myself.

'Your old inmate's gone,' Shenton states.

'George Petty? OK... so what?'

'Elkins is scared. Petty leaving shows the system's working. You going back to Elkins and seeming to jump to conclusions without him even opening his mouth makes him feel like you might work it all out. "She did it with Petty, what if she does it to me?" – he'll be thinking.'

I blank, barely able to keep my face neutral, never mind answer out loud. Chi, Robbie, Mum, even *I* hadn't come up with such an obvious explanation for Elkins' outburst. And this strange stick insect sees through it all like a toddler's lie. It's the sheer clarity with which he says it as well. The words aren't just believable, they're logical, like he's had a lifetime to think about them, not three seconds.

'Why are you here, Miss Rose?' That stare is stuck to me, his ravenous curiosity eating me up and spitting me out. He can't know about Sam.

I need to listen back to his analysis of Elkins ten times – listen to it, interpret it, unpack it, work out how to use it.

It's been eons since I last spoke at this point. I make sure to ignore Shenton's recurring question. 'Elkins is worried we're making progress... It's a theory, I suppose. Anyway, we're here to talk about Andrew Stride.'

His eyes finally move off me to the clock on the wall behind. 'I think eight minutes is long enough for a first meeting, Miss Rose.'

I laugh even louder than last time. 'Got somewhere else to be?'

'I like you, Miss Rose. But that's enough for today.'

'If you want to clear your name, refusing to talk isn't a good start,' I say with teacher-like wisdom.

'Oh, we will clear my name. But not today. You need to get to know me first.' There's a hint of patronising patience as his head tilts to the side and he looks down at his arms.

'I need to get to know you... but you won't talk,' I mock.

Unflappable, he smirks. 'You still haven't answered my question.'

'Why am I here? To get answers for the families,' I state. But my insistence on maintaining eye contact only confirms to him that I'm lying.

He can't know anything. He hasn't actually said anything specific, he's just good at pressing buttons. Some people are like that. They wind you up and you can't articulate how, but they do.

Shenton observes me, head still tilted, as if appreciating a Picasso. Then he looks away, and yet somehow, I know he must speak next – it's the only way to avoid accidentally revealing any more than I already have.

He pushes his tongue out enough to moisten his lips, then adjusts in his seat and looks into the mid-distance next to me. 'I was driving once,' he begins. 'Countryside, early-ish, Sunday morning. No traffic about. I was enjoying the sweep and sway of speeding around the narrow lanes. Out of nowhere, a black cat, little more than a kitten, darts into the road. My front wheel goes over it.' He lets his foot pat down on the floor to recreate the bump, glancing at me, before returning to his scene. 'I stop, get out, and there it is, the kitten, just months old. I always remember its little pink nose for some reason,' he pauses as if reliving the episode in real time. 'This thing is now clawing along the edge of the road.' He lets both feet pat on the floor quickly to imitate running. 'Its eyes, above that tiny pink nose are enormous, bulging. It knows it's dying. And yet it carries on moving, fast front legs like a sprinter. Its back half, however...' He shakes his head, taking a fortifying breath. 'Its back half is monstrous. Hind legs, lower back, tail, all slithering from side to side along the ground.' He sways, as if mimicking the movement. 'Front half scrabbling onwards, the scrape of limp flesh and crushed bone behind. It wrenches itself all the way back to my car – the very thing that has broken its spine – then disappears underneath the chassis. I crouch down. It's curled up in a wheel rim. Literally in the act of dying, half-paralysed, its impulse is still to move out of sight. Why?'

I feel queasy. The detail and composure of his storytelling leaves me in no doubt this really happened.

'Why does the kitten hide, Miss Rose?'

'To make sure predators can't see it,' I try, not sure at all why I'm humouring this tale. 'It's wounded but might not know it's dying. It wants to get to safety, then decide what to do next.'

'But it dragged itself *back* to the thing that had hit it. Its killer,' he states with more feeling, admonishing me.

I shrug, swallowing hard as sickly saliva builds in my mouth.

'The kitten hides because it is ashamed, Miss Rose.' He observes me as I listen. 'It doesn't want the world seeing it unnatural and broken. And once it is in that wheel, it won't come out. Because at least, now, no one can see how futile it has become.'

I hold his gaze but refuse to reply. There's no sympathy or pain in his expression, but an earnest will for me to understand his point.

'You remind me of that kitten, Miss Rose.' His eyes narrow as if X-raying my soul. 'The most interesting question remains, however. Why would such an attractive, smart, successful young woman hide here, reeking of such fatal resignation?'

'Tim! Talk about hobbits and unicorns for all I care. It's not going to help you at trial. We *must* discuss the case.'

'As I said, Miss Rose. Not today.' And with that, Shenton slips both arms out of the circular clamps he's supposed to be locked into at the sides of his chair.

Terror-struck, I slam my feet down, shunt my chair backwards and plant my body against the wall furthest away from him. Eyes fixed on the inmate, I flail for the door handle to my right. A mouse in the corner of a cobra's cage.

The locks on each side of the chair were never fastened. I've been left unguarded with a potential sadistic killer.

Noticing my explosion of fear, he raises his unshackled hands in surrender, then moves his own chair back and stands up.

'Stay away!' I scream as I find the door handle and open it, still not sure I can get out and shut him in again before he reaches me.

He lets out a breathy chuckle to suggest I'm overreacting. 'I look forward to talking again soon, Miss Rose.'

I dart out, banging the door shut so hard the echo rattles down the corridor.

Why are you here, Miss Rose?

11

For goodness' sake! What has Joe done wrong? Why does Emy punish him like this?

Tim Shenton only arrived four days ago, but she's had time to speak to *him* on top of all the rendezvous with Frank.

Does she not understand how much Joe cares about her? How much it means to him when they do have their lovely long chats? Maybe he should go on hunger strike. But then he'd basically be forcing her to give him attention. That defeats the point. Their relationship isn't a thrill because she *has* to speak with him, it's beautiful because she *wants* to spend time with him. Except now, apparently she doesn't, and Joe's had just about enough of it.

He looks over at Frank, sitting in his usual seat, reading his big book. In some ways Joe is envious. Frank seems content with next to nothing; he doesn't crave friendship, that's for sure.

Needy, that's what girls used to say about Joe at school. *You're too needy, Joe.* He hated that, hated the way they'd turn his loving, caring nature into a negative. So many cruel voices, so many painful memories. Lucky old Frank, who looks like he doesn't feel anything at all.

Footsteps and raised voices approach from outside the common room. The door crashes open and Tim Shenton is flung back over the threshold, amid angry cusses from the two guards.

They slam the door shut again and Tim springs back to his feet like a deck of cards falling in reverse.

'What was that?' Joe calls over. He's seen inmates given the rough treatment at other prisons, but never at Beeswell.

Tim pulls his blue tracksuit top back down straight so it hangs over the front of his jogging bottoms. He blanks his concerned cellmate and instead gazes at Frank. After a pause he wanders over to the third prisoner, pulls out a chair and sits down.

He's going to get short shrift if he tries to interrupt Frank's reading.

'Need your advice,' Tim says, keeping his voice low, but still clear enough for the room to hear.

Frank wrenches his eyes off the pages in front of him and stares at this personal space invader. He has scary eyes, does Frank. Light, icy blue. When they freeze on you, there's an effortless stare that crushes all, leaves you a centimetre tall and desperate to scuttle away, anything to escape him looking at you any longer.

But then, to Joe's astonishment, Frank puts his book face down, splayed open on the page he's reading, and leans in too.

'That Emy Rose, she's doing my nut in,' Tim says. 'Rude bitch. How do you handle her?'

Handle. Joe recoils. It's too graphic a word, it conjures up impossible images of them holding her, embracing her. The idea either of these men would touch his Emy is repulsive.

Frank's round shoulders stay hunched into the middle of the table. He takes Tim in, a Great Dane contemplating whether to maul the Chihuahua puppy in front of him or slink off to his own kennel.

'Just zone out while you're in there,' Frank grunts.

It's not much of an answer, true. But how on earth has Tim got any sense out of Frank at all? It's more of a response than Joe's had from him in months.

'She's out of line. Trying to manipulate emotions. I see right through her,' Tim gabbles, unaware he's already got as much out of Frank as he's ever likely to get. Quit while you're ahead, mate!

But he doesn't. He just keeps on rabbiting. 'I mean, you've got your secrets, I've got my secrets, fuck face over there probably has twice as many.' Tim nods over at Joe as he says this, and to Joe's horror, the name-calling elicits a tiny smile from Frank.

'But she's not that clever,' Tim persists, curling his long brown hair back behind his ear. 'I'm just worried that if she got Petty, she'll trick the rest of us eventually, y'know.'

'Not me,' Frank grunts with a single shake of his head, seemingly more intrigued than irritated.

'I wish I was as confident as you,' Tim admits.

Joe's not buying this. Not one bit. Tim was plenty confident enough when he ordered Joe out of his cell on his first day. He was plenty confident enough when he ruined all the puzzle pages – something he's gone on to do *every* day since. Tim Shenton isn't some weak little dweeb. And yet Frank looks like he's genuinely interested in the newbie.

Tim asks Frank a question about the book he's reading and gets another response.

What's going on? Why does nobody want to be Joe's friend?

He's the nice one! He actually feels things. But, yet again, it's Joe out in the cold. Joe all alone. Joe whom nobody loves.

'Maybe we could start a book club?' he says, standing up and walking towards his comrades.

They both stare up at him and don't recommence their conversation until he's walked away again.

Joe lets his cell door slam shut and throws himself face down onto his mattress, the weak corner of the bedframe shunting slightly and squeaking as he buries his head in the pillow. He thinks of his girls. His perfect girls. They are the only pure moments of joy in his life. No cruel looks, no cold words. Just precious time spent together when he could love like he's always wanted to love.

When all else is pain and desolation, he still has them. He will always have them. That was the whole point of killing them.

12

I give the Hive's security detail a long, well-deserved bollocking. Apparently, Shenton was taken to the interview room by a new, green warder who fell hook, line and sinker for his lies about being exempt from needing restraints.

I order Robbie to type up the transcript of my first interaction with the new inmate – with no delay. I wait for his reaction when Shenton finally pulls his arms up and stands uninvited in the interview room. Robbie chokes on his BBQ McCoy's. Knew he would.

'Plays into the theatrical streak we are looking for in Andrew Stride's killer,' Chi observes, once we've been through the interview as a trio.

I give a deliberate nod. She's damn right.

'Send it straight to Harrington,' I instruct Robbie. 'Give him a taste of the crap he's putting us through. Oh yeah, and had either of you noticed that thing with the string Shenton mentioned about Elkins, wrapping it round items he wants to brand his own?'

'Oh yeah, I'd seen that!' Robbie claims with pride. 'He's done it on a few things.'

'And you never raised it?' I decry.

'What d'you want me to say? It's not of any importance to the case and...'

'You don't know that. We can't leave any stone unturned.'

He loses his usual easy-going swagger. 'So you want me to tell you every tiny little thing any of them does, even though you have access to all the same cameras I do?'

'Yeah! Why wouldn't you mention it?'

'Alright. Well, he also wipes his arse after he shits, and sleeps with his head on a pillow.'

I look to Chi. Urgh, she's looking at me as if I should cut *him* some slack, and to be fair, if I've ruffled ray-of-sunshine Robbie then I probably have gone too far. 'Let's forget it, but anything out of the ordinary with any of them from now on, we *must* bring up. Nothing too small. OK?'

He grunts agreement, fishing a four-finger KitKat out of his bag but not offering us any.

'Talking of not ignoring things...' Chi huffs. 'I've had *another* email from *The Times* saying they've been promised an interview and pushing for when you're going to do it.' She makes it sound like I'm the bad guy rather than horrible Harrington.

'*Mañana.*' I shrug.

'No Em, you can't outrun this.'

'Oh ye of little faith,' I shoot back with a wink she doesn't appreciate.

'There's another clip we could send to Harrington by the way,' Robbie interjects – already trying to make up for his previous lack of disclosure, bless him. 'Shenton was bitching about you.'

'In what way?'

Robbie turns back to his computer and rewinds the latest common room footage.

Shenton is chucked back into the bull-pen and walks straight over to Elkins, pulling up a seat like no one ever has before. The time stamp on the recording would put it directly after our interview.

Robbie tries to narrate: 'Shenton starts whinging, not very nice. Calls you a bi—'

'Shh!' I hiss, wanting to hear the actual interaction play out.

'Need your advice,' Shenton starts. 'That Emy Rose, she's doing my nut in. Rude bitch...'

'Told you it wasn't very nice...' Robbie interrupts again.

I slam my hand down in mid-air to make him shut up.

'I can see right through her...' Shenton continues.

I watch Elkins. He's immediately engaged in a way he never is in the interview room. Eyes lively, engrossed by Shenton's hyperactivity. Not bored, not annoyed, somehow interested in this bizarre buzzing specimen in front of him.

Shenton goes on. 'She's not that clever. I'm just worried that if she got Petty, she'll trick the rest of us eventually, y'know.'

'Not me,' says Elkins. Classic response. Vile human.

The pair move off the topic of me and Beeswell and on to philosophy. Shenton still manages to keep Elkins talking, but the conversation feels less poignant. It's that initial interaction that tantalises.

We watch it back a couple more times.

'Another inmate you've got your work cut out with,' Robbie proclaims. 'Already hates you. That's why you should be working more on Joe, he's our best bet at another win, trust me.' Of course he's making this about Joe – his tacit chess coach.

'I don't think Shenton does hate me,' I posit, confident my hunch is right but unsure why.

I turn to Chi. Can she articulate my thoughts for me? It wouldn't be the first time.

She's got that steely, won't-be-defeated look in her eye. That *we're not leaving until we've got to the bottom of this* energy.

'Play the clip again,' she requests. We watch the first couple of minutes of the interaction once more, Chi consulting her transcript of my interview with Shenton at the same time.

'I think he's trying to prove he can get through to Elkins,' she states.

'Why? To impress me?'

'Yeah,' she says, warming to her theory. 'You complained about Elkins being hard work. This was Shenton showing *he* can break him down.'

I feel my own thoughts slotting into place like Tetris pieces but let her keep flowing.

'Him acting like he hates you, that didn't seem convincing. It was a prop to get to Elkins, which is sort of scary: how quickly he knows what he needs to do to manipulate you over Elkins, and vice versa... Elkins over you.'

Chi may not have formal psychological training but her emotional literacy is off the charts.

'It's the way he knows exactly how to disarm Elkins, arguably one of the most guarded people he'll have ever met,' I ponder. 'Those first words, "Need your advice". He's making himself seem dumb and harmless. Then obviously trying to pretend his views align with Elkins, knowing there's no love lost between me and Elkins, so nurturing that resentment with him.'

'Surely Elkins would see right through it, though?' Robbie says. 'He's so mistrustful of anything you or Joe says. Why the sudden change with Shenton?'

'There is something transfixing about Tim Shenton,' I think out loud. 'He's so consummate at reading people, unravelling them. Even when I was speaking to him, it was as if he could see through every bit of body language, read between every line. It gave me a horrible chill, and I'd only just met him.'

'Oh shit, Cialdini's unity principle too,' Robbie says as if he can't believe it's taken so long to occur to him.

I open my hands and nod. 'Makes so much sense.'

'Wait, what's Calzone's principle?' Chi checks, purposefully getting the name wrong.

'Robert Cialdini's idea is that if you can convince someone that you and they are on the same team, have the same goals, or the same purpose, it makes them far easier to manipulate and influence,' I explain.

'Wait, so is Tim Shenton doing that to you or to Elkins?' Chi asks.

'Elkins!' Robbie cries, plucking out a packet of Minstrels from his bottomless bag and ripping off the top to celebrate his tangible contribution to the discussion. McCoy's, KitKat, now Minstrels, all in the space of an hour! Who's his nutritionist, Homer Simpson?

But I'm glad he's replied so quickly. It covers for me; I don't want to answer because Chi's question is far more astute than either of them realise. If Tim Shenton is trying to prove to me that he can get through to Frank Elkins, it suggests he already knows far more about me than he should. And someone playing mind games that devious is never doing it out of altruism.

Why are you here, Miss Rose?

We carry on discussing the interactions, what we've learned about Tim Shenton so far, and also the little extra light it's shed on Elkins. Robbie is also concerned about the nasty way Shenton has been treating Joe Okorie.

We all agree that being a manipulator with a penchant for the dramatic in no way precludes Shenton from being a child-

'Or maybe Barnaby Harrington just told me,' he adds with a fresh grin, showing off his neat white teeth.

'What's your angle then? You want to know more about the project?'

'You, the project, the progress. Everything,' he says with enthusiasm, getting his phone out, putting it on the table and setting it to record. Am I the inmate now? Detained under duress to answer myriad questions?

I shrug my shoulders and raise my palms to the ceiling – let's get this over with.

'Why didn't you want to speak to me?'

'I'm busy.'

'Some good PR might help you keep your centre open if the Tim Shenton gamble doesn't work.'

'Who says we won't stay open anyway?' I ask.

'A source I've got in Whitehall. Not Harrington.'

'The only good PR we need is convincing these men to give up their victims.'

'I think we both know that's overly simplistic,' he chuckles.

'If you know what we both think, then can I go? Leave you to write up both sides of whatever this is?' I say, keeping the conversational thermostat at absolute zero.

He still seems amused. 'How did you come up with the idea for a project like this?'

'Watch inmates, plot ways to open them up, rinse, repeat. It's not that complicated.'

'You're being too modest, Emy. Is it OK if I call you Emy?'

'You can call me Twatty McTwat-Face if it means this ends quicker,' I tell him.

He laughs. 'Why isn't every psychologist doing a scheme like this then?' His warm brown eyes trace me the whole time.

'It costs a ton of money. And most people in my field rightly want to work with subjects they can rehabilitate. My inmates... most of my inmates, at least... will never get parole, so aren't particularly fulfilling cases to a lot of psychologists.'

'But they are to you?'

'Yeah.'

'What is it about real beasts that captures your imagination?'

Thoughts of Sam flash before me. The bad thoughts: what Elkins inflicted on him, which bout finally killed him, where his malnourished body is dumped. 'I don't know,' I reply. 'But can I just say, that's a bugbear of mine. Calling them "beasts". People love doing that, calling killers "animals" or "monsters", because it puts a distance between us and them. These men aren't beasts. Cold-blooded murder is as unique to humans as calorie counting and bikini waxes. Beasts are far less cruel.'

'Wow,' he says, producing another toothy grin. 'You make—'

'And don't go writing a headline like "Emy Rose says murderers aren't monsters". What the guys in here have done is horrific. Beyond horrific. But it's still human. Pretending they're feral helps no one.'

'Is that why they get extra privileges? You want to treat them humanely?'

'The press went way overboard with that stuff. We're not a soft touch. Each man is allowed one bonus benefit. Joe Okorie has his chess set; Frank Elkins has a new book delivered once a week. It's not the Ritz. But if it makes them a millimetre more amenable to cooperating, then it's the right thing to do. All evidence shows that 100 per cent unremitting punishment doesn't work, whether you're negotiating with a toddler or for the Treaty of Versailles.'

Leon grunts in agreement. 'Maybe you've got more to get off your chest than you thought?'

I respond by not responding.

'Are you having to treat Tim Shenton differently since he still claims to be innocent?'

'We aren't assuming guilt, so it's a longer process. No updates to report though. Way too soon.'

'What about the other two then?' Leon probes. 'Six months and we've heard very little except for information sent out to families of the victims.'

'Joe is chattier than Elkins. But both are coming along fine.'

'Give me a little more. Specificity is everything. Something you've got out of one of them... just in case Barnaby Harrington happens to be reading this.'

I stare at the reporter, not wanting to answer. But to my own bitter disappointment I find myself faintly reflecting his infectious smile. 'You're annoying.'

'Sorry, sorry,' he bumbles. 'Just *one* little glimpse, then we can move on. Promise.'

I roll my eyes and don't hide a huge sigh. 'Erm... Joe's got into this habit where he won't tell us anything outright, but he will always tell us if we have got something right or wrong. We've used that to get further down the line of his murders than anyone had before.'

'Joseph Okorie? Kidnapped women from their homes and they never showed up again?'

'Joe. The Ghost Killer, yeah.'

'So what did he do?'

'I was about to tell you... Basically, the girls never got home. He'd flag them down late at night while they were driving. Then force them into the boot of his car. He'd then drive *their* car back to their own home and leave it there. Before walking all the way back to his own car with the woman still in the boot.'

'Bloody hell,' Leon says, furrowing his brow at the sudden

tsunami of gruesome detail. 'Were they still alive when he got back to his own car?'

I remind him he'd vowed to move on if I answered him properly and he's as good as his word. 'What tactics do you use to prise this information out of them?' he asks instead.

'That's got to be off the record,' I state. 'If any of them start getting wind of the finer points of how we operate then their guard shoots up immediately. But for instance, with George Petty, it was so obvious that he loved the notoriety of talking about his crimes that we just fed that: put extra cameras up, started doing more sessions with him, dropped hints that people were hanging on his every word in the outside world. Then one day, we took it all away again. Cold turkey. He suddenly felt so deprived of attention that he blew his load within forty-eight hours. Like an addict would sell anything for their next hit, he sold his secrets for one last volley of headlines. But, as I say, that's all off the record. They can't know that's how we're thinking.'

'Understood,' Leon says. 'I'm surprised he fell for that though.'

'We try dozens of things; we just need one to work. That's the beauty of having the time and resources here.'

'So impressive,' he extols.

'You're very cheery, considering this is a quick chat about very dark things.'

'Who said it's going to be quick?' he replies.

'You're not as clever as you think you are.'

'No, but you are.'

My eyes lock with his and my cheeks begin to flush. 'Are we done?'

'Not at all. Talk me through your team. Chiyoko Aoki and Robbie O'Brien...'

'She'll kill you if you print *Chiyoko*.'

'She's in the right place then,' he fires back without missing a beat.

'They're brilliant. Chi liaises with the families, deals with the press – usually – does all the paperwork. Basically keeps my mind clear to focus on the inmates. It's helpful having a non-scientist in the room when we're discussing things too. Brings emotion back to clinical conversations.'

'And Mr O'Brien?'

'A PhD student. Does all the transcripts, a good heart. Very observant with patterns and stuff.'

'What stuff?'

'Confidential stuff.'

Leon smells good. I hadn't noticed at first, but having spent so much time in here with multiple aging men who care little about personal hygiene, Leon's mellow aftershave is starting to permeate, cleansing the room with citrus and spice.

'I've got some quick-fire questions I was wondering if you could respond to,' he goes on.

I blow my cheeks out. 'Go on then.'

'Age?'

'Thirty-four.'

'Worst thing about the job?'

'The woman in charge is a tyrant.'

'How do you switch off after work?'

'I read your articles – they're powerful... like sedatives.'

He snorts and smiles again. Why is he so chipper? Secret day-drinker, I bet.

'What made you want to be a psychologist?'

'The glamour.'

Flicking over a page in his notepad, he glances down then

goes on: 'What's the difference between a sociopath and a psychopath?'

'Books sell better if you put "psychopath" in the title.'

'Are you enjoying this interview?'

'Not as much as you.'

'What was the last lie you told?'

'When I said, "Nice to meet you".' I'm hoping for another smirk. He obliges.

'One quote that sticks in your mind from your time here?'

I pause and grit my teeth, annoyed I can't summon another instant riposte. A memory drops in quickly enough, however, and I let out a loud bark of laughter. 'George Petty told me he wanted "My Way" played at his funeral. Like he's just your average unassuming guy who's faced tough times and come out the other side. That, more than anything else, sums up these men.'

'That's quite the laugh you've got there, Emy.'

'Thank you.'

There's a prolonged pause which ends with him leaning forward to tilt his phone towards himself. 'I think I might have enough there,' he says.

I raise my eyebrows as we both get to our feet. 'I thought you'd try harder for some juicy exclusives. That wasn't much of a grilling.'

'Coming from the woman who's taken six months to get one decent confession out of three inmates... I think I've got plenty.' He speaks softly and reaches for the door handle.

I restrain from answering, unsure if I've genuinely pissed him off.

'Just one more question then.' He clears his throat and takes his hand off the door, turning back to face me.

'Oh yeah?' I punch.
'Can I take you out to dinner?'

14

Foisting Tim Shenton on me was a head-fuck enough. Now Harrington's wasted more precious time making me answer questions from a Fleet Street rapscallion, albeit one with warm brown eyes... but that's not the point! I'm drowning under layers and layers of men; it's the world's worst trifle.

My car is my haven, the drive home always an opportunity for ordering thoughts and letting off steam with my foot down.

There is the little Elkins update to tell Mum about today, at least. Anything, or – in this case with Tim Shenton – *anyone* that gets Elkins saying more words out loud is a positive. Might mention the string habit too. I probably was a bit harsh on Robbie for not revealing that, but at the same time he and Chi just don't approach the whole project with enough intensity.

There's still something not right about Shenton too. That question: *Why are you here, Miss Rose?* keeps rattling around my head. It felt as if he was asking but answering it too. Posed with fascination, but with no compassion for me whatsoever. I don't have the words to articulate the contradictions, but it's stayed with me.

I'll see what Mum has to say. She's always good at re-grounding things around Sam – clear thinking in the maelstrom.

My stomach growls and I squeeze the accelerator down a touch harder. Mum was going to the butcher's today, wasn't she? That should mean sausages and mash tonight. I really hope it does. My tummy squeals in agreement. It was always three sausages per plate growing up, but I insist on her cooking four nowadays. Minimum.

Parked up, I shiver against the evening breeze as I pace from the car to the house. Definitely time to dig out a thicker jacket now September's rolling in.

I twist the key and bundle in. The warm air from the radiator is a hug as I shut the door behind me. No waft of onion gravy though; no kitchen smells at all. Coat off and into the lounge. Maybe...

I stop.

'MUM!'

Panic drenches me like scalding water.

Mum is on the floor, face down. A half-empty bottle of prescription painkillers lies spilled next to her tiny, motionless hand.

15

A paramedic in the back of the ambulance is explaining we're almost at the hospital when I notice her blink.

'Mum! Mum!' I squeeze the hand I haven't stopped holding.

'Mrs Whirberth, can you hear me?' the male medic asks.

A little nod.

The shattering relief cleaves me open. I'm not sure if it's fifteen or twenty times I thank that young man. Even amid the tears and drowning emotion, I can sense his relief at getting to pass this mad, soggy woman and her mother on to the doctors inside.

I scurry after them as they wheel her trolley around a corridor labyrinth, into a room for more checks, staff in blue shirts and white coats milling around.

They think she's broken her wrist, but nothing more serious. No head injuries. And to see Mum's eyes, wide and observant as she traces the kerfuffle around her, it feels to me like they're right.

X-ray: fracture confirmed. Left arm rather than right. Thank goodness! Her world's small enough without losing the ability to write.

Off to a ward where she must wait for a doctor to talk us through next steps. We are finally alone.

'Did you try to take all your Tramadol?' I ask immediately. She deserves time to settle, to come to terms with what's just happened. But I cannot wait.

She doesn't shake her head. But her eyes scream *NO* and also *How could you even ask me that?*

'The bottle was on the floor,' I tell her.

She raises her good arm and sticks up her index finger. One. She means she took one tablet.

'You tripped while walking?' I suggest.

She shrugs: *I don't remember.*

'I honestly thought you...' The words are too hard to say, my throat thickens and closes. I drag my chair right up next to her and put my forehead on her shoulder. Her left hand is all bandaged up but it could have been so much worse. She strokes the back of my hand with her other thumb.

I sleep in the chair next to her bed all night. OK, that's a lie. I sit in the chair next to her bed all night, not sleeping, petrified by how close we were to the worst. The hard chair doesn't help either – it's about as comfortable as rickets. And the smells! Whiffs of alcohol gel, chlorine and patients' involuntary bowel movements all take turns to invade my nostrils.

Mum has a precautionary scan in the morning to double-check there's still no bleed on her brain. I contemplate asking a couple of young, strong porters to wheel me in after her, see if they can spot any permanent damage done to my back from that bloody chair.

A middle-aged female doctor speaks to me bluntly while I'm waiting for Mum to be discharged. 'The wrist will heal. But if this happens again and she breaks something more serious, the chances of recovery plummet. No one likes losing independence, but if she doesn't take care, to be brutal, the next fall may be her last.'

We get a taxi home, both as silent as each other. Once back, I half-carry her up to bed and text Chi explaining I have to stay home today and look after Mum. Then I collapse into my own bed, exhausted. And yet sleep still doesn't come. Useless, circular questions orbit my mind. What if she had died? What if it happens again? What if tomorrow's not the day? The doctor's words haunt me too: 'The next fall may be her last.'

I've been so focused on Harrington's threats, I've been ignoring the other way this all ends: in desolation. The worst way.

Anxiety crushes me, borrowed time closing in on all sides. I cannot afford a day off. I get back up, tiptoe into the spare room and pull open a large ring binder of evidence from Elkins' case.

16

'How's your mum?' Chi asks, taking a big swig of her Sauvignon blanc.

'OK. Struggling to sign with a broken wrist but... OK,' I reply.

We're at our favourite bougie bar – Ava's – with its huge windows showing off a panoramic view of the Tyne and waiters in tight black shirts and ridiculous cream bow ties endlessly offering us olives and come-hither smiles. At the centre of our spotless, white marble table is a candle radiating a warm scent of lemongrass. My Chianti, served in a glass the size of a cauldron, is so moreish I might marry it.

'You going to take tomorrow off too?' She checks. 'You should.'

'Two days is definitely enough. Time ain't stopping.'

Chi traces her finger around the top of her glass, passing judgement but not comment.

I shouldn't even really have come out for a drink, but we'd booked it weeks ago and Mum's been upset with herself, feeling like she's a burden to me. I've reassured her a million times it's not the case, but with Tuesday's fall on top of everything else, she's more fragile emotionally than usual, so when I hinted I was going to skip tonight's drinkies she basically pleaded with me to go. If me sipping wine with my best friend is going to make my mum happy, then I'll do it. I'm such a bloody trooper!

And to be honest, now I'm here, I'm so glad I did come. The change of scene, the lack of demands, the excuse to get dressed up... I can feel my mind taking a well overdue gasp of breath.

I still can't stop myself talking shop, though. 'Have I missed much?'

Chi shakes her head. 'Shenton's still bullying Joe, but talking to Elkins. Gets a bit out of him but nothing juicy.'

'Is Robbie...?'

'Yessss, Robbie typed up all the transcripts for you to read.' She rolls her eyes. I'm so predictable.

I chink my humongous glass against hers and beam.

'Finding your mum like that must have been horrendous,' Chi poses, much more serious.

I meet her eye and nod. I don't want to relive it. She gets that. 'We just need to find Sam,' I add to conclude the silent conversation.

She clinks her glass against mine the same way I did to her. 'D'you want a distraction?'

'Always.'

She smirks, but only for a second. 'There's actually something I've been wanting to talk to you about, Em.'

'I'm not doing shots on a Thursday, babes.'

No smirk this time. 'You know in London, when you went back to the hotel room?'

'Yeah.'

'And I stayed at the bar?'

'Look,' I state, putting my hands up in surrender. 'If this is some sex confession let's just take it as read. What happens between a desperate woman and two consenting cockneys is none of...'

'I didn't sleep with them! Eww!' She snaps, looking at me as if I'm an idiot.

'Alright, what then?'

'I didn't sleep with *them*,' she says deliberately.

'You just slept with one of them?'

She shakes her head and twizzles her glass round, fixated on the stem. Glancing up to see my face asking *who then?* she mutters: 'Someone else.'

'Who?' I demand, taking another sip and slouching back.

Another peek up from her glass. My gaze is fixed on her.

She doesn't speak.

'Who?'

She peers round the plush lounge, as if an MI5 agent might be recording every word. 'Don't make me say it,' she whispers, her eyes lost between mischief and guilt.

I study her. Why the weirdness? This isn't like Chi. Who on earth could she have slept with that she's so worried I'll judge her about?

Unless...

'No,' I whisper back, shaking my head at a frantic speed.

She contorts her face as if bracing for a punch.

'*No*, Chi. Please. No. Not...'

'Don't say it!' she begs.

'Harrington!' I explode.

Her mouth twists, sucking an invisible lemon; she manages a tiny nod of admission.

'I'm going to be sick,' I tell her, not even half joking. 'What the *actual*...'

'Don't!' she says, pointing her index finger up to stop me.

Downing the rest of her wine, she readjusts, sits up and prepares her rebuttal. 'He called saying he was still at his members' club in Soho. Invited me to join him.'

Lost for words, I listen, trying to work out if this is just a hideous story for the ages or if it actually has any ramifications for the project and Elkins.

'So, I used it as an excuse to ditch those two dweebs at the bar. Three or four drinks later and he's saying he's booked a room upstairs. Asks if I want to go up and have another drink.'

I don't think this is a problem for the Hive. I mean, if anything, it's good. The organ grinder in thrall to one of the monkeys. We can use that. He'll be more amenable, maybe. Except he wasn't to me on Zoom. He was drooling over Chi, though. I noticed that. A tsunami of drool.

'He was charming,' Chi goes on, increasingly defensive as I fail to find any words in the whole English language. 'When you're not provoking him, he can be fun.'

'He's got a wife and kids,' I finally spew, recrimination saturated in condemnation.

'That's just for the cameras. The marriage is over.'

'Oh, Chi, come on!'

'It was a one-off, it's not an affair,' she returns to a whisper, though a far more scorned one. 'I'm just saying, I don't think she's going to be bothered.'

'He's absolute slime. Did he pressure you?'

'No! He was very chilled. Before anything happened, he said he'd call me a cab if I wanted. Said he'd had a great evening regardless,' she informs me.

'But erections speak louder than words?'

'Well...' She pauses, eyes aflame. 'Yeah!'

She giggles; I don't.

'You are literally unbelievable,' I conclude.

'Oh, please. No more sanctimonious rubbish. I did it. It's over.' You can see in her eyes that she's relieved to have told me.

'Has he been OK with you since?'

'Yeah, really nice.'

'Of course he has. Urgh, grim,' I fume. 'I bet he's hung like a seahorse.'

'Actually, he was pretty impressive when it comes to all...'

'My bad, my bad! I immediately regret asking.' Draining my Chianti, I turn around. 'I need another one for the shock.'

The bar manager spots me and comes over to top us both up.

I turn back to Chi. 'I suppose if you can tell me something that heinous, I'll fess too. You know that reporter bloke from *The Times*? He sort of asked for my number after the interview.'

'No!' She inflates with excitement. 'And did you give it to him?'

'I got him to put his number in my phone. Said I'd think about it.'

'And?'

'Yeah... I don't have time.'

'Em. Make time!' Chi orders, tugging at the silver crescent moon-shaped pendant on her necklace.

'I literally can't. If we're shut down, I'll have all the time. But right now – nah.'

'You *need* distracting right now. Go for a coffee, at least.'

'I don't even think I like him. He's a bit annoying, like... he probably still does Wordle every day. That kinda vibe.'

'Oh, stop! Message him.'

I grunt to signal I won't be doing that.

'How long is it since you last, y'know...?'

'None of your business.'

'Exactly. Too long.' Chi grins.

'So we've gone from coffee to sex in ten seconds?'

'Can you imagine! Not even Harrington's that good.'

I let out a bark of laughter, drawing the silent ire of far more subdued tables around us.

'Shagging is not the answer to everything.'

'Neither's chastity.'

'He probably lives in London, anyway. It's a non-starter.'

I get up and announce I'm going to the loo – give my would-be pimp a beat to cool down.

When I get back to the table, however, she's got a dreadful, sheepish smirk superglued to her face.

'What?'

'I've done something,' she admits – unnerving simper still intact.

'What?'

She slides her phone towards me. Except it's not her phone – it's mine. I must have left it on the table.

'No! No Chi, you can't just...'

'It's not my fault your password's 1-2-3-4,' she remonstrates. 'I got it on the second try.'

Guessing at what she's done, I open WhatsApp and feel my heartrate accelerate into the ceiling as I'm proved right.

I read the message out loud: 'Hi Leon, how about dinner? Marlow's in Gateshead is nice if you're bringing your wallet. Winky face.'

'Whoops!' Chi says, beaming like a Cheshire prat.

'Winky face! This is *not* funny.'

Drowning in laughter, Chi tells me it is, in fact, very funny.

I should text him straight back. Apologise and explain it was a prank.

But I don't.

17

My arrival in the interview room goes unacknowledged by Elkins.

Assuming his natural form – hunched forward, staring at the floor – the jagged scar on top of his bald head looks almost too deep to be real.

'Your father gave you that, yes?' I nod at his scalp.

Those cadaverous eyes look up. 'Just as much as last time you asked.'

'When did the physical abuse start?'

'I don't remember a time without it.'

Engagement, good.

'How did your mum deal with it?'

'With him hitting me or her?'

'Both,' I clarify.

'He'd hit her, but not beat her. With me, she'd pretend she hadn't heard or seen,' he says, taking a deep breath and shuffling in his chair, sitting up straighter.

'Did she tend to you afterwards? The cuts and bruises?'

He snaps into that high-pitched squeak he uses to imitate

his mother. '*Ooh have you fallen over again? Poor thing, poor thing. A hot bath for you I think.*'

A shiver slips down my spine. His eyes roll up in his head as he does it, as if he's genuinely lost in the memory for a moment. It's hard not to wonder if he ever fell into the alter ego when Sam was with him; how terrifying that must have been, locked up, alone with this unhinged man, screeching in an old woman's voice.

'Did you ever tell her what your dad had done?' I maintain my tone, hoping he'll continue living in the mirage of his past a second longer, but he's already back in the room.

'If he wasn't in earshot, yeah. Changed nothing.'

'You were fifteen when she died?'

'Why ask me questions you already—'

'How did your father react to her dying?' I continue.

'Badly.'

'How did he show that?'

'Drank more, got hot more.'

'Hot?'

'Angry,' he mutters.

'But you'd already started coming back later after school, spending time at the library.'

'If I timed it right the library would close at 8 p.m., I'd pick up a couple of sarnies they'd chucked out at Safeway and get home to him already passed out.'

Sustaining these rare open exchanges long enough to unearth something pertinent to Sam is so fraught – like racing towards the last train home and never quite making it to the carriage before the doors close. I daren't ask him anything about any of the tiny potential clues we might have. He'd know we were spotting things – and shut down completely. But trying to join dots while not alerting him to any of them is as painstaking as it is inefficient.

'I've been very honest with you before about the affective psychopathic traits you display. Do you think the absence of your mother in your teens informs the way you approach relationships now?'

'You've decided for me,' he derides.

'What do *you* think though?'

He shrugs, a gesture I usually see far earlier.

Mustn't lose him. 'How did you get on with your brother?'

'I loved him.'

Wasn't expecting that. 'But then you killed him?' I probe.

'It's complicated,' he grunts.

'Enlighten me.'

Shake of the head.

Quick... another line... 'What kinds of books did you read at the library?'

'Fiction at first. Got through stuff quick, they got to know me. By sixteen it was history, biographies.'

To teach himself in this way, to seek out and absorb complicated information so naturally without tutoring is extraordinary. Such autodidacticism is so rare and so daunting to go up against. 'You picked up philosophy too...'

'Eventually,' he says, eyes glued to his lap again, the scar on his head staring straight at me.

'Nietzsche specifically?'

'At some point,' he replies, weary.

'I was reading a bit of his stuff,' I explain. A whopper of an understatement. I've consumed enough Nietzsche to give a Reith Lecture on the man. He's the closest thing Elkins has to a spiritual guru. '"The world is will to power and nothing besides",' I quote. 'Is that something you believe?'

Another shrug.

'Was that why you took them? The ultimate pow—'

'It's not power over others, it's power over self,' he growls, a peeved glance up, his arms fidgeting for the first time in their restraints as his face flushes.

Too direct, too confrontational. Move on.

'So, you were going to the library after school. Where was your brother?'

'At home.'

'Did your dad beat him too?'

He stops twitching. No answer. Eyes back down. I let the question hang. But even by his own high standards, he is resolute to offer no hint whatsoever.

'Did your dad always drink?'

'Yeah.'

'Always get aggressive afterwards?'

'Mm-hmm.'

'What was he angry about?'

Those weak, emaciated shoulders twitch up and down once more.

'Try harder,' I tell him.

His eyes flash red. '*You* try harder.'

'What are we talking? Beer? Wine?'

'Well, he wasn't gargling crème de menthe in the bathroom, was he?' he quips, letting out a snort.

I hate it when he laughs. Sam doesn't get to laugh. Sam doesn't get to enjoy company or memories or funny asides. I want to scream at Elkins so loud it drowns out that snigger and any other joke he'd ever dare to tell for the rest of his life.

Instead, I squeeze my jaw closed so tightly my molars ache.

Looking up, he drops the half smile and answers again: 'Spirits and lager mostly.'

'Alone?' I murmur, barely keeping it all inside.

'Yeah.'

'Did you ever give *them* alcohol?'

Silence.

Don't get in your own way! You'll lose him.

'How much did your dad drink a day? A bottle of spirits? More?'

He shuts his eyes and swallows. 'Being an alcoholic isn't drinking a bottle of vodka a day, it's needing to know there's another bottle in the cupboard. That's what I observed anyway.'

'Did he ever do anything else to you except hit you?'

'Like what?' he says, insulted. 'Sexual? No.'

'What about put you in a cage?'

'We're done here.'

Voice rising in pitch and volume, I lean as far forward as I can: 'Did you beat them – the same way your father beat you?'

Silence and navel-gazing.

'Your dad beat you, you beat your brother, it went too far, and you've been replacing him over and over ever since.'

Nothing.

Groundhog Day. Groundhog Week. Groundhog Month.

* * *

I want to go back into the office, go through the transcript, catch up with my colleagues, check if Elkins has said anything else to Shenton in my absence. But no sooner have I stepped through the door, Chi is marching me back out to the security room, ordering the warders to fetch Tim Shenton, then marching me back to the interview room. 'After what happened to your mum, I don't think you should be working at all,' she says. 'But it's Friday, so since you are here, there's no way I'm going home for the weekend without a recording to send Harrington. He'll bollock us both, otherwise.'

'I thought you liked him disciplining you,' I quip.

She gives me the finger and leaves me to my fate.

'I'm surprised not to have seen more of you, Miss Rose,' Shenton says in his oddly well-spoken accent, once he's in and I've triple-checked the guards have handcuffed him properly this time. He sits very loosely, thin arms dangling in their restraints, bright eyes hinting at a good night's sleep.

'We thought we'd give you a chance to get to know your fellow inmates,' I make up.

A small, demure smile curls up his lips which he holds just long enough to feel creepy.

'But you're a bully,' I tell him, looking past him to my mental portraits of Sam on the back wall. *Just get some conversation out, whizz through a few questions; no need to get emotionally involved. Get the recording to Harrington, then we can get back to Elkins.*

'I don't think that's fair, Miss Rose,' he says, overly sincere.

'The way you treat Joe isn't fair.'

'He tried to lump me with the worst cell. I owe him nothing,' Tim states, grimacing as if he's trodden in dog dirt. 'And he's too clingy. Growing up in state institutions, the clingy kids were always best avoided. Give them an inch and they take a mile.'

'A mile of what?'

'My time, my space, my anything. I'm not an emotional support blanket. What's in it for me?'

None of us in the office have witnessed Tim using his shower since he joined Beeswell. His dark greasy hair reflects the white light above us even more than last time. He flicks his neck to get the fringe out of his eyes so he can look at me more intently, then he goes on: 'He's also guilty of eight murders. I shouldn't be in here. It's a huge injustice to me, huge!'

'We don't allow musical instruments in Beeswell, so you can put away the tiny violin.'

'You're a unique communicator, Miss Rose.'

Tim Shenton most definitely treats people based on what he can extract from them. Classic antisocial behaviour disorder. Joe can offer him nothing, so is ostracised. I, on the other hand, could give his trial defence a real boost, so am treated with mild reverence.

'Yet you're civil with Elkins. Chatty even.'

'You noticed,' he smirks. 'I'm glad.'

'Why?'

'Because I said I can read people and you doubted me.'

'Did I?' I query, unimpressed.

'You could use me, Miss Rose. I'm a real team player.' His voice is at its most courteous and heartfelt. The diction clear, the tone precise, it's as if he's in a job interview, focussed 100 per cent on convincing me he's the right man for the role.

'You're a convicted paedophile. I'm here to work out if you killed Andrew Stride. I can't see much to work on together, unless it's a confession.'

'Short-sighted, Miss Rose,' he states, dropping the deference for a split-second.

I study him but make no comment. What's he getting at? His words sound like he wants attention and relational contact. But his demeanour, his look, his impassive self-ease all make me feel like he doesn't have any human connection to me whatsoever.

Why are you here, Miss Rose?

That horrible question hits afresh, because it had been delivered with that exact same surface-level concern atop an ocean of apathy. If it is all social mirroring – learned behaviour without any true emotion underneath – then he may be one of the most psychologically extraordinary individuals I've ever met. The media would label him a true psychopath. Traits he would most likely possess would be a complete lack of compunction for hurting people and excellent social observation skills, but all emotions would be fabricated, made up in the moment with the sole aim of extracting whatever he wants. An arch-manipulator, a compulsive liar, and a terrifying person to get on the wrong side of. Could he be that odious? I'm still testing the theory in my head when he loses patience and speaks again.

'I've decided what I'd like as my benefit.'

'Your benefit?' I double-check, confused.

'Yes. Frank Elkins gets his books. Joe Okorie has his chessboard. I am due a benefit also, am I not?'

'Go on.'

'I don't want to be chained to this chair when we chat. It's uncomfortable.'

'You are chained there for my protection as well as to keep the parameters of the study consistent for each inmate.'

'Any consistency is already compromised by giving Elkins and Okorie personalised benefits. Don't make weak excuses Miss Rose. And anyway, I pose no threat.'

'You've been charged with murder.'

'Of which I am innocent.'

'Tim, you're a convicted paedophile at the very least. I can't have you unrestrained in here alone with me. You can have your *arms* free from next time onwards. Final offer.'

'So be it.' He looks off to the side for a second. 'Are you aware of the link between abuse as a child and unorthodox attraction patterns in adulthood?' There's a whiff of annoyance at my lack of effort to engage, or maybe it's frustration that his superficial charm hasn't quite got him what he'd wanted.

'Some victims of child abuse become paedophiles. Yes, the correlation can be significant.'

'My tastes have been affected by actions perpetrated on me as a child. I can't help that any more than you can help being heterosexual.'

'Trying to blame your decision to watch child porn as anyone's fault except your own is not clever psychology, it's spineless. And how do you know I'm heterosexual?'

'I keep telling you, I'm perceptive.'

I let out a loud laugh. 'And modest too.'

Missing the dig, he visibly sits up taller at the fact he's sparked any kind of reaction. 'I like people-watching.'

'Why?'

'I'm good at it.'

'You like seeing other people give stuff away through body language. Meanwhile, you're more adept at hiding your secrets, yes?'

'Miss Rose, I am innocent.'

'You've blamed your paedophilia on the fact you were abused. I'm not sure that alone has convinced me that you are innocent of murder.'

'What will convince you?' He purrs, his cool intact.

'I will make a psychological assessment based on our observations of you over the next few weeks. I will stick to my role. So, let's get back to it, shall we? Andrew Stride. Your stepsister's little boy.'

'Miss Rose. This is still a topic I struggle with.'

'You know we have to go there.'

'Not today, Miss Rose. Maybe after a few more...'

'Why do you get so nervous talking about him?'

He pauses, looking at me. It's a horrible look, choosing

when, not if, to crush me. Omniscient and forensic at the same time. *Why are you here, Miss Rose?*

Fine. If he refuses to talk about it, I'm not wasting any more time. Harrington can hear I tried. That's it for the day.

I break his gaze and get up to leave. Take the power back.

'You use sarcasm and put-downs to provoke us.' Tim's voice is assertive, his stare unwavering as he draws me back in. 'But you're also harsh because it forces you to stay sharp. No room for complacency when you're so critical of others.'

I stay standing but don't want to interrupt or leave for fear any sort of action will confirm he's right. But then does staying silent make me look even more defeated?

He goes on: 'You've worked out that being mean makes people like you more in a world where no one says what they actually think. Rudeness equals honesty, so people trust you. You also know that human nature is to seek approval, so the harsher you are, the harder we'll try to impress you, to tell you what you want to hear. You are compelling, Miss Rose; single-minded. And humble too. You are the only doctor I know who insists on being called *Miss*.'

'Cheap route to equivalence,' I tell him.

'Of course,' he nods, appreciative of my candour.

Then his eyes open too wide. He knows something, he has something. And somehow just from looking at me he understands that I know he's getting through too. An airless freeze clamps my chest. He can't know. Yet he does.

Roused by raw instinct, I move to the door and hit a lonely button on the wall – the switch that stops the relay from the interview room to the office. Whatever this man has to say next, I want it contained within these four walls.

I turn back to Tim Shenton.

And then he says it. No more than a whisper but it hits like a cannon. 'Who did Elkins kill?'

His mouth curls into a gentle smile and he finally looks away, his performance complete.

I look away too, fearing he'll notice my eyes begin to reflect the harsh lights above. But my photos hanging on the walls have vanished. I can't reach them in the panic.

'Your father? But he liked them young, didn't he? Boyfriend? Hmm, not sure you'd show this kind of resolve for a callow sweetheart.' His eyes fizz again. 'Brother.'

I'm trapped, terrified this is profoundly bad for my search for Sam, but not able to articulate why.

'It's your laugh, you see,' Tim explains, luxuriating. 'It clatters down the corridor from what I assume is your office; it booms around this room. It rattles around the whole complex if I'm honest. But never with Elkins. And yet you spend *so* much time with him. I ask... why? And why couldn't you say his nickname the first time we met? Okorie was the Ghost Killer, but you couldn't bring yourself to say Elkins was The Dentist. And yet you wanted to know everything I thought about him. Now it makes sense.'

'I got your predecessor, Petty; I can focus on more than one man.'

'You're shaking, Miss Rose,' he observes.

'I'm not!' I snap, regretting everything about the reaction the millisecond it's out.

Shenton continues to leer. I look away again. Those horrible dark eyes bore too deep.

Then he lands his second devastating blow, in that same, self-assured undertone. 'Elkins doesn't know, does he? You're the sister of a victim but you're keeping it from him.'

I need to play it down, act unaffected, but the whirring in my head is accelerating and I can feel the blood plummeting out of my face. Shenton sees it, knows it, exploits it. I realise now that's what Tim Shenton does, what he is. But it's all too late.

'Understanding people isn't about science, Miss Rose. You can have all the modern tools in the world but the best thing for getting under the skin is still a scalpel. I am a scalpel.'

'You're deeply manipulative and I'm not playing,' I clarify, reaching for the door and pulling at the handle.

Tim's voice is cold: 'So I can tell Elkins about you?'

I stay facing the door but don't move. My hand grips the handle, tremors whipping up my arm as I stand, impotent and beaten.

I turn back. 'Please don't. My mum needs...' I catch myself. This man will use *anything*. The faintest vulnerability. I swallow hard. I can barely generate the power to beg: 'Please don't tell him. We can sort this out. Just... please.'

I stalk out – a torrent of nausea almost beating me to the toilet cubicle.

18

If anything is going to take my mind off that horrific encounter with Tim Shenton, it's going to be sharp, immediate physical pain. I choose that in the form of trying to get into an old pair of heels.

Agony! Trotters squashed into thimbles.

Mum's amused at least, as I rock and roll around the sofa trying to pull them on. She picks up a mini whiteboard, leaning her strapped-up wrist on top to keep it steady as she scribbles:

What's his name?

'Whose name? I'm seeing Chi.'
Scribble, scribble. Holds board up.

Heels, full make-up…

Damn it, Mum. Always too observant by half.

'Mmm,' I grumble, utterly rumbled. 'Leon Courtney-Peltz. The journalist who I did the chat with.'

Scribble.

Is he posh?

'Not as posh as he sounds.'
Scribble, scribble.

Is he trying to get a story?

'I hope not,' I say, having had the same thought myself. 'If it does seem like that, I won't see him again.'
Mum puts the board down on the coffee table to write something a little longer. I get off the sofa, having finally coerced my shoes on and read the message over her shoulder as she writes.

He could do a special report appealing for info about Sam.

I rub my hand over her back but have to look away as her hopeful eyes peer up. 'Yeah, maybe,' I offer. I feel bad for leading her on; but that is not the particular agenda I have in mind for Leon Courtney-Peltz.

* * *

Chi really is outrageous. Marlow's – the restaurant she suggested Leon take me to – demands the kinds of prices only royalty and TikTok influencers can afford. I wonder which one Leon secretly is.

I arrive bang on 7.30 p.m. but he's already sitting at a table on the far side of the room, wearing a smart grey jacket over a casual white shirt. He gets up to herald my arrival, revealing a pair of well-cut jeans and a tan-brown belt that matches his shoes.

'Hey,' he says brightly, putting a soft hand on each of my hips and kissing me on the cheek. He moves a step back then adds: 'You look amazing.'

I glance down at my cute black wrap dress and then back at him. 'Thanks.'

Chi gave me a pep talk earlier about my tendency towards constant belittlement and emasculation and how – funnily enough – men don't really like that on first dates. It's not the first time she's had to remind me of this. I want to tell Leon that leaving a second button open on his shirt screams 'divorced dad on holiday'. I want to tell him I only date black belts. I want to tell him his hair makes Boris Johnson's thatch look tidy. But Chi's made me promise. So I take my seat, give another smile, and wait for him to summon a more socially palatable topic.

'Not sure where to start,' he says, tracing his index finger and thumb along the sides of his chin.

'Alcohol, usually,' I reply, plucking the wine list from the middle of the small, immaculately laid table.

He laughs. 'I mean I don't know what to say first.'

'A drink might loosen the tongue, so...' I waggle the wine list in the air.

'I get the hint.'

Like he's got some telepathic agreement with the waiters, he looks towards one and they scurry over. They recommend two 'full-bodied reds'. Leon picks the more expensive one then turns back to me.

'Was half expecting you to stand me up,' he admits.

'Just doing my bit for charity.' Chi wouldn't approve of the joke, but I want to have *a bit* of fun this evening.

Leon's less cocksure than I'd expected in a romantic setting.

It's disarming, removes the need to be on acerbic top form myself. I feel my guard lower a smidge.

'Why don't I jump straight to what I was going to say?' I suggest, warming to my role as the more confident, forthright individual at the table.

'Interesting,' he says, gesturing for me to continue.

'But this is 100 per cent, totally only between us. This isn't a story. At least our conversation isn't.'

He nods his head in agreement as the expensive vino arrives. The waiter takes out the cork and pours a dram into Leon's glass. Why do the men always get to see if the wine's corked? Why aren't women's mouths deemed suitably evolved to notice chunks of solid floating in their Pinot noir? Anyway, Leon gives it the nod and two hearty glasses are poured.

'It's Tim Shenton,' I explain.

'Is he guilty?' Leon fires back.

'Don't know,' I say, dismissive of the interruption. 'But you might be able to find out.'

'How so?'

'Harrington's admitted to me... and again this is all off the record. But Harrington's basically admitted the case against Shenton is weak. Police didn't pass enough on to the CPS. Bit slapdash. So he wants me to do the heavy lifting for them. Get a confession without the trial. Save the investigation's blushes.'

Leon tries to butt in. 'Yeah, I know. But that's not why Harrington wants to avoid a trial...'

I'm not done though. 'I can't uncover hard evidence through my work at Beeswell unless Shenton's forthcoming. And he very much isn't. But Harrington's threatening us with closure if we don't get him sent down. So I was thinking... Hold on. Did you say you already know all this?'

'Yeah...' Leon shrugs. His smirk an equal and opposite reaction to my befuddlement.

'How?'

'Because I know why Harrington's so obsessed with this Tim Shenton case.'

'Why?'

'Whoever killed Andrew Stride filmed it, right?' he asks, clearly knowing the answer.

'Yeah.'

'Do you know how it came to the authorities' attention, that video?'

'It was sent to the poor mum.'

He shakes his head. 'Before that.'

'Just tell me,' I snap.

'It was downloaded off the dark web onto one of Harrington's government-issued devices – by his son.'

My eyeballs come a fraction away from breaching their sockets.

'I know,' Leon says. 'His son's got previous for underage downloads, but Harrington's always got it brushed away. It was one of his old work phones or something this time, he'd passed it on to his lad months earlier. Obviously, the son thought it'd had any tracking stuff uninstalled or whatever, but he was dead wrong. So he starts streaming all this dodgy, violent shit and it raises a whopping red flag. Some MI5 spook spots it, seizes the device and they find the Andrew Stride video downloaded on there.'

'How do you know all this?' I ask, unsure whether I want it to be true or merely a vicious morsel of gossip.

'Colleague of mine was at Shenton's plea and case management hearing for the Andrew Stride murder. The origin of the video came up. It was already under tight reporting restrictions.

Harrington had got an injunction for his son early doors, so we were forbidden from printing a word of it. The judge then clarified, though, that the video is still admissible as evidence. If it is used by the prosecution, which obviously it will be, then the injunction will be lifted so it doesn't interfere with a fair trial.'

'So the only way for Harrington to keep his son's role out of the news is to avoid a trial all together?' I clarify.

Leon leans back, lifts his wine with a cultured swirl of the glass, dips his nose over the rim for a second to embrace the aroma, then allows himself a measured sip.

I, on the other hand, knock the whole glass-worth back. What does this mean for the project? Maybe it's good news. Harrington could get the sack. A new Justice Secretary might be kinder, more human. But what if we fail to get a confession and Harrington just closes us out of spite before the trial even starts. His obsession with Shenton's case makes so much more sense now. He's got skin in the game – does that make him more dangerous? I need a week to process it all. I need to tell Mum, I need to tell Chi. I need to lie down. All of those options are sadly unavailable, so instead I refill my glass and take another large gulp.

The waiter comes back over to take our food order. With so little headspace left I default to the safest, tastiest meal known to humanity: rib-eye. Rare. Triple-cooked chips. Peppercorn sauce.

Leon swills his own wine again. 'You're right that the police investigation was slap-dash though. Because Harrington had tried to sabotage that too. He hoped if there wasn't enough to charge Shenton then there'd be no case *or* trial, making it easier to keep the injunction in place. But he underestimated how easy it was to get evidence on Shenton, so it's gone ahead anyway.

Leaving him where he is now, praying that you get him a confession.'

I feel logic filtering back into my mind, one grain at a time. 'Can't you just report all this anyway? It's absolutely disgusting.'

'He's *the* justice sec *and* he's got an injunction. We'd be the ones breaking the law. The only hope is, as I said, the judge lifting the restrictions at trial.'

'Vile,' I whisper.

'I know, right?'

'But it does mean...' I pause, working out my thought process afresh. 'That what I was going to pitch to you still kind of stands.'

'Pitch?' Leon leans forward on his elbows. The move brings with it a waft of his aftershave, sweet but masculine. I lean closer too.

'Two pitches actually,' I tease, feeling it easier all of a sudden to park Leon's absolute bombshell. That's a problem for tomorrow's Emy. Right now, my mission remains the same.

'Two pitches, now?'

'Yeah. Pitch one: we need more wine.' I pour us both another glass and jiggle the empty bottle in the air in that way one only does when one's enjoyed the lion's share of said bottle.

'Of course,' he states in pretend-earnest concern. He glances at the mind-reading waiter again, who scuttles over and a fresh bottle of the same wine is ordered. 'And the second pitch?' Leon asks, resting his cupped fists under his stubbly chin.

'I've already got my work cut out at Beeswell without trying to crack an inmate who refuses to admit he's done anything wrong. What if you were to do some digging on Shenton? You could unearth some extra evidence. You pass that on to me, I pretend to Barnaby Harrington it's stuff we've unearthed at the project, makes it look like we're making progress. I could also use any extra evidence to strongarm Tim Shenton, make him feel he's better off confessing now than going into a trial he'll inevitably lose that will lead to a longer sentence.'

'What if he's innocent?' Leon rightly asks.

'It can work the same. You might find evidence that weakens the case so much it collapses. Harrington's happy, I get Shenton off my books. Basically, I just need someone to offload the Shenton case on so I can show Harrington we're making headway one way or the other, but so it doesn't derail the actual *progress* we're making with the original inmates.'

'So I do your job for you. What's in it for me?' Leon again rightly asks.

'Whether Shenton confesses or the trial gets canned, you can run a story highlighting the deficiencies in the original investigation either way. OK, I didn't know Harrington was to blame, but you don't even need to report that. You'd have an exposé on how murder investigations aren't fit for purpose, and – whether it boosts the case or kills it – how a half-decent journalist was able to find out more than the police.'

'Half-decent?' There's a slow upwards curl at the edges of his mouth.

'Sorry, quarter-decent.'

He sits back to contemplate.

'Dream scenario,' I go on, sensing I've not yet sealed the deal, 'You give me some banged to rights evidence that proves Shenton did it. I put said evidence to Shenton in such a way that convinces him to confess. You then get to write an exclusive piece about how this paedophile, child rapist is behind bars because of *The Times*' investigation. You don't need to mention the Harrington angle at all, but if, in the fallout that will inevitably follow, it does come out that his son was wrapped up in the Shenton case, then so be it. However you cut it, *The Times* and you come out with a golden egg.'

The waiter arrives with our food on pristine china plates, steam rising from the succulent beef.

'Considering you've only just heard the full story, you're thinking very fast,' Leon says.

I cut a hearty piece off my steak, raise it in a cheers-like action on my fork in front of him and eat it. It's exquisite, by the way.

He nods in the direction of my food. 'That steak's so rare it should be put up for auction.'

I look down at his plate. He ordered the same as me but wanted the meat cooked far longer. 'Yours is so well done it's basically "congratulations".'

He smirks; I smirk back.

A lull in conversation as we eat leaves my mind time to spin afresh. Harrington is just doing everything possible to protect his flesh and blood. Mum and I are doing the same. I sort of get his desperation to bury this case. The thought solidifies and I shudder. Stop that. Any empathy with Barnaby C. Harrington is, by definition, wrong.

'So what d'you think, Nancy Drew?' I check as I put down my knife and fork. 'Do some digging and if you find anything we both win. At the very worst you find nothing. No harm, no foul.'

'And there was me thinking you were just here for my electrifying company.'

'I get my fix of lunatics at work.'

'Have you ever thought about going into comedy?' He doesn't leave me space to reply. 'You shouldn't.'

I boom with laughter.

'There's a good chance that even if I do find something and

we publish it, Harrington will have the power to bury it and get us both sent to Siberia,' he adds.

'Feeling lucky, punk?'

He likes that. The corners of his eyes crease. We have a deal!

I swallow my delight, not wanting to give him the satisfaction. His brown eyes are alluring though. I'm still not sold on the thick, chaotic barnet, but that second button undone on his shirt looks more and more interesting. I take a daintier sip of my fresh glass of wine.

'After your interrogation of me the other day, I've got some quick-fire questions of my own for you,' I inform him.

'Only fair,' he says, raising his eyebrows and opening his arms to welcome the challenge.

'Age?'

'Forty-one.'

'Where do you live?'

'Up here, North-East. But I go down to London most weeks for the paper.'

'Sounds glam.'

'Fleet Street's not what it used to be.'

'When's your feature on me coming out?'

'Day after tomorrow. *Sunday Times Magazine*.'

I nod. 'Is it kind?'

'Buy a copy and see.'

'What if we don't uncover anything about Tim Shenton?'

'Then I've still had a lovely evening,' he says. Those dark eyes stay locked on me, waiting to see if I've got anything else to throw at him. A silence builds, neither of us wanting to look away.

We polish off the wine and skip dessert.

I don't sleep with him on our first date, however.

I sleep with him twenty minutes later, once we're back at his place.

19

Castling is the book move. Get the rook active and protect the king. Of course, if the computer then pushes the D pawn, Joe's lost another central square and his white-squared bishop becomes impotent. He could sacrifice the bishop and ruin the computer's pawn structure, but being down material so early in the game would be reckless. No – smarter to keep things simple. Always give your victim no need to worry until it's too late to escape. Joe plays the book move.

He takes a mental picture of the board, gets up from the table and walks towards the water cooler.

Tim is sitting at Frank's table, jabbering on about a sore tooth as he scribbles endlessly over empty squares on a crossword.

Joe desperately misses working his way through the puzzle pages each morning. He could ask Emy for a Sudoku book to keep under his bed. But part of the joy had been the routine, the sense of satisfaction when all the day's brainteasers had been beaten. And what has he done so wrong to be punished by Emy this way? Both Frank and Tim have been summoned to see her numerous times – but Joe? Nothing. Maybe he should request a meeting. He could say it was about the puzzles but really he just needs to be with her, to get a fresh waft of her perfume, to see those lovely, clever eyes looking at him. Her full attention devoted to him, and his to her.

For his part – despite being known as The Dentist – Frank is mostly ignoring Tim's wittering about teeth and trying to read his book. But if Joe ever tries to speak to Frank he gets told in no uncertain terms that he is not welcome. And yet he won't tell nasty Tim to shove off. Why?

Joe carries on towards the cooler and picks up a paper cup. 'Anyone want water?' he asks the room.

Frank, back turned, shakes his head. Tim doesn't respond but heaves himself up and walks over to the unattended chessboard.

'Doesn't look like you're doing very well,' he sneers.

'No, no, early stages yet,' Joe says, stalking back towards his seat as he sees his compatriot reach out at the screen.

He is too late, however. Tim taps several times on the electronic board and by the time Joe has swiped the intruding arm away, he has lost the white-squared bishop and also allowed the computer to fork his queen and king's side rook.

Joe slams a fist down on the table. 'NO! Come on!'

'What are you talking about? I've helped you out.' Tim pushes out a snicker.

'Why did you do that?' Joe pleads, his cry rising as it goes.

'Do what?' Tim scoffs, slinking away. 'If you were that good you'd still win.'

Joe picks up his cup of water and hurls it at his tormentor. The cup flies past Tim, however, and splashes at Frank's feet, causing him to snap round and swear.

'Sorry Frank, sorry Frank,' Joe gabbles.

'It's a game of chess, you twat,' Frank spits. 'Calm down.'

'He's doing it to upset me,' Joe replies, exasperated.

Tim retakes his own seat – a tennis umpire ready to adjudicate in a match he's just organised.

'Stop smirking!' Joe shouts at Tim, his voice wobbling.

'Calm down!' Frank growls.

'Oh yeah, take his side.' Joe stays standing, hands in the pockets of his tracksuit bottoms, nails digging into his thighs like eagle talons.

Frank turns back to his book, muttering under his breath. '"Let the doors be shut upon him, that he may play the fool nowhere but in his own house."'

'What was that?' Joe calls, indignation fuelling courage.

'It's from *Hamlet*.'

'Quoting things doesn't make you smarter than me,' Joe proclaims, nails still clamped tight to flesh in his pockets. '"Hatred stirs up conflict, but love covers over all wrongs." We can all quote things. It doesn't make—'

'Proverbs 10:12?' Frank interrupts with a patronising chuckle, not even deigning to turn and look at his adversary any more.

'Oh, you know the bible? Try acting like it then.' Defeat is already thick in Joe's throat.

Frank finally spins round to face Joe. 'How many women did you kill?'

'Eight,' Tim snipes from the sidelines.

'Exactly,' Frank says. '"Take the plank out of your own eye." Matthew 7:5.'

If this was a chess match, Joe would be knocking his king over right about now. His glassy eyes stare back, tensed jaw twitching but mouth clamped shut.

'Nothing? That's what I thought,' Frank adds. Tim tries to

share a nod with Frank but is ignored as the bigger man shifts back around and reopens his book.

Be cool, Joe. Be cool.

20

The three of us crowd around the screen with the wide-view angle of the common room, transfixed by the inmates' Monday morning contest.

'I thought Elkins was going to lamp Joe after he threw the water!' Robbie claims. His podgy knuckles rest on the desk as Chi and I stand with our arms crossed.

'It was weird what Elkins was saying to Shenton though, wasn't it?' I ponder.

'What?'

'Shenton asks Elkins the best way to remove a tooth and Elkins responds as if he has no idea.'

'*That's* what you got from all that just happened?' Robbie exclaims. 'They're bullying Joe left, right and centre. You need to get him in, reassure him.'

I block Robbie out. Tim Shenton was complaining about supposed toothache... he asked Elkins how to pull a tooth out... and Elkins acted as if he didn't know how to do it. Literally his signature. It was only for a second, then he changed his tune and gave Shenton a proper answer. But that pause, the immediate reaction, was as if he genuinely didn't know. Evidently the most ponderable and fascinating moment of this morning's Hive drama has whooshed right over my colleagues' heads.

'Please get Joe in, he'll be more than happy to see you.' Robbie grins. 'He must be busting by now.'

I grimace. Robbie's talent for spotting patterns in our inmates' behaviour is a curse rather than a blessing on this occasion. Precisely, he's spotted habits in the nocturnal habits of all the inmates. George Petty – and Tim Shenton, albeit based on fewer days observed – both like to pleasure themselves on a nightly basis. Elkins hasn't indulged at all – not once. But worst of all, Joe Okorie only seems to masturbate on evenings after I've interviewed him during the day. If knowledge is power, make me powerless!

'I need to get Elkins in, grill him on why he was playing dumb about the teeth,' I decide.

Robbie mutters something and slumps back into his seat. He plucks out some Hula Hoops from his bag, tears open the top and down both sides of the packet, then splays it open in a flat, silver-foil platter of salty, starchy goodness on the table. Turning away from us, he refocuses on Joe's Chess Cam, writing down the moves in his notebook as the inmate embarks on a new game.

I turn to Chi. *Is he annoyed?* my eyes ask.

She shrugs.

'We should get a transcript of all that aggro between them this morning,' I state emptily, waiting to see how Robbie responds.

He is unmoved, the crunch of Hula Hoops and the scratch of his pencil his only replies.

Chi throws her pen at him. 'Oi, grand master. The boss wants to brainstorm.'

'What's even the point of writing down his chess moves?' I ask. It's 9.43 a.m. on Monday morning and I'm already losing patience with him for the week.

'So I get a feel for what openings he uses, what his middle games are like, his strengths and weaknesses when he's playing with the black pieces,' Robbie explains as if it's obvious, not looking up.

Neither Chi nor I know what to say.

'I could watch him all day,' he adds.

'That *is* what you do.' The words slip out before I can stop them.

'Well somebody has to,' he fires back. I've lit the powder keg.

'And by that you mean...?'

'You ignore him constantly!' His hands white-tight as he snaps round. 'It's all Elkins, Elkins, fucking Elkins.'

'OK, so what have you got on Joe then?' I remonstrate, a little too high-pitched.

'What have *you* got?' He throws a disconsolate arm up. 'When was the last time you looked over his case, or read back over his transcripts, or downloaded a journal article to get some fresh ideas, or organised a call with an expert in borderline personality disorder to...'

'OK, Robbie,' Chi pacifies.

'No, let him go on,' I order.

He does. 'If time is running out here, stop focussing on the others. Joe is far more responsive. Plus, Elkins has fewer victims and one of them's already been found and another's his own brother. Joe has *eight* bodies not found. We could get the families answers. But you don't give a shit about that.'

The room falls silent, besides Robbie's shallow panting.

Maintaining eye contact, I swallow hard and keep my tone steady. 'I hear what you're saying Robbie. Thank you for being honest.' My one-two punch of the understanding words and dominating body language could mollify a starving piranha. 'Ten-minute breather, OK?'

Robbie pulls out his inhaler and puffs on it twice.

'Oh, but Robbie?' I call back as I reach the door to the office.

He looks up, sheepish.

'You will never know how much I care about the families of the victims.' I swing open the door and let it bang shut behind me.

I go outside to the car park to clear my head. Chi doesn't come immediately, which is good. She *should* check Robbie's OK. But eventually she joins me on a bench by the entrance to our unit.

There isn't a cloud in the sky but a stiff breeze sees her scrunch up her shoulders and snuggle up to me as she sits down.

'You should tell him about Sam,' she says softly. 'He'd get it. He's nice.'

'The more people who know, the harder it gets to...'

'You always say that, but if anyone deserves to know, it's Robbie,' she reasons.

I can't tell him. End of discussion.

'You underestimate him, y'know,' Chi says. 'When has he ever filed a transcript late, or failed to contribute to a group discussion?'

'He doesn't talk like a psychologist; he needs to learn.'

'I don't talk like a psychologist,' she points out.

'You're not meant to. He misses things because he's so focussed on Joe. Like when he forgot to mention Elkins using string to mark things.' I take in a huge breath and force it out hard.

'He still spotted it though, didn't he? But you put him down too much.'

'No, I don't!'

'Em, you put *everyone* down. You put *me* down all the time.'

'Not all the time... Sometimes I'm sleeping.'

Chi smiles but shakes her head. 'You must know that being positive is more likely to get the best out of him.'

'This is the first-date advice all over again.'

'Yeah, and the way you bounced into the office this morning, I can guess how well that went.'

I hold out a second longer as she raises her eyebrows with a filthy hint of mischief. My stern look crumbles and we burst out laughing. I kiss her on the cheek.

'Whatever you did with Leon, it worked,' she continues. 'Harrington was pleased with the article in the Sunday Times.'

'Urgh gross! Leon had already written it by the time we met up,' I correct her. I think about telling her that I gave Leon information regarding Tim Shenton; the challenge I set him. I think even more about telling her Harrington's ulterior motive – his son's complicity in the case. But can I mention any of it? She's slept with Harrington. She's slept with *Harrington*!

The grotesque news hits me afresh. Harrington – the enemy. The worst human outside of Beeswell. I can't help but fear there's 1 per cent of Chi that's now compromised. What if he calls for a booty call? What if she gets drunk and spills a secret? I want to tell her everything, but maybe I can't.

'Call in Joe,' she says on a completely different wavelength, rubbing my arm. 'Robbie could do with the win today.'

Not that you'd know it listening to Chi, but I made a big effort to improve my man-management skills prior to the Hive opening. I read several biographies of successful leaders in all sorts of fields: Barack Obama, Coco Chanel, Jürgen Klopp, Bill Gates, Emmeline Pankhurst.

In Obama's memoir he said one of the key features of his leadership was having a strong Number Two in Joe Biden and how during briefings with experts he'd make sure Biden was always the last voice in the room giving him forthright counsel, be it hopeful or harsh. Chi may be flawed, but she's still my last voice in the room.

I let out a long sigh and nod.

Robbie's all over Joe Okorie; Leon's digging into Tim Shenton.

I'd betray both good men for a single, concrete clue from Frank Elkins about my brother.

21

He can't help it... He must say it... The words whistle out of him like rose-petal blow darts. 'I've missed you, Emy!'

'Hello Joe,' she says with characteristic demure control as the interview room door shuts behind her.

'How are you, my love?'

'We've talked about this, Joe. Boundaries.'

Her dirty-blonde hair is pristine; that tight blue shirt and pin-striped jacket suit her figure so well. Joe thinks about telling her, but knows she gets funny and bashful when he showers her with too many compliments.

Be cool, Joe. Be cool.

He leans forward in his chair to meet her scent as it floats across the table. Lemons and lavender. She is breathtaking. The fabric below his waistband begins to shift. Unable to cross his legs – which are locked to the chair – he decides the best way to cover his protuberance is to stay hunched forward.

'We've got so much to catch up on,' he adds, grinning in hope of reciprocation.

'Yes, sorry. Been a busy time with the new inmate,' Emy explains. 'But here we are now, so...'

'I have to tell you my lov—Emy. I have to say I don't like Tim Shenton. I've been very low.'

'I saw what happened this morning with Shenton ruining your chess game,' she says.

Of course she did. No wonder she called him in here – it's to cheer him up. She's so kind and loving like that. The two weeks of agony and self-doubt that have tormented him as he waited for a fresh chat – a 'fresh date' as Joe secretly calls it in his head – has all washed away, replaced with a frenzied current of eros.

'You still haven't answered my question... How you are?' He teases, a playful timbre to his voice.

'I'm fine, thank you,' she confirms, matter-of-factly. 'Shall we begin?'

'Wherever you want.' He feels so comfortable, like he's in a warm bath luxuriating in the bubbles; safe, content, loved.

'At school, did you have much luck with the ladies?' she quizzes.

The question is a little abrupt, jolting Joe. 'Yeah, I did fine.' What else is a man supposed to say to such a question?

'Tell me about them. Your first kiss, your first love.'

He hates lying to her. He can't do it. Is this one of those games women play where you think they're genuinely interested in your answer but actually they're testing you, to see if you speak more warmly about another woman than you do about them? Joe's read about that in the paper before, in a dating column.

'You can be honest if you didn't actually have much luck with girls, Joe,' she says into his silence – soft, understanding. Maybe it's a relief to her that Joe wasn't so promiscuous growing up.

He gives a little nod at the floor, ashamed at having fibbed, worried Emy will be annoyed.

'There's no judgment,' she soothes, sweet as honey. 'I was desperate for a boyfriend at school and didn't have one at any point. I think it might have been similar for you too, yes?'

He nods again.

She keeps probing. 'Did you try really hard with crushes but they never seemed to appreciate it?'

Eyes stern now, he's watching memories of girls giggling at him in the park, him trying to kiss one, her boyfriend calling him racist names.

'I don't think you grew up dreaming of killing women, did you?'

Shakes head.

'But you got upset that they never gave you a chance?'

'It wasn't just that. They'd get scared,' he says, the gusts of wind that swelled his sails when Emy first entered now suddenly lost.

'And that made it feel hopeless that you'd ever get a normal girlfriend?' Her eyes are full of that feminine concern he adores so deeply.

'I've never connected with anyone the way I do with you, Emy,' he whispers.

She ignores the tender words, which hurts.

Glancing away, she perseveres with her own thoughts: 'There's one thing you've got to help me with, Joe. How do such intense feelings of love for women you *did* know turn into such brutal acts against ones you didn't?'

'It wasn't brutal,' he snaps, offended. 'I've never told you how I did it so how would you even know?'

'You've said they were dead by the time you put them in the car, that sounds brutal to me.'

'Like there was a nice way to do it!' He barks the words at her. 'There's plenty of ways that would've left less blood, y'know. Would have left fewer clues for police. But I didn't want them suffering, my girls. They weren't frightened before I did it, then maybe it hurt for thirty seconds, then they were OK.'

'Joe, they were dead.'

'They were at peace!'

'Thirty seconds, that suggests knife or blunt force,' she probes, speaking louder, empathy vanishing. 'So which was it?'

'I did it the quickest way I could!' He bellows. Why is she not understanding? She is supposed to *get* him – they have a connection. How on earth could she think what he did was brutal? It was not. It was not. IT WAS NOT!

Joe usually loves sparring with Emy, flirting around conversations together until she deserves a treat – another clue to how he did it, how he captured all his beautiful girlfriends, where he left them, how he never got caught. He knows that's what she wants and usually the verbal foreplay, that tantalising tug-of-war which precedes the latest admissions is spectacular. But Joe is too upset for fun games now; he just wants this to be over.

'I used a paring knife to sever the aorta. Every time. It was *very* quick. Every time. They did not suffer! I wouldn't make my loves suffer.'

She nods and lets her chest fall gently. 'Thank you for being truthful.'

'I've had such a horrible time lately and I thought you'd be the *one* person who understood,' he whimpers, nudging his cheeks against his shoulders to rub away the tears.

'I'm sorry, Joe. I know it's been tough. But you *are* at Beeswell to talk about what you did.'

'And what I did was not brutal!' he calls out, very ready to leave. 'I loved them. I still love them!'

'OK, OK, they didn't suffer,' she pacifies. 'Here's a different topic. Why do you think Elkins doesn't shoo Shenton away all the time like he always did with you and George Petty?'

Joe shrugs.

'I don't know either,' Emy admits, eyes roving around the room as she thinks.

Joe feels calmer now, drawn once more into the gravitational pull of her emerald eyes, those sexy scarlet lips. He was being silly before. Of course he doesn't want to leave. So much better being in here with beautiful Emy than being back out in the bull-pen with that ruddy idiot Tim Shenton and boring bozo Frank Elkins. He should say something so she doesn't leave. But what?

Oh Joe, why did you get so angry? Why can you never just be cool?

'That's enough for today, Joe. I hope you'll be OK, I didn't mean to upset you.'

No... stay! Think of something, Joe! Think! Tim and Frank, what was her question? Say something. Anything!

'Erm, they look a bit alike, kinda.' *Quick, keep talking.* 'If Tim was older, they'd look alike I mean. Erm, maybe Tim reminds Frank of his own family and that makes Frank happy.'

Emy stares at him, unblinking.

'Sorry, sorry,' he spurts. 'I'll try harder...'

'No, Joe.' She has a small life-giving smile fixed especially for him. 'That is a really intelligent thought. Thank you.'

Joe, you son-of-a-gun! She's pleased with you! She's so, so pleased. Look at her gorgeous, perfect face. You were cool, Joe! Look what happens when you're cool!

22

The atmosphere is febrile as we run through my latest chat with Joe.

Robbie bounces about the office like a space hopper, knuckle-deep in a bag of Revels, interrupting every other word of the interview to sling out ideas as we watch it back.

'The way his mood swings one way and the other – classic Borderline trait,' he fizzes. Not particularly helpful since we ascertained Joe had the personality disorder months ago.

'Robbie, you've done your 10,000 steps. Sit down,' Chi pleads.

'I think he honestly believes he did nothing wrong,' he fires again, slouching back in his chair. Three fingers plunge back into the bag like a claw in an arcade game.

The chocolatey obstacles won't stop him yakking. 'He wasn't killing for dominance; he was killing for domesticity. He still loves those women, he doesn't despise them, so any idea he hurt them will be hard to accept. What a good day! As Churchill said, "Success is not final, failure is not fatal. It's the courage to continue that counts." And man, did we show courage today.'

The needless historic quote makes me want to chew my own tongue off. But instead, I tell Robbie he's doing a good job of understanding Joe's state of mind, making sure Chi clocks my generous praise. Robbie himself misses the compliment, however, as his restless eyes land back on Joe in the common room with his little electric chess set.

'He's so messed up,' Chi murmurs, the yin to Robbie's yang. 'I don't know what to say to the families in the next newsletter. It's going to be of zero comfort to them that the throats were cut.' She exhales hard at the ground and tucks her knees up to her tummy.

'Well, shows they weren't kept as slaves for months at least,' I remonstrate, trying to sound positive but failing as thoughts of Sam in captivity descend on my mind like flint arrows.

She sees all that play out in my demeanour so is sensitive in reply. 'I agree with you, but he'd already admitted they were dead before he got them in his car. The parents knew their daughters died relatively quickly. All they get from today is a more visceral image of the actual killing. You did great navigating that interview, Em, but I can't deliver that to families like some kind of victory.'

I hear Chi's point but can't process it any further. It's the other thing Joe said – about Elkins seeing Shenton like family. The longer I dwell on it, the more nervous excitement prickles my chest. Random thoughts that have been rolling around my head like loose rocks suddenly feel more like stepping stones to some kind of plan.

Robbie's all over Joe Okorie... Leon's digging into Tim Shenton...

Maybe there can be someone working Elkins over too...

* * *

The next six hours crawl by – as if I've been forced to hold my breath the entire time while I wait for my colleagues to leave. But now they are leaving.

Chi clocks me not putting my jacket on as she and Robbie log off.

'Need to speak to Arthur quickly, nothing major,' I tell her. Not entirely untrue, I will be speaking to the security team very shortly.

She buys it and they're gone.

Spreading the pictures from little Andrew Stride's crime scene across the table, I stare. Can I do this? Tim Shenton may very well have killed this boy.

My fingers twizzle the locket around my neck, Sam's and my dad's faces spinning inside a silver-clasped heart shell. I don't always wear it; but I'm glad I did today. What would they have done in my situation? Mum would think it was wrong. *What about the little boy's family?* she'd probably point out. But maybe that's why I'm here – doing the dirty work so she can stay clean. Morality laundering.

I pick up my iPhone and stare into the black glass of the blank screen. I don't like the face reflecting back at me.

This is what sociopaths do – they get you to need their help, then they use it to exploit you. Tim's certainly trying that. Am I any better?

The harsh overhead lights bounce off the glossy A4 photographs of the Stride crime scene, obscuring some of the horrors. I move my head to different angles so the glare moves across the pictures, bleaching different areas of each frame and revealing others. We don't even have this much to go on as to what Sam's death looked like. No answers. No nothing.

I catch myself. Is that truly what I've become? A grieving

sister so bereft of closure I can look at the murder of an innocent child with a jealous eye?

Elkins' wretched face stampedes through my consciousness afresh. His apathy. His silence. His cruelty. My fingers twizzle the locket a little faster.

Tomorrow could be the day.

I buzz through to the security team. 'Arthur, bring Tim Shenton into the interview room immediately please.'

Arthur assures me he will.

I tilt my phone's black glass so I can see my eyes in it again, then turn it over to face the table.

23

'Miss Rose,' Tim says with outstretched arms as I enter. Speaking first to assert dominance, hands out to remind me that the last time he wanted something and I'd opposed it, he'd got his way.

Subliminal tricks are my speciality, mate. Nice try.

Clicking the button on the wall of the interview room so the conversation isn't recorded, I choose not to respond to him until I'm seated, resetting the conversation on my terms.

'I need to speak to you,' I start.

'A little small talk first, surely?' He pretends to be hurt.

I take a loud, deep huff in and out through my nose then raise my eyebrows, inviting him to get the mind games out of his system.

'I must say I'm enjoying staying here, Miss Rose. So thank you for that. A room to myself really is a relief. My cellmate at Strangeways had Fregoli syndrome – decided I was his mother waiting to smother him while he slept. Actually, he was far more compliant once I started pretending I *was* his mother. Funny man. But I prefer the peace and quiet at Beeswell.'

He waits for me to engage, unblinking – those all-engulfing jet-black pupils devouring me. I refuse to be cowed and say nothing.

'All fuck, no foreplay. My, my, you must be a hit with the boys.'

My continued silence finally gets through; he drops the faux smile. 'You want to talk about something Elkins-related, I assume.'

I take another beat before answering and stare at the back wall, at my mind-portraits. There's one off to the left of the four of us: Mum, Dad, Sam and me, all smiling, all dressed smartly – a cousin's christening. There are cookie crumbs down the front of my custard-yellow frilly dress, Sam's eyes are hyper from his fourth cup of squash. Dad's big hands are draped on my shoulders for protection. I miss that. A scene that is the utter antithesis of this hope-forsaken interview room.

'Elkins seems to like you,' I eventually state.

Shenton shifts in his seat, dark greasy hair – well overdue a trim – curled behind both ears today rather than pushed to one side as he often prefers. His cupped hands, as per his previous request, rest freely on the table, his thumbs tapping together like he's a benevolent bank manager about to grant me a loan.

'Miss Rose,' he starts in a voice so calm and slack that it croaks. 'If I can't unravel Frank Elkins then you'll have the peace of mind that no one can.'

'Arrogant words butter no parsnips.'

'You may be miserly with praise, but you *were* impressed by my insights into you yourself, Miss Rose. I could tell.' He leans forward and lowers his tone further to a patronising, heavy whisper. 'And let's be clear, if this conversation was just business as usual, you wouldn't have waited until after 5 p.m. when I assume your colleagues will have left the building, yes?'

The way he deduces things with such precision is alarming. And yet that is why I'm here. I keep my face neutral, desperate not to show any glimmer of being impressed by this unhygienic, imperious twig of a man. 'He might talk to you, open up. His guard will be down more with you than me.'

'So that's my assignment. Speak to Elkins, get him talking without realising it...'

I confirm it is.

'What's in it for me?'

I've dreaded this. The moment of no return, where harmless chat crosses the threshold into criminal collusion. I look at those invisible pictures on the walls again and remember Mum's ghostly eyes looking up at me from her hospital bed.

I stay assertive: 'I give you an easy ride. Frame questions in a way that makes you sound innocent.'

'Testify for the defence at my trial.' He's not asking, he's instructing.

I bite my lip hard, he knows exactly what he wants and how to extort it. My heart crashes against my ribs so hard it could crack them. And I keep my hands off the table, so he doesn't see them fluttering like flags.

'Easy ride for now, I'll testify if we actually find my brother's body before the trial.'

He looks sceptical, as if to say, *You'll ditch me the second you find the corpse.*

'If I tried to screw you, you could go to the press, tell them about this conversation and end my career in a second,' I add, genuinely.

Shenton can read emotions like no one I've ever met. He reads mine and is satisfied, shutting his eyes, knitting his hands behind his head. 'Mutual destruction bound by a nuclear deterrent. Clever.'

'Deal?'

'Where do I sign?'

'You're not the Svengali you think you are,' I stab, already repulsed by my new business partner. 'My theory is you remind Elkins of his brother. The boy died as a teenager and you don't look much older than that, even though you are.'

'Elkins killed him,' Shenton clarifies, eyes shut, rocking gently in his chair.

'Whatever they had together was complicated. He loved him, he hated him. He cared for him, he killed him. Whatever it was, you may tap into it.'

'You do me a disservice, Miss Rose.'

I tut. 'Find out where my brother is and I'll give you a Blue Peter badge. How's that sound? And anything that strikes you in the meantime: ideas, inklings, you bring them back to me and we discuss them. But only after 5 p.m. We must make no mention of this in our daytime interviews, for both our sakes.'

'Ah so you *do* think I can bring insight as well as a familiar face,' he smirks.

'Oh, my goodness, is your ego *that* fragile?'

'You hadn't even spotted the way he ties knots round his possessions. Not very impressive of you, really.'

'My team *had* already spotted that,' I mock, spying my chance to leave.

He reads my micro-movement towards the door and trumps it. 'You're not asking the one question that matters most... *why* is he hiding what he did?'

Easy to answer. I don't miss a beat: 'Basic offence-paralleling. Replace the power over his victims with power over their families.'

'For what? Come on, Miss Rose. Has Elkins demonstrated a hint of being power-hungry since he's been here?'

'He's got what he wants. He left the teeth for police to find. Just enough evidence to be convicted without needing to give any details.'

'Or just enough evidence to stop police following any other leads, and seemingly tricking you too.' Shenton is very animated now. Hands twitching as he talks, he's sitting ramrod straight and stiff, an electric current surging up his spine. 'But you still haven't answered *why* he'd hide all this,' he adds.

'I have... For the power, the feeling that we are all waiting on his every word.'

'Is that how it seems when you interview him?' Shenton challenges. 'Because I can't imagine Frank Elkins giving any more than 5 per cent of his attention to any answer, whether it's about our sludgy dinners or about your brother.'

I don't answer. Months of glacial adjustments and readjustments getting nothing out of Elkins replaced with a million-mile-an-hour tornado of new theories and angles. My armpits are roaring hot and my cheeks are burning but I daren't take off my jacket for fear Shenton'll read through that too and turn it against me. The joy he is already getting from the exchange and his chance to show off how astute he thinks he is at reading people is unnerving.

And yet it's everything I need. I trace over a hundred prosaic conversations I've had with Chi and Robbie off the back of my interviews with Elkins: they can't rouse themselves, they can't artificially manufacture enthusiasm. You can't fake desperation. But Shenton's appetite to be freed isn't fake – the hungry wolf runs faster.

'You've been trying to make him fit preconceived ideas of what you think he is. Blinded by hate,' Shenton goes on lecturing. 'Open your eyes, Miss Rose!' He slams a palm on the table in intense encouragement. 'You're better than that. From tonight, we start from scratch.'

As much as I dislike the man, his energy is terrific – an unnegotiable insistence that we *will* break Elkins by whatever means possible. I just need to make sure I don't mention in passing that I've got a national newspaper journalist looking into his case on the sly – definite buzz-killer to this illicit partnership.

His mind keeps crackling. 'Also, if Elkins is so desperate to have power over the families, why no trial? Why not put them through that so he could bask in it? And then we come back to the *why*. Why keep all this secret? That's maybe something we should both ponder ahead of our next chat,' he suggests, with the audacity to assume he gets to choose when this meeting is over.

His witless, self-aggrandising patter renews my desire to get out. I get up to leave.

'Miss Rose, I owe you an apology,' he says – his calm ease is creepy again now he's less animated. 'Hubris got the better of me the last time we talked. I compared myself to a scalpel. I've been thinking about that, and I believe a better comparison would, in fact, be a syringe. I don't slice through skin, I get under it. What's more, a syringe can contain either venom or vaccine. You have chosen the latter, and I am so grateful.'

'The more you boast about being so calculating, the more I think you're the kind of person capable of hiding the fact you raped and killed a little boy,' I reply.

'We're way past needing to worry about whether you think I'm guilty or not, Miss Rose.'

'Keep digging!'

'I am innocent. But to win a hand of poker, you don't simply wait to play the cards you're dealt...'

'You rig the deck first, right?' I predict, unimpressed.

'No, Miss Rose.' He shakes his head, bemused that I've not understood. 'You don't rig the deck. You make sure you own the dealer.'

The callous look of deranged bliss he shoots me sparks a cold spidery sweat at the back of my neck.

This is a dance with the devil. I must not trip.

24

Leon wanted another fancy meal out, I wanted Domino's and corner-shop wine. Sipping my room temperature, Spar-donnay now, I wish he'd been more assertive.

There's an odd atmosphere as we scroll endlessly through Netflix options on the sofa. It doesn't matter that we knocked boots last time I was here, we're acquaintances at best. Keeping strictly to our own separate sides of the sofa, our glasses are still half full, but I top them up anyway.

'You're probably wondering if I've got any further digging into Tim Shenton for you,' he says at one point.

I should tell him about my pact with Shenton. But, of course, I won't. I definitely should have told Chi and Mum. All week I've been making up reasons for staying late at the Hive – Chi's almost certainly suspicious despite my creative excuses. Then making up equally questionable reasons for why I've got home late has been perplexing to Mum too. Bottom line: lying is the worst. After five days of it, the deception is clinging to me like poison ivy, making me itch. And what have I got to show for it? Nothing.

'Or maybe you're not wondering what I've found at all...' Leon adds, a little hurt at my complete failure to respond.

'No, no, sorry. Yes! I'd meant to ask straight away. Hit me,' I say, smiling encouragement. The wine's beginning to dull the anxiety that's been cleaving my mind apart all week.

'I spoke to Andrew Stride's mum.'

'Really?' I check.

He gives a smug nod.

'That's beyond the call of duty, I'd say.'

'I'm not above death knocks,' he replies, slightly defensive.

'She let you in?'

'Mm-hmm,' he hums, nodding again.

I rotate my index finger forwards so he'll hurry the story up.

'I think Shenton had bad blood with her,' he states.

'How so?' I'm sitting up straight now, eyes glued to my host.

'I thought she was being shy at first. She didn't want to talk much about it, understandably. But then I realised she was holding back.'

'Holding back?'

'Less shy, more... coy,' he clarifies.

I had thought before about the horrific position the mum would be in. She wants to know what happened to her son Andrew, but she also has to contend with the fact her own stepbrother might be the perpetrator. 'She might be terrified of Shenton, of what he'll do if he gets out and she's trash-talked him.'

Leon presses his lips together and squashes his eyebrows down as he shakes his head. 'Mmm, it wasn't that. It was more like she couldn't bring herself to admit it could be Shenton.'

'Interesting,' I acknowledge, taking a big swig and wincing at the warmth of the white wine as it goes down – not that it'll stop me drinking it, I'm no quitter. 'Like she genuinely doesn't believe it's him? That would make her an incredible witness for Shenton.'

Leon rubs at his stubble. 'No, it wasn't quite that. I don't know how to put it, it's as if she won't let herself accept that...'

A picture of that poor mum settles in my mind, a broken soul emerging from a magic-eye pattern. I understand her completely. 'She won't let herself acknowledge she may have booked the babysitter who killed her son. It's easier to think it was someone random.'

'Yes!' Leon calls out, satisfied that we're both on the same page. 'And I think that's where the police probably stopped. Asked her the basic questions: timings, background on her son, how they knew Shenton. But if she wasn't offering up anything about him being suspicious, it doesn't sound like they dug any deeper into their past together.'

'She'd have been in no state to give that much information in the days and weeks afterwards, anyway,' I empathise. 'A single mum, her only child...'

'Fair enough,' he agrees. 'But it made me think, if the police weren't forcing the issue, which let's be honest, appears to be a flaw throughout the case, and the mum is happy to tell herself it wasn't Shenton, then none of them were properly testing whether Shenton really did have a motive, it's a real weakness of the prosecution case. It's not to say he did do it, but whoever did this had obviously studied the house, chosen the little boy specifically. And right now, the only person who *may* have any sort of personal motive is the man who was supposed to be looking after him at the time.'

I force down another sip of painfully acidic vino, wince and fail to hide it.

'I was delicate,' he states. 'But I tried to see if she and Shenton had ever had a falling out of any sort.'

There's an endearing innocence to the way Leon speaks. He's obviously intelligent, but unlike most sharp, successful men, he appears oblivious to his own talents. Either that or he's very modest, it's too soon to read. But it's nice to have an engaging conversation with an adult male who doesn't whiff of deluded omniscience.

'She said they'd fallen out as teenagers,' he explains. 'But then about six months before the murder he'd randomly got back in touch, said there were no hard feelings and he wanted to reconnect.'

I scrunch my eyebrows together. 'Fishy!'

'I know. I pushed her and it turns out she complained to her mum about some of Shenton's behaviour at the time. She wouldn't say what, but it led to him being moved on when they were both about fourteen,' Leon explains, washing back his own white wine vinegar with a lot less drama than me.

'Shit,' I mutter. 'Blaming her for the fact he had to leave the family could fit as a motive.'

'Bit extreme, isn't it? Falling out almost a decade ago, then finally coming back and killing her son.'

'For a normal person yes, but if he has APD…'

'APD?'

'Antisocial personality disorder. It covers lots of things but in extreme cases would include…'

'Psychopaths,' Leon finishes the sentence.

We stare at each other for a second as we let the details sink in.

'And the police didn't get that out of her?' I check.

'Don't think so. It was as if after she'd explained all that stuff about the falling out, she realised the significance of it and clammed right up. Like she'd never put two and two together before, and was scared she'd said it out loud.'

'Still doesn't make Shenton a definite killer,' I remind him. 'Food for thought, though. A bone to throw Harrington at the very least if he asks. A motive. And to be honest, Shenton holding onto a grudge for years wouldn't surprise me one bit.'

'One other thing she said is she remembers a friend Shenton used to have. A fellow orphan who used to come round and play sometimes. How Shenton was always talking about him, crying when the boy had to go home, was absolutely devoted to him,' Leon adds. 'But when Shenton got back in touch more recently and his stepsister asked about that friend, he pretended the boy had never existed.'

'Weird,' I conclude. 'She give you his name?'

'She couldn't remember. Annoying. But I'll keep digging.'

The conversation peters out but that initial unease has melted away and we grin at each other, both comfortable with the extended eye contact. Those dark brown eyes get more delicious every time I see him, or is it just the more I drink?

He's got broad, swimmer's shoulders too – something I hadn't noticed until I was ripping his shirt off last weekend. I can't work out what I like more: his impressive frame, or the fact he's secure enough not to show it off at every single opportunity.

Reading my mind, he shuffles along, sweeps up the wine bottle on the floor at my end of the sofa, tops us both up again, then puts one of those strong arms around me. Smooth.

'Erm, what's wrong with your side of the sofa?' I demand.

'You're so mean,' he replies, amused.

'I've told the justice secretary he's a moron to his face, don't flatter yourself that I'm only mean to you.'

'The meaner the better, in my books,' Leon says, his thick arm still squeezing me to him.

'Pervert.'

We pick a semi-engaging true crime documentary to watch

but it's not long before he's opening the second bottle of wine – chilled this time, mercifully – and we're wrapped around each other, kissing.

He carries me to his room. There isn't time to take off my top as we race through the gears. I cling to fistfuls of that dark hair, my grip aching as I clasp tighter and tighter.

Afterwards we lie for a minute – breathless, facing the ceiling – coming back down to earth.

'You can sleep here if you like,' he says, justifying my decision to pop a toothbrush and deodorant in my handbag before I left home.

I kiss him on the cheek.

'Want to hang out tomorrow?' he suggests, shifting on to his side to look at me. His forehead's glistening: I trace a finger around the edge of his dewy hairline and down the curve of his jaw.

'Can't. Got plans with Mum.'

His smile is accepting. 'What you doing?'

Well, usually we go out touring the farmlands of North Yorkshire looking for the impossible-to-find remains of my dead brother. But since she broke her wrist, I'll be pushing her round in a wheelchair, building up the kind of stamina in my thighs usually reserved for marathon runners and porn stars.

Obviously I can't say that, but what can I say? I'm a spider trapped in the criss-crossing web of my own duplicity. 'Nothing much, a walk, a bite to eat.'

'Maybe I could join you.'

'Woah there!' I groan. 'Meet my family? What next? Matching tattoos?'

He snorts and places his finger over my lips, shaking his head at the immature girl in front of him.

* * *

I wake with a jolt. Leon stirs; I tell him to go back to sleep. I've already lost a clear grasp on what the dream was about, but what I do know is that Tim Shenton's cold, conniving eyes are now front-and-centre in my mind. It is pitch black. I wish I could turn on a light, the image of Shenton staring unblinking at me feels like it is just out of reach in the darkness. Out of my reach, not his.

Leon shifts closer, folds his arm round me and leans his body against mine. 'It's OK,' he says, kissing me on the back of the head. It doesn't take long for him to drift back off as I lie stuck in position and wide awake. Shenton isn't going anywhere.

Shenton won't tell Elkins about me, will he? He mustn't! It's essential Elkins doesn't know I'm Sam's sister. What about the Goal Theory? It's so important to keep that detail away from him. Critical.

Or am I overreacting? Elkins has had months of not knowing my identity and still hasn't admitted a thing. Maybe discovering the truth would somehow unlock him? But my gut doesn't feel like that will work. He's obviously holding back the burial sites to retain power over the families, regardless of what Shenton says. Having me there, for him to see my anguish in the flesh, and to know he caused it, he'd thrive on that. It's not going to suddenly spawn sympathy in him, is it?

Or even worse, the revelation could spark a more drastic reaction. Knowing my identity could panic him. The inmates are compelled to stay at Beeswell, but they can't be forced to enter the interview room or speak to me, to that they must acquiesce at the very least. He could refuse to ever come out of his cell again until he gets moved on. I have no recourse to stop him. Then that would be it. That would be the best opportunity to ever find Sam's body gone. Over. Destroyed.

But why does a man so eager to keep his secrets continue trudging into my interview room whenever I request it? Why? That's a fair question Shenton has posed.

I lie awake, the circular saw of my post-work conversations with Shenton slicing through me again and again.

What's the earliest I can leave Leon's without it seeming rude? It gets to 7 a.m. and I decide that's plenty. There's light swelling around the curtains as he squints at me. I plant a kiss on his cheek and tell him I'll see him soon. He grunts and I'm gone.

25

Mum's already up and dressed when I get home; I knew she would be. I tell her I stayed at Chi's. Too awkward to admit anything else. Downing a quick coffee over the sink I can feel her eyeing me with suspicion, but she doesn't probe. Anyway, what's another lie on the bonfire at this point? I'm a terrible person, there's nothing more to it.

We decide there's no use in waiting around so set off for North Yorkshire, onward to this week's futile quest. Mum's decided she wants to start the trail at a car park next to a copse on the A61, actually nearer Thirsk than Bedale. She's visited the area before of course but not in years and feels it would be a natural place to bring a body if you didn't want to be disturbed.

The car is the most difficult place to communicate with Mum. Sign language, written messages, even facial expressions are all hard to assimilate when driving. She doesn't try to make any conversation either. I don't know which journey is worse each week – the way over, where she harbours a speck of genuine hope that this will be the time she finds Sam's resting place, or the journey home when that speck of hope has been snatched away again.

We reach the car park and I realise I recognise the area myself. We convened here with a couple of other victims' relatives once and went on a search together. It is not a destination that will be fun to push a wheelchair around. But Mum was never going to agree to stop going on our weekly hunts, even though the uneven ground is such a hazard. This is the compromise. I retrieve the NHS-issued chair from the boot, unfold it, open Mum's door and help her into it. This is going to be an absolute slog.

She points the way she wants to go as I'm still doing my jacket up against the drizzle. Then she twiddles her index and middle fingers in mid-air, miming legs walking, impatient to get going.

'Yeah, give me a minute! Or d'you want to push yourself?' I snap.

She whips round and scolds me with her eyes. I hate myself even more. Getting short with most people is warranted, overdue often. But not with Mum, never with Mum.

'Sorry,' I mumble. We push off, the grind of the wheels against the damp, muddy gravel grating on me immediately.

Sometimes I wonder if Mum's voice would even come back if we recovered Sam's body. Would it come back straight away? Would it come back after we buried him? Would it be a few words or full sentences, or just noises? In some ways it doesn't even matter if she talks again – it wouldn't heal the pain of the last eighteen years. It wouldn't bring him back to life. And yet it would give us closure. Is all this worth that? Would we be better off going back to trying to counsel the pain away, or could antidepressants give Mum a moment's respite from the torture of not knowing where her son is? I know what her answer would be – anything like that would be to start putting Sam behind us, and that is something she cannot contemplate.

I see the exact same trait in myself, sadly. She cannot let go of looking for Sam, and I cannot let go of helping her. I took up a new profession from scratch in my mid-twenties, haven't been able to afford to live on my own ever since, mothballed all other areas of my life – all in pursuit of a brother who no longer exists in any present and meaningful way. Even spending the night at Leon's made me feel guilty – how can I have nights off when Sam is still out there? I don't think I will ever be able to leave the hunt behind; not while Mum's still around.

The copse we initially explore is smaller than I had remembered and we skirt the whole perimeter in less than half an hour. We always check along the walled or fenced edges most – no self-respecting body-burier would dig a hole in the middle of a field or wood, rather than use the barriers at the side which conceal their actions from at least 180 degrees of view. Plus, the one Elkins body found, Ollie Vaughn's, was close up to a long length of privet hedge demarcating one farmer's field from the next.

For a while Mum used to look specifically for walls with barbed wire circling over them, in the beyond-negligible hope that a fragment of Sam's clothing might have been caught on it. Can you imagine? The probability of not only any fabric snagging, but then surviving all these years and Mum spotting it? The chances are... well, I've got more chance of joining Chi and Harrington in a three-way, let's put it that way. But these are the microscopic details Mum comes up with.

Right now, she decides we should cross to another clump of trees about 100 metres away.

Lots of space and flat ground, she tries to sign one handed.

We trudge through the field, lanky wet grass slapping across my trainers with the moisture seeping through to my increasingly cold, damp toes. Mum sits in her chair, hands clasped together under a blanket. Eyes fixed on the next destination, she insists she is more than warm enough to continue.

When we reach the new woodland, it is just as Mum predicted – lots of open space and flat ground. Her ability to recall almost any detail of the terrain, surroundings or structure in the areas that she has searched all these years is astonishing. I bet you could show her a picture of any gate, any dirt path, any road sign in a fifteen-mile radius and she could take you straight to it. It's extraordinary. London cabbies have the Knowledge; Mum has the name of every blade of grass in North Yorkshire.

We trudge around the new area for a while, my thighs of steel and upper arms dealing with the wheelchair's adventure over bumpy roots and through sludgy puddles better than I'd expected, though I'm dripping with sweat.

On to another almost identical crop of trees. No luck. Then around the edge of a farmer's field, full of sandy-golden wheat ripe for harvesting. Mum looks across the expanse, as if waiting for the kernels to all loll in the same direction, pointing the way to Sam. Instead the crops dance in the breeze, this way, that way, no way at all.

Then the heavens really open. Our coats are no match for the fat globs splatting down, intent on soaking us through. Half-prepared I open a small umbrella and try to hold it over us both while still pushing the chair. Mum offers to hold it but with one arm out of action, she hasn't got the strength in her other alone to hold it high enough for both of us.

I stop, take back the umbrella and lean forward. 'We need to go back. The main road's over there, it'll be easier going back along it,' I yell over the din of the downpour.

She looks round, her small, blameless face defeated. Those

wide, fragile eyes know I'm right but she can't quite bring herself to admit it. I kiss her cheek. She doesn't need to admit anything.

'I'll get us back,' I call.

The smell of earth being pockmarked with bullets of rain is musty, heavy. It's a relief to be back on the main road and by the time we reach the car park the shower has passed and the clouds are brightening.

Mum looks as deflated as I knew she would. I give her a big hug; I wish I could tell her that we do at least now have Shenton working 24/7 to help as well, even if it is to save his own skin. That would probably perk Mum up.

No. It's too risky a gamble with Shenton; I don't want to stress her out.

'Tomorrow could be the day,' I say instead once we're back in the car. She wipes away the tears, nods and we have a longer hug. By the time we break hold, all the car's windows have steamed up. Together, alone, unable to see in any direction – what a metaphor.

26

I see Sunday before it sees me. Awake at six. Lying in bed, staring at the ceiling. I haven't got a hope in hell's chance of keeping the intrusive thoughts at bay for another twenty-four hours – or more like thirty-six hours if I want to wait until Chi and Robbie have left the Hive too.

What have Shenton and Elkins discussed in my absence? What might have come to Shenton as he wrestles to help me out of pure self-interest? This last week, indulging in our late afternoon briefings, I've quickly become reliant on that daily dopamine hit of hope; a glimmer, however small, that the conversation might be lucrative. A new appreciation of Mum's addiction to visiting the fields around Elkins' home hits me. It's one last delve into the cookie jar, it's one last scratch of the insect bite, one last go on the fruit machine. It's never the last one.

I'd leave for work right away if the inmates were up this early. Instead, I lie there, willing *myself* to come up with a fresh angle of attack. For all my desperation to touch base with Shenton, our tête-à-têtes have so far yielded zilch.

What if that continues? What if Elkins doesn't actually see his brother in him? Or gets bored of Shenton's overly familiar patter? What if Shenton blackmails me? *I'll tell Elkins who you really are if you don't testify at my trial.* That's the kind of switch he could make if he loses trust in me. Maybe that's part of my impulse to meet so often: a modicum of reassurance he's still onboard.

Mum potters downstairs at about 7.30 a.m. Who gets up that early on a Sunday on purpose? Mad woman. I follow her down and we have a silent cup of tea in our dressing gowns. Her eyes are set at a point on the wall beyond me. I wonder if she has mind-portraits hung around the house the same way I do in the interview room? I've never asked her; I've never asked anyone if they do that.

Once we're both finished, I collect the empty mugs and rinse them, looking out of the window above the sink. 'Need to pop into the office for a bit. Just some annoying tech updates and organising papers before sending Harrington fresh stuff tomorrow.'

I glance round. *I wasn't born yesterday* – that's what Mum's expression screams.

'What?'

She pulls a whiteboard across the kitchen table with her good arm, bites the lid off a pen and scribbles. Drying my hands, I wander over and read out loud over her shoulder: 'You don't have to hide it, you've been seeing that journalist.'

She thinks she's got me rumbled: the late nights at the office, sleeping elsewhere on Friday night, making excuses to absent myself on Sunday. I'm out the whole time with Leon... she thinks.

And she's not *totally* wrong. That persistent little terrier has already texted me about meeting again on Tuesday. Says he's got more on Shenton's case. I must admit, it does feel fun to have another date in the diary, and not just because I need fresh updates for Harrington. But that is not today's agenda. I must be the first daughter in history to get an odd thrill from tricking my parent into thinking I *am* going out to meet a handsome rascal when, in fact, I'm heading into work.

'OK,' I tell her, not able to look her in the eye as I do it. 'I'm meeting up with Leon. But y'know what I'm like. No interrogations, no nothing, please. I'll be back by lunchtime, OK?'

I kiss her on the cheek and run upstairs to get dressed.

The way she looks at me as I plod back down and pull my coat on, I'm sure she's more amused than irked by the mystery she thinks she's solved.

'No questions when I get back,' I reiterate, pointing at her with my best Alan-Sugar-You're-Fired finger.

* * *

'Not at church on a Sunday?' Shenton questions as I sit down in the interview room. 'Heathen.'

'I'm getting Elkins in early tomorrow, what have we got? What's your hunch? Next moves etc.'

He's not ready for business yet and takes off on a soliloquy about how once his murder charge is quashed he'll still be an outcast because of the child porn conviction on file and his new-found notoriety. How poor old him is going to have a very tough life when he gets out.

I can't engage with the vile self-pity. If anything, it just underlines his narcissistic tendencies.

Focus on your pictures, Emy. Focus on Sam, on Mum, on Dad. I look off to the left corner of the room. The invisible photograph of Sam at a pub with his friends for his eighteenth birthday.

Tiny V-neck T-shirt that looks dreadful on him, uber-tanned at the end of the summer, leaning on his pals for support, huge grin, pint sloshing out of the side of his glass.

'You're nervous this won't work,' Tim says suddenly as I zone back in.

'Don't try getting in here.' I tap the side of my head.

'I don't usually wait for permission.' He leans forward in his chair, resting his chin on his cupped hands – ever reminding me of his unchained arms.

'Elkins. That's what we're here about.'

'That's what *you're* here about,' he half jokes, as if I'm insulting him. He brushes his fringe out of his face, those big eyes gaping too wide as they stay latched onto mine. There's a horrible, inescapable feeling to his stare, like he's got you until he chooses to relinquish you again.

My eyes return to the wall behind him. Maybe I shouldn't have told him all this, his impulse to exploit is so deep-seated.

'So you haven't got one decent insight into Elkins then,' I goad.

'There's a difference between not revealing and not noticing,' he replies in his slow, annoying-as-hell dreamy riddle voice.

'Thoughts, then?' I begin before clarifying: 'On Elkins.'

'Does he ever...' Shenton stops, the right words not forming as quickly as usual for him, 'talk to himself?'

The bemused posing of the question leaves me in no doubt what he's referring to. 'As if he's playing out conversations from his past out loud? Yes. Sometimes.'

'I take it you've not seen or heard any of our chats over the weekend yet?'

'No, we go through all that on the Monday.'

'I'll save you time scouring, it was 2.35 p.m. yesterday afternoon,' he says with no further comment.

I bite like a shark. 'What was?'

'I was trying to engage him on burying bodies, very obliquely of course. It troubles me how one body could be found so easily, and the other four stay so cleverly hidden. I hinted that he'd obviously honed his skills over the years if none of the more recent ones were found.'

'Right,' I say, impatient for actual content.

'And he burst into this high-pitched character, eyes rolling and roving everywhere.'

'Yep, that's what happens. Some sort of dissociative trauma mechanism.' My hands are gripped in my lap. 'I've never seen it in anyone else.'

'You could have warned me, Miss Rose,' Shenton chuckles, sounding playful, trying to torment me by demonstrating how unaffected he is by my brother's killer. A separate thought sparks: that mean streak, that basking in others' pain – was that what drove him to kill Andrew Stride? Not just the child's suffering, but the eternal agony it would inflict on his own stepsister?

I grit my teeth and squeeze my hands tighter so they quiver. 'Tell me what he said, Tim.'

And out of nowhere comes an uncanny impression of Elkins' terrifying, dissociated voice: *'I can do it, I can do it, I don't need any help from youuuuuuuuuu!'*

The last word contorts out of his mouth and flies towards the ceiling in a horrid, twisted howl, ripping me in two with fear.

Back to himself, Shenton inhales through his nose and pins those black eyes back on me. He's smiling and placid as he says it. 'I think he had help burying the bodies.'

27

Down hair, down! If I wet it any more it'll just poof up later in an act of self-sabotaging spite. How can it have got into such a mess when I was lying rigid and awake until dawn? Sleep was impossible after what Shenton told me.

Of course, I'm not even supposed to know yet. As far as Chi and Robbie know, I wasn't at the Hive yesterday. Can't tell Mum yet either, since she thinks I was off with Prince Charming. So the only route to discussing Elkins' slip-up is to watch it back with my colleagues as if for the first time, which involves me reaching the office – a task at which I am failing most miserably.

I check my watch: fifteen minutes to make the forty-minute drive to Beeswell.

My hair's mutiny persists.

A hat. It's going to have to be. What's least conspicuous? My Newcastle United baseball cap? No, not to work – it reminds me of Sam.

Mum's green bucket hat she wears for gardening? Please! I'm not at Glastonbury.

I'm digging into my old wardrobe, elbow deep in a forest floor of forgotten finery. I'll reach Narnia if delve any further.

I pull out a wide-brimmed straw sun hat from yesteryear, floppy and flattened. Hmm. I could style that out on my way into the office, but it'd be ridiculous to keep it on after that. Then I'd be left with hat hair too.

Twelve minutes left to get to work.

I swear under my breath.

One last dive into the clothes chasm. I come out grasping a denim cap – bought when I had a secret teenage girl-crush on Keira Knightley in her *Love Actually* butter-wouldn't-melt days. I squeeze the hideous blue bastard in my fist. It's going to have to be.

Pulling it down over my rebellious barnet, I rush out. The key to wearing a hat is to forget you're wearing it – casual nonchalance. If I ooze enough confidence Chi might not mention it.

* * *

She nods at the hat with an enormous smirk the second I walk in. 'Bad hair day?'

Panting from jogging across the car park, I give her the finger and drop my bag on to my desk with a heavy thud.

I've not even logged on before Robbie is up and standing next to me, chewing his nail rather than a snack for a change.

'I've had a thought about Joe,' he starts. 'He's obviously not happy and hates it in the main cell block. How about I start playing chess with him in the interview room? He's desperate for a proper game and I play all the time. It'll get him away from the others; I could build a rapport with him. Might lead to more confessions.'

I give him a reproachful look. 'Do you want the long answer or the short answer?'

'Short answer.'

'No.'

'What was the long answer?'

'Fuck no.'

He lets out a petulant bleat. 'It's actually a good idea. I don't get why you—'

'Robbie. This is, first of all, a scientific experiment – yes? We are seeing if constant observation paired with regular contact with a single outside source is an effective way of making headway in—'

'The families don't care which of us is talking to the men or whether we keep to test conditions.' He pushes his shoulders back and glances at Chi for backup. Wisely, she stays looking at her own computer.

'Secondly,' I say in an undertone to bring temperatures back down, 'the relationship I've been building with Joe over the last few months is delicate. If all of a sudden we chuck you in there every day, it will make him feel like I'm palming him off to a junior colleague. In fact, that's exactly what I'd be doing. It'd tarnish the bond he thinks we have.'

'You could still see him just as much!' he pleads.

'Thirdly, what would the other inmates say when he told them? They'd want extra time out of the block too, extra people to meet, extra privileges. It's a can of worms. We are making progress with Joe, slowly but surely. There's no need to risk it by being impatient.'

'He's going to shut down, refuse to go in the interview room at all if we don't change things, or he could flip out completely.' He sits back down, plonks an elbow on the table and leans his chin on his fist, his back to us.

Chi chooses now to turn around. *Be nice*, she says with her urgent, piercing glare. I roll my eyes back at her.

'Love the energy, Robbie. Let's just keep some pretence of order, yeah?'

'Yeah, yeah,' he echoes, defeated. '"If you mean to profit, learn to please."'

'Churchill?' I guess.

'Ohhh yessss,' he chirps back. More like the dog from the adverts than the prime minister.

I force out a loud laugh the quip doesn't deserve; Robbie looks round with a rueful smile. He never stays cross for long, poor little emotional goldfish.

'Found anything from the weekend cuts?' I enquire, suitably subtle.

'Still running through them.' He pops his headphones back on to continue listening to the recordings.

I've made clear to the security team that they do not need to log Shenton's extracurricular invitations to the interview room on the overnight and weekend logs – and they've adhered to the request. The package of potentially noteworthy out-of-hours footage they aggregate and send to Robbie for him to trawl through each morning doesn't show any hint of Shenton ever leaving the main cell block. Long must this continue. But after my impromptu chat with Shenton yesterday I came straight back to the office and watched that interaction he'd had with Elkins at least forty times by myself. Not that Chi and Robbie know this. I'm going to have to act shocked if and when Robbie does flag the conversation.

I stare at his screen, trying to work out if he'll have reached the key moment yet...

'One thing stood out,' he says, absent-mindedly lifting one

headphone off his ear. 'Elkins did that weird voice thing with Shenton.'

A current rushes through me. 'Saying what?' I'm as blasé as my sleep-deprived, impatient mind can muster.

'Ahh it's easier to show you when we go through it,' Robbie concludes, underwhelmed.

How on earth could he hear what Elkins had said and not be bouncing off the walls? All he cared about was asking to play chess against Joe. Wake up, Roberto!

The extra half-hour wait for him to complete the transcript of the weekend's in-house highlights may as well take ten years – that's how much I age in the meantime.

Finally. Finally! He potters over to the printer, picks up three warm copies and drops one on each of Chi and my desks.

'It's taking longer and longer to type these up now Shenton's in there, chatter-boxing,' he observes.

We crawl through the first couple of pages, our eyes flicking between the transcript and the playback of the video feed – Shenton doing an admirable job of covertly prodding at Elkins, waiting for replies, angling for a reaction. Critically, he pretends to be so preoccupied as he prattles that it's almost as if he doesn't care if Elkins responds. It's clever. Manipulative but clever. He's embodying the jabbering younger brother, playing to the familial weak point we discussed. And the less he seems to care about their interactions – the more self-obsessed he appears – then subliminally, the less it will seem to matter to Elkins when he does engage. Not a trick I can employ. No one would buy me building the most expensive square footage of prison in the country and then acting like I didn't care what the inmates had to say. But Shenton's performance is a masterclass; probing but not pissing off the monosyllabic monolith. None of us three in the office say much in the early exchanges.

And then it comes.

Shenton throws out a metaphor about burying a hatchet. 'Mind you,' he adds, 'you're no stranger to burying shit, are you, Frank?'

Elkins' shoulders twitch as he lets out a light, single snigger. 'Physically or mentally?' He asks back.

'Except that one time,' Shenton goes on, ignoring the interruption. I wonder whether he is making this conversation up on the fly or whether he'd planned it out. He can't have anticipated the climax, but the rest almost seems choreographed. 'How did you manage to bury four so well and yet the other one was found in like a day! You got sloppy, Frankie-Boy.'

The CCTV footage isn't high res, but you can see a lowering of Elkins' brow. 'That was an error,' he growls. He's hurtling into a memory fast, but Shenton's just as quick.

'D'you get interrupted?' he asks, throwing the question away perfectly.

Elkins' shoulders contort, as if embodying someone else. And then it comes. *'I can do it, I can do it, I don't need any help from youuuuuuuuuu!'* he screeches. The same way he did every time I watched the clip yesterday.

'What was that?' Chi squeals, and I love her for it.

Her reaction makes Robbie jump.

I tell him to play the segment again; this time it sinks in for him too. His eyes bulge to mirror Chi's. I try to mirror them both.

I blurt out the words that have been pinned to my tongue for the last twenty-four hours. 'What if he had help burying the bodies?'

'It sounds like it, doesn't it?' Robbie agrees, jaw hitting the floor like an anchor crashing to the seabed.

'We have to go straight in and confront him on it,' Chi asserts.

'I'm not sure,' I caution. 'I still don't know whether he realises he's doing that stuff, remembering things out loud. And even if he does realise, if we call him out for letting something slip, he might go even more into his shell.' The frisson of excitement between us is electric.

Robbie's already pulling a packet of pickled onion Monster Munch out of his bag in celebration. He pops it open and offers them round. We both decline.

'You've got fear paralysis.' Chi pulls up the sleeves on her black Boohoo crop top. 'We never have anything strong to go off with him, and we get nowhere. Now we *have* got something, don't waste the momentum. Hit him with it! He might unravel. Turn the screw.'

I look at her, both of us unable to keep the smiles from our faces. Chiyoko Aoki, always my last voice in the room.

* * *

The interview room is as icy as the office was ablaze.

Elkins' head is slumped forward and lolling to the side as he looks at the floor. If you'd never met him, and someone told you he'd been lobotomised, you'd believe them based on 90 per cent of his movements.

'Can you look up?' I provoke.

He tilts back a fraction and meets my eyes.

'Here's one I've never asked you before,' I toy. 'Have you ever told anyone where the bodies are? A cellmate? A warder? Just to get it off your chest?'

'Nope.'

'No, of course not. I mean, even if you had, it's in your best interest to say you haven't, so we don't go back and find everyone you've shared cells with, try to get round you that way. Silly question really.'

No response, barely listening again.

'But someone else knows about the bodies, don't they?'

His eyes are up, crushing me all of a sudden. My pulse quickens as the stare intensifies.

'Quite the physical feat to lug a body about all on your own and bury it, all in the one night,' I push.

Eyes stuck on me, he shakes his head.

'Much easier with help.'

Slow shake this time.

'That would be a *real* reason to keep quiet all these years, wouldn't it?'

My heart pounds. Everything feels ultra real: the hum of white lights above, the still air clinging to my goosebumped forearms, every plosive that pops on my lips. This is everything this place was intended to be.

Elkins' eyes are wider than I've ever seen them before. He swallows hard before replying in a low, certain rumble. 'I was alone.'

'The second one, Ollie Vaughn. That didn't go to plan, did it? Didn't go to *your* plan at least. How else to explain such a shoddy job when all the others were so well hidden? Did the other person take the lead on that one?'

No answer, but his grinding teeth give away an unfamiliar panic. He's broken eye contact, his gaze darting around the floor as if following a mouse scurrying back and forth along the tiles. The tells are minor, but by Elkins' standards they're colossal.

'There's someone else still alive who knows about those bodies, isn't there?'

Something childlike and terrified bubbles up in his haggard, blotchy face. Then a brutal jolt forward, and another, his arms jerking as they remain pinned at his sides. Is he trying to escape? I push my own chair a foot back, unnerved by his spasming chest, realising too late what's happening. His mouth snaps open – vomit cascades out. Warm, gluey spots of it bounce off the table, splatter and cool on my cheeks as I belatedly retreat from the splash zone.

He doesn't say another word. He doesn't have to.

28

Joe hears the block's main entry door open but doesn't get up from his bed. His cell feels smaller and smaller these days, which is a great sadness since he's spending more and more time in it. His chessboard is the only reason to use the common room, but even then he has to psyche himself up to go in there, to ignore anything horrible Tim Shenton might say or do.

So Joe stays lying down, nudging back and forth, the crooked leg of the bedframe by his right foot squeaking as the welding stretches and strains at a different angle to the other three legs. If it snaps, they'll be forced to sort it out at long last.

'What's happened to you?' Tim enquires in the common room – it sounds like Frank's back from yet another session with Emy.

Tim's always trying to suck up to Frank. It's pathetic. Frank's so cold and unfriendly. Joe and Tim could have been good pals. But Tim has hated Joe from the start, treated him like rubbish.

At least George Petty treated everyone the same, he was even quite chatty on a good day. Frank's a boring oaf, obviously. But Tim... he's something else – nasty, twisting things, overblowing things, making drama out of absolutely ruddy nothing. At first Joe blamed himself: the bed thing, then maybe trying *too* hard to be Tim's friend. But now he thinks differently. Joe's done nothing to Tim. Nothing. He reckons Tim's just like those girls that used to pick on him at school. Joe wishes he could teach him a lesson, show Tim he's not a wimp, not someone to be laughed at. Teach him a real lesson. Just like he always dreamed of doing to those school bullies. Yeah, that'd be so good.

'Hey, Frank! What's happened?' he hears Tim call again.

'Shut up,' Joe whispers under his breath, making sure the riposte is nowhere near loud enough to be overheard.

Frank doesn't respond to Tim, however. All Joe can hear is Frank's heavy gait padding quickly back to his own cell and shutting the door so hard a tremor reaches Joe's cell door.

Then it's all very quiet. The distant hiss of Frank turning his shower on is the only change. Joe begins to lose interest and is just about to return to his rocking when the common door clicks open again.

Frank's already back in, Tim's obviously in. Must be a guard entering. But they've already served up breakfast. Maybe they've come to ask for Joe. Maybe it's time for that next chat with Emy that she promised!

Springing up from the brittle bedframe, Joe can't help but investigate.

'What's happened?' he hears Tim ask the warder this time as Joe reaches the door of his cell.

'Elkins isn't feeling well. Giving him some fresh clothes,' says the guard – Danny – one of the sweeter, more friendly security staff.

'Was that sick all over his front?' Tim asks, revelling in the drama.

'Is he OK?' Joe asks Danny, his feet still in his cell but his head peering round the door.

'He'll be fine,' Danny smiles before knocking on Frank's cell door and calling in. 'I'll leave your fresh clothes out here, Frank, for after your shower. Just leave the old ones in the laundry bin as usual.'

No response inside the cell.

'Is it something we've eaten? Could I have a bug too?' Tim asks.

Tim is so self-centred; Joe hates him.

'I doubt it,' Danny says, clearly desperate to leave.

This is highly unusual.

Danny departs. Joe creeps out of his own cell towards Frank's, making as little noise as possible so Tim will have no reason to snarl at him.

Tapping his knuckles on Frank's door, he says: 'Everything OK in there? Bit of an accident, was it? Would you like some water?'

No response – from Frank at least.

'He's not going to reply to *you*, is he?' Tim mocks, still seated at Frank's usual table.

Joe wants to scream. Tim just makes him so angry. He takes a deep breath.

Be cool, Joe. Be cool.

'If you aren't feeling well later then please let me know, I can get you some help,' Joe keeps talking through the cell door to Frank.

Tim lets out a disparaging snort. 'There're cameras everywhere, why would *you* need to raise the alarm?'

Shut up, shut up, shut up, shut up, shut up, shut up. Keep it in, Joe. Come on!

'I'll just be in my room if you do need me for anything, Frank, OK?' Joe ends, turning and making for his own room.

Tim's forcing out fake guffaws of mean laughter. 'He's fobbed you right off, soft lad.'

'I'm being nice!' Joe shrieks, swinging back round to face the stupid man and his stupid face sitting on his stupid chair. In fact, Joe notices Tim is sitting in Frank's usual seat, the one with the string tied around the leg. Who does this man think he is?

'Don't be pathetic,' Tim smirks. 'He's not three. My goodness. No wonder Miss Rose never asks to see you if you're this much of a pussy all the time.'

'I get on better with her than you *ever* will!' Joe yells.

'Oh yeah, then how come she never wants to talk to you?' Tim flops back with his arms behind his head.

Joe doesn't know what to say. He'd hoped no one had noticed Emy hadn't called for him much recently. 'We speak as much as anyone,' he claims, convincing no one.

'No you don't. And she lets me have my arms free in the interview room. Not pinned to the chair like you, y'idiot. Why? Because she actually *likes* me.'

'Stop lying!' Joe clenches his fists so tightly they jitter by his sides.

'Ask her next time she invites you in... not that it'll be any time soon. We should see who she calls for next. I bet it's me,' Tim gloats, winking.

'Leave me alone!' Joe cries, his voice wobbling.

Tim changes tone, as if he's talking to a baby: 'Awww, what? You gonna cry?' Then he pushes out another laugh and adds, 'You really are a pussy!'

Joe scurries back behind his cell door and slams it shut.

Slapping his lamp off his bedside table, he plants his head face down into his pillow and screams. This has to stop.

29

I dreamt about Sam last night. I'm not sure if that's a good thing – that in some way I'm feeling closer to him. Or is it just the mind resorting to self-flagellation?

He was still only about nineteen in the dream, immortally stuck in adolescence. And yet as we talked, I never questioned why my brother – born only three years after me – still looked like a teenager while I am now almost twice his age.

The dream wasn't horrible or nightmarish. It didn't cross my mind that he'd been kidnapped and killed. We were just in a car – not even one I recognise – driving, listening to Queen and laughing. I can't remember what we talked about, but I remember the feeling, the ease, the naturalness with which we sat revelling in each other's company. It was an intuitive happiness you have with those few people who truly *know* you; we shared an absent-minded, impossible-to-articulate relational DNA, one you never properly appreciate when it's happening because you're too busy enjoying it, living nowhere except in that immediate moment of unbridled unanimity – we have that, at least we did. And still do in my dreams.

Then I woke up.

Back to an existence which he no longer shares. With only the faint hope we'll reconvene another night soon, for a hazy, scriptless exchange that is already fading like steam by the time I wake.

I haven't told Mum about my dream, I never do. But I have told her about the new theory of Elkins having an accomplice; in fact, I told her last night. She didn't take it well. Too much to comprehend in one go, is my guess. She needs time. She barely interacted with me all evening.

Leon's asked if I fancy dinner this evening – says he's got fresh intel on Shenton. I accept. Two hours' respite from the febrile storms of home and office may just keep me sane. Plus, Harrington was badgering Chi this morning, whinging about the lack of progress on Shenton's case. These fresh crumbs could be most useful.

Might be *a bit* awkward though, what with me deciding I'm going to break up with him this evening as well...

* * *

I sit alone at Leon's dining table while he beavers away in the kitchen. We're half talking, half shouting through the wall at each other in a bid to maintain conversation. I'm no couples counsellor, but I'm pretty sure dead-heading a relationship via scream while your partner stands over a pot of penne pasta in an adjacent room is frowned upon.

I don't know why he's trying to impress me with his culinary skills anyway, I'd rather date a sommelier than a chef.

He did at least fix me his 'house drink' when I arrived – a Whiskey Cee-Zee, he called it. Turns out it's just a whiskey and

Coke Zero, which to be fair, is pretty funny. But I've finished my fancy cocktail now.

I try poking my head round the door but he escorts me back to my seat promising that the feast is about to begin.

None of my chair's legs are the same length so I sit there rocking back and forth, wondering why the walls are so bare, why there's no rug or carpet on the floor, and he hasn't even bothered to buy curtains for the lounge window. What does that say about a man? That he's boring? That he needs a woman to come in and make his house a home? That he's recently committed murder and had to dispose of all soft furnishings as they were contaminated with the victim's blood?

None of the potential explanations are particularly inspiring.

'Sorry, sorry!' he exclaims, rushing in with a huge bowl of said pasta that he plonks in the middle of the table. 'Here it is!'

Half his flat block probably feels the ground quake as my stomach grumbles in anticipation. The food smells divine. There's a very good chance I'm going to get sauce over my chin, nose and shirt. That might be a perfect performance, y'know! Surely he won't want to keep dating me if I eat like a toddler.

'This better be good,' I say as he passes me a large spoon and I scoop out bucketfuls of cheesy, tomatoey, chorizo-y pasta onto the warm plate that has just appeared in front of me.

'If you don't like it, I'll waive the service charge,' he says.

I give his dad-joke a titter of encouragement, mainly because he is now – finally – opening a bottle of white wine.

'So... how have you been?' he asks as he settles into another rickety chair opposite and ladles out his own portion of pasta.

I've got a pact with a potential child-killing rapist that I haven't told you about, and it might be starting to reap rewards with the man who killed my brother – which I also haven't told you about.

'Weekend with Mum then just back at Beeswell. Pretty dull,' I say instead, inspired by his living room décor.

'Busy couple of days at work?'

What *can* I tell him? 'Yeah, busy as always.'

'Any breakthroughs? Off the record, obviously.'

'Maybe... A few chinks of light... nothing concrete,' I'm shovelling in the warm, gooey penne – it's so damn good. No way I can waste a drop of it by eating sloppily. That was a terrible plan. Plus, the fuller my mouth is with that delectable sauce, the harder it is to answer these prying questions on the Hive. That's just science.

'Blimey, I've seen boa constrictors chew more!'

I shrug in apology and keep shovelling.

'I know we joked about it last time but I would like to meet your mum eventually,' he states. He's holding his cutlery above his dinner like the knife – and fork – of Damocles but isn't eating, instead looking at me and waiting for me to peer up too so he can make some meaningful eye contact. I take a very brief respite from gorging to gulp down some wine and tell him truthfully how scrumptious the meal is. Hopefully that's enough to stop him asking about my mother again. When am I going to do this, when do I deliver the fatal blow? I've had my fair share of dumpings, but I'm usually on the receiving end – wankers, all of them, by the way.

Yet here I sit, opposite a man I actually like, whose one crime is being kind and nice and generous to me at a time when my life is in bedlam. But while the distraction is so, so good, Mum and Sam don't leave room for a partner, even if I must forego my Shenton sleuth and our conjugal visits. Stupid, lovely, ignorant, amazing Leon. I can't lead him on. That said, ending it is going to be like putting a pillow over a puppy's face. Can I do that?

'What about you and Tim Shenton?' I mumble with my

mouth full – trying to focus on the grub instead. I'm starting to get some smoky garlic hints coming through now. Magnificent chef-ing.

'More goss as promised.' His eyebrows raise in pride. 'From this woman who worked at one of the orphanages he stayed at. Apparently, she came forward to the police offering evidence against Shenton but they fobbed her off because she'd been sacked. Using the orphanage's credit card on personal items, or something. Anyway, she was still worth chatting to. It's mind-blowing how much the police overlooked. If I could break half of it in the paper, Harrington would be done for, even without bringing up his son. But it could take months to get a legally watertight version. He's perfectly placed to snuff out any stories he wants, I've never seen a justice secretary use their powers so obviously to undermine justice before.'

'I despise that man.' I shake my head.

Leon agrees. He looks a bit dishevelled today, no sweet scent on him, stubble three or four days old. The warm, generous smile is still there, at least.

'Go on then,' I say, seeing he's bursting to tell me. 'This woman from the orphanage. What was her deal?'

'Ah well, very interesting,' he replies, trying his usual technique of pausing in the hope I'll beg him to carry on.

I just widen my eyes and give my head a tiny wobble of impatience.

'She hadn't got a good word to say about Tim Shenton, even as a kid. Said he was cruel, sneaky, would lie all the time, bullied weaker kids, stole things.'

'We know he's troubled. Kind of all fits the pattern. Doesn't make him a killer though. I've got to file my next report to Harrington tomorrow and I'm pretty sure I'm going to say there's no way I could offer myself as a prosecution witness. If anything, I'd do a better job for the defence.'

He's as bemused as I knew he would be, and that's not even the bombshell I've come to strike him with.

'That's... What?'

I shrug. 'I don't see the requisite violence or anger in him to be able to perpetrate the crime.'

'He's an arch-manipulator, you've said it yourself.' Leon double-takes. 'He'll wear whatever mask it takes to convince you he's not guilty. That's a red flag in itself.'

'Sorry, which one of us is the trained psychologist?' I fire back, riled by the condescension.

'Yeah, but... listen to what I'm telling you. A woman who worked with him as a child saw a cruel streak, a bullying streak, a lack of compunction for lying and stealing. He's using the same tricks now.'

'Not necessarily.'

Leon goes quiet and the lack of back and forth gives me a moment to reflect. I don't truly believe the things I'm saying. Even a half-arsed, meddled-with police investigation found enough evidence to prosecute Shenton, and Leon's built on that foundation further himself in the last two weeks. And yet I somehow have to make it seem reasonable and legitimate when I send a pathetic report to Harrington saying Shenton could well be innocent. Those are the terms of the pact. Chi's definitely suspicious now of why I'm staying late in the office every night too. If she has a grain of distrust about my intentions with Shenton already, she'll have a whole beach by the time she reads my next report. I've thought about fessing all to her, but now she's buttered Harrington's biscuit there's just this 1 per cent of me that fears she'd blab to him. Why, oh why, oh why, did she do it? I will never have a justifiable answer.

'Just my opinion,' I chirp up, back in the room with Leon, trying to be conciliatory. 'Did this woman mention any specific incidents?'

'Said that no one ever wanted to bunk with Shenton or share a room with him, but it was very hard getting the kids to explain why. Also said he came back from walking in the woods in the orphanage grounds on several occasions with dead animals: birds, squirrels, a fox once. Said she never got to the bottom of whether he'd just found them dead or if it was something more sinister, but it gave all the staff the creeps how interested he was in the bodies.'

Bloody hell, why didn't he lead with that? Morbid fascination with death and high probability of having perpetrated animal cruelty in childhood. Those traits often manifest sexually in adulthood among people with antisocial personality disorder. Not that I can let Leon know any of that.

'It's common for witnesses to subconsciously adjust memories years after the fact, if it makes them fit better with what they believe in the present. Sounds like her imagination's probably got away from her slightly, off the back of what she's heard about Tim in the news.'

'Why would she do...? If you'd been there with me, you'd have seen how genuine she was.' He's not touched his food since I started disagreeing with him, but his hand taps the stem of his wine glass over and over.

Can I really end my connection with this man? He's so smart and astute and pure and, well... yeah, hot! I want to make this work, tell him *everything*, spend way more time with him and not think about work, just let him hug me and drink wine with me and plot a life away from the Hive with me. But I can't. I'm trapped and the only way out is to brutally rip myself from one of the few genuine, beautiful, relatable men I have ever met.

'You said she got done for using company accounts to pay for her own stuff,' I restate, trying to keep on topic. 'I wouldn't take her word as gospel.'

If I don't break up with Leon, how much longer will I have to force myself to contradict his growing evidence? I feel so sorry for him. Who made gaslighting so onerous?

No matter! Mum and Sam are the priority. Always. And Shenton is the best route to Elkins right now. Next, we need to work out who this accomplice might be. That's the primary concern.

And in all honesty, I didn't expect Leon to be so relentless in his pursuit of Shenton. I must seem so contrary: I ask him to find dirt on Shenton, he does find dirt, I pass it off as nothing.

Bewilderment is writ large on Leon's face. 'Well, even if you're not convinced, I'm going to keep digging. Still need to find that one friend he supposedly had. This woman mentioned him too, but hadn't got a name either.'

I stare at my plate, shovelling more pasta in.

'Change of subject,' he announces. 'Not this Saturday but the next one, it's my birthday.'

'The big five-oh?' I tease, not really knowing why.

'Har-har,' he says. 'Forty-two, actually. I'll be going for brunch with some friends and I'd love you to come.'

This is my moment – U-turn right away from romance. That's it, that's all I have to do, say once and for all... look Leon Matey-Boy, it's been fun but it's over.

'Yes,' I tell him. 'I'll be there for sure.'

Why can't I say it? Why? Go on! Just say it! It's over! Do the whole Monty Python 'dead parrot' routine if you have to... This relationship is no more, it has ceased to be, it is an ex-relationship. He'll understand, you aren't doing it because he's dull or weird or bad in bed. Certainly not! You're letting him go because your life is a basket case and it wouldn't be fair to give him 20 per cent when he deserves 100. Go on... tell him!

Yet... I don't.

A small, relieved smile returns to his face and little dimples pop up in his cheeks as I fail to talk.

Ergh! Since when was I such a people pleaser?! I'm going soft in my old age and now I have an unwanted bruncheon date to navigate. And on a Saturday too, when I'm supposed to be out with Mum.

The rest of the evening is suitably excruciating. Pudding is homemade crème brûlée. He caramelises the sugar with a blow torch in front of me. My guilt at not coming clean almost distracts from how tasty the dessert is – almost. Somehow, I soldier on.

Afterwards he goes to open a second bottle but I stop him and suggest I'm going to head home. He doesn't flinch or put any pressure on, he accepts my underwhelming response like the classy gent he is.

'That's OK.' He smiles in his usual breezy way. 'I still need to do my Wordle for the day, anyway.'

Ha! I knew it! I *so* knew it!

'Em,' he says as he's getting my jacket. 'Be careful standing up to Harrington over Tim Shenton. If Harrington wants him found guilty, he probably will be, and if you don't toe the line, from what I've seen of the man, he wouldn't think twice about canning your project.'

'Oh, I know, he tells me that every time we speak.'

'So given all the evidence on Shenton, it might be best if you at least don't actively fight the guilty narrative with Harrington, for self-preservation if nothing else.'

Oh Leon, you annoyingly thoughtful man, if only my world were that simple.

30

Another Saturday, another expedition to the innumerable fields of North Yorkshire for the county's bleakest walking club – where only one of us is still walking at this point.

The rest of this week has been painfully underwhelming. Elkins has refused to come out of his cell so I haven't been able to drill any deeper there. And without the man himself to talk to, Shenton's unique selling point has been severely curtailed.

Meanwhile, at home, Mum's still refusing to countenance the idea there even was an accomplice: I explain over and over how Ollie Vaughn's grave appeared to be dug by a different person to the others; I remind her again and again of Elkins' vomitous reaction when I raised the idea; I relay time after time the incriminating line Elkins blurted to Shenton when they were discussing digging the holes. She's having none of it.

This morning is the first day she's brightened up since I brought up the new theory – her mood always rises on the outward journey.

She's typing on her phone in the passenger seat – sloth-slow with one arm still in a sling – then hands me the mobile as we wait at some traffic lights. *When will I get to meet this boy?*

'Boy?' I laugh. 'Mum, he's over forty.'

She's tapping away for a while after that and I don't get the chance to read it until we've parked up:

> You need to find a nice boy/man. Someone who understands the pressures you're under and is willing to be patient with your job for now. But once we've found Sam you'll have more time on your hands, and it would be nice to have someone handsome and loving there to share it with.

I glance up from the message at Mum's sweet, smiling face, grasp her small, fragile hand tight and kiss her on the cheek. I turn to my driver's side door so she doesn't see me welling up.

Then, dry as you like, I add: 'You just want a grandkid.'

She slaps me on the thigh and we share a goofy grin.

Wheelchair out, Mum settles in and we begin our trek. At least it's sunny today. T-shirt and shorts weather.

My thighs have only just recovered from last weekend's exertions, but they feel a little stronger this Saturday.

We stop for our cheddar and Branston pickle sandwiches – two each – around midday and both feel happy to push on as the sun continues to beat down. I speak about Beeswell mainly, every detail I can summon, every exchange I can remember, delicately peppering in the new accomplice theory hoping Mum will warm to it – and to my eternal relief, there is a little bit of quiet nodding coming from her as we drift along. Progress.

We make our way along yet another thin, dusty perimeter of a verdant meadow. A couple walks the other way holding hands, their golden retriever bounding in zigzags ahead of them, snapping at butterflies, sniffing at buttercups.

As always on these outings, Mum's eyes are scanning the vicinity. The single question *Where is he?* silently pulsing from her every movement like the bleep of a sonar.

I'm nauseous thinking about it. We do seem a step closer to the truth after all these years, but that truth is not going to be comforting, it is going to be atrocious.

A rogue midge bounces off my forearm, pulling me out of my funk as I slap it dead against my skin.

Mum mimes rubbing her own arms then points at the sun to suggest I should put on more sun cream.

'Nah, I'll be fine,' I reply.

She shakes her head.

'It's been funny not having Elkins in the common room for days,' I jabber. 'Seeing how different they all are. Shenton spotted that Elkins had tied string around the leg of his favourite chair so Joe won't dare use it. But Shenton makes a point of sitting in it specifically now Elkins is sulking in his cell. Wonder what that says about them all?'

Mum looks round.

'I told you, didn't I? Shenton spotted it – Elkins tied string around a couple of things so the others all know they're his.'

Mum's looking up at me, perplexed, as if I've just told her I've soiled myself. We slow to a stop.

'What? The string thing Elkins does... I had a go at Robbie for not raising it as soon as he spotted it himself. I mentioned it... didn't I?'

Her petite, brittle fingers are twitching like spiders' legs but I don't recognise any sign language.

She huffs and takes out her phone.

'What is it?' I half chuckle.

Her thumb pushes at the keyboard on her screen with a dismal lack of pace. I take in our surroundings. The next field rolls up towards a country lane. I might suggest we follow that back down towards the car, it's getting too hot with less breeze now. I check the time, 3.20 p.m. Yeah, definitely been out long enough.

She's still typing, slowly but deliberately.

Pulling the water bottle out of my backpack, I spin off the top and take a long slug. 'Is this a novel?' I ask, feeling a bit more human after my drink.

Finally she hands me the phone.

Elkins ties string to things to mark them as his? I've seen stones in walls with string tied round them before. What knot does he use? The stones have double constrictor knots.

I read the message three times without replying. How on earth would anyone notice something like this? It's a level of observation so unfathomable it cannot be real.

Yet if there's anyone in the whole world who would spot such a microscopic detail, it's Mum.

'I don't know what knot it is,' I say apologetically. 'Can you show me the rocks? Where are they? How many are there?'

There are two apparently. The nearest is on a farm about three miles west of Elkins' old house. Her next message reads:

What if Elkins used the string as markers?

'Markers for what? For graves?'

Mum shrugs as if to say *maybe*.

It's a long shot – a very long shot – but given the complete lack of hope these excursions usually provide, I'm forced to admit this is at least worth investigating.

Back at the car, she plucks a map off the floor and slaps a

confident finger on the area she thinks the offending string is to be found.

***

The drive takes about twenty minutes. We pull up in the courtyard of the farmhouse. Mum assures me there is no problem with parking up next to the owners' muddy Land Rovers.

I'm still undoing my seatbelt as I see her stalking off towards the front door.

'Mum!' I cry through the windscreen. 'I'll get the wheelchair out of... urgh!'

I get out and rush after her. My trainers, that had survived unsullied on the original cross-country walk over sun-baked dry land, are already flecked with wet clay-like mud spatters from the filthy track up to the house.

Knocking with as much strength as her little knuckles can muster, the door is already open before I make it up to join her.

"Ello Mimi,' comes the warm Yorkshire welcome from the hearty woman who answers. Instinctively, she leans in and gives my mum a generous hug. 'Having a wander round, is it? D'you fancy a glass o' somethin' before you go? Oh no, what happened to your arm?'

The friendly woman, complete in flowery apron, glances up at me. 'This your friend, Mimi?'

She sticks a plump reddish hand out to me and I shake it. Blimey, the grip of the woman! She almost tears my arm off.

'Oh, I'm Mimi's daughter.'

'Is that right?' the woman nods before turning to call back into the house. 'Bill... BILL... Mimi's here with her daughter!'

'Who?' a muffled shout bounces back.

'MIMI.'

Footsteps follow and a rosy-cheeked man, about sixty and plump like a Toby jug, appears in the doorway, brushing pastry flakes off the front of his gilet like savoury dandruff.

"Ello Mimi,' he says in exactly the same way as the woman, who I now assume is his wife.

What on earth is going on? Have I just walked into an alternate reality where Mum is head of the Yorkshire farming mafia? Maybe that's why she hasn't spoken all these years – it's not trauma, it's omertà.

Of course, she stands there in silence throughout this bizarre scene leaving me to explain our unexpected arrival. 'Mum thinks there might be a wall on the farm somewhere with a piece of string tied round some rock she'd like me to see.' I cringe as I say the words out loud. This couple must think we're complete crackpots.

'String on a wall, y'say?' the man repeats, trying and failing to recollect the detail himself but taking the revelation much more seriously than I'd expected. 'OK, where is it? I can zip y'over there. Be quicker.'

Mum nods and smiles. Not to be left out, Mrs Farmer Woman follows as the man leads us over to the closer of the two Land Rovers.

'Which field y'thinking of, Mimi?' Mr Farmer Man asks. His name was Bill, wasn't it? Was that what his wife yelled? I'm struggling to take in half of what's going on.

Let's call him Bill.

Bill lists about a dozen fields and Mum finally nods again when she hears the name of the one she wants us to go to.

We get in the car and he accelerates across the drive, bumping along the uneven ground past the farmhouse and through a gate into one of the surrounding fields.

'What's y'name, sorry love?' The wife asks, leaning round to speak to me from the front passenger seat.

'Oh, Emy. Pleased to meet you. Sorry for the inconvenience.'

'No! Not at all. I'm Gladys and this is Bill. We've known y'mum a long time, she's been coming round the fields for years, haven't y'Mimi? Frank Elkins used to work for us on and off y'see, and after everything that happened, we just always wanted to help.'

Mum smiles in agreement.

'We were just sitting down for a bit of a breather so this is a nice surprise,' Gladys goes on, warm and genuine.

It takes about ten minutes, then Bill announces we've arrived and Mum leans forward into the gap between the seats, gesturing to the bit of wall she wants to stop by.

The Land Rover trundles over, Bill cranks the handbrake then takes his keys out of the ignition.

Once again Mum's out of the car first, door flung open, letting horrible wafts of cow pats infiltrate my nostrils before I'm ready. She stoops down, looks along the wall then stops and snaps out a finger, pointing about two feet above the floor.

I skip after her. There, as predicted, is a rock – among the thousands that make up this one wall – with brown twine tied repeatedly around it.

'Your mum's got a cracking memory,' says Bill. 'Never doubted she'd be right.' He gets down on his haunches and inspects the rock. 'Y'know, I'd never ever noticed that before.'

The last half an hour has been so bewildering that I stall. And despite my present company my first reaction is one of shame. I told Robbie off for not telling me about Elkins' habit with string, and yet somehow, I never even passed the detail on to Mum. What a hypocrite! I try to re-engage with the matter at hand. 'So *you* didn't put that string there?' I ask Bill.

'No, no, why would ya?'

I look at Mum; she's looking at me. I glance at Gladys; she's also staring at me, understandably rather confused.

'Mum thinks Frank Elkins might have tied the string round the rock there as a marker for where a body's buried. Says there's another one at another farm too. So it's not an agricultural thing, tying string to stuff?' I check again.

Bill shakes his head, the glare of the sun beating off his short white halo of hair. 'Not on a random rock, and not a double constrictor knot.'

'Yeah, Mum said it was... that.' I crouch down next to him as he continues tracing a finger over the string. 'Is it easy enough to get any of these rocks out of the wall?' I enquire, giving the stone a pathetic little nudge.

'Most will be jammed in, but the odd one might be loose.' With that, Bill grips the edges of the same rock with his spade-like hands and pulls it from side to side. It comes out within two seconds. 'Yeah, like that y'see.' He turns it over in his hands; apart from the string and the fact it slipped out of the wall like a loose Jenga piece, there doesn't seem to be anything remarkable about it.

I turn to Mum. Her eyes are strained and wide, she must have a hundred follow-up questions she can't get out. She's relying on me. What else do I ask? 'Just speaking hypothetically, do you think it would be at all possible for someone to get into this area of the farm and bury a body? Or would you have noticed it, with all the churned-up earth and everything?'

Bill stands back up again and strokes his chin, the scratch of stubble against those coarse hands making a soft scraping noise as he ponders. 'I mean the longest I'd not be in the field would be two or three weeks, bit o' rain, the earth put back in flat and neat, I reckon it's not *impossible*.'

'OK.' Think brain, think. What else can I ask?

A horrible thought strikes. If Elkins did have an accomplice, could it be this farmer, Bill? Hide the body on his own land, almost no chance of it being discovered. Elkins worked for all the local landowners as a farmhand. Could he have got this man involved? I look across at Bill, he crouches back down next to me, I can smell his musk, a mixture of overworking and undershowering. He doesn't look panicked like you would if you knew someone had just discovered a burial site on your land. He looks puzzled, like the rest of us. And he brought us straight here, no funny business or leaving us to find it ourselves. My gut kicks in: this man is no ally of Elkins'.

'That knot you mentioned, Bill,' Gladys pipes up. 'Is that a common one, or is it from the navy or something?'

'Not from the forces that I know of,' he tells his wife. 'Not the most common though, not one everyone would know, I'd say that.'

I grunt. 'I need to go back to Beeswell, see if Elkins' ones match this...'

Brainwave!

'Hang on.' I pull out my phone. This is exactly the kind of useless knowledge Robbie might retain.

> Hi sorry it's a Saturday. Do you know the kind of knot Elkins tied in the string on his chair in the common room?

'Just texted someone at work in case he knows,' I explain. 'He's good with patterns and stuff like that.' The couple nod in support.

'How did you even ever spot that string, Mum?' I ask in awe, aware she can't respond but feeling uncomfortable at the lack of conversation. 'And how did you know it was that double constrictor knot?'

She gives a humble, nervous shrug.

The silence resumes and I think about suggesting we all head back up to the farmhouse, apologising for taking up this couple's precious time, but at least having given Mum her chance to show me the offending article.

I check my phone one last time. 'Oh, he's typing!' Those three little dots tap along under my message. It probably takes five seconds for Robbie to reply but it feels like a lifetime.

> Yeah I think so.

Comes the first message.
More typing. Another eternity. And then...

> It's a double constrictor knot.

31

I read Robbie's text message aloud and stare at Mum. Her eyes flick and flitter around spots on the ground, trying to comprehend.

Bill and Gladys share a gasp of their own and choose not to speak either.

I'm suddenly super aware of the heartbeat crashing in my chest, the pulse thumping against the right side of my neck. Need to keep calm. It's a piece of string, not a tag with Sam's name on it. But what if... What if he's right underneath us? Right here. With us now.

I'm sweating, breathing heavily, reeling between nervous and dizzy. The heat of the sun is blocked out by the tense pinch of what could be.

No! Stop it! No thinking like that. Not yet. Coincidences ten times more astounding than this come and go every day and we don't think anything of them. It's just a knot in some twine – for now.

'You said there were two of these rocks, Mum.' I swallow hard. 'Should we go and check the other one's still there too?'

She nods, dazed. I can stall myself from running away with the hope that we've found Sam, but Mum is clearly bounding down that chain of thought far too quickly for me to stop her.

Usually she's quiet. OK, always she's quiet. But right now, she's bursting with ideas, questions, observations. I can tell. Her jaw is jutting and twitching, on the edge of blurting it all out. Then she looks up through the coming tears and motions back up the slope. She wants to find the other field.

I take several pictures of the offending stone then Bill drives us back to the farmhouse and he and Gladys both make clear they are happy to call the police or have officers come on to the property whenever necessary, if it comes to that. I thank them over and over.

And will it come to that? Police coming to inspect the wall? I suppose it will. This is a potential clue to a quintet of murders that has baffled law enforcement for too many years.

Mum pulls another map out from the back seat as we get back into my car. She finds the other farm and we work out the route.

'I'll try calling Detective Miller on the way. She might have some thoughts,' I suggest to more nods from Mum.

Detective Miller is the chief superintendent at North Yorkshire Police who led the initial investigation into Sam and the other missing men and finally caught Elkins. I've not seen her in almost a decade but I know she keeps in touch with Mum and has always retained a genuine sense of regret at not having found the other bodies.

Mum texts me her number and I try it on the way over to the second farm. No answer. Annoying.

The dynamic at the second farm follows a similar pattern to our time with Bill and Gladys. They recognise Mum, embrace her warmly, I explain why we're there, they take us down to the field. Mum inevitably remembers correctly again exactly what she's looking for and there it is: another of those rocks, low down in a wall with string tied in one of those double constrictor knots. Nothing else on it, nothing even in the wall behind the rock. I take more pictures of this one too. Could Sam be *here*? Under the ground at *this* farm? Under my feet right *now*?

No! Stop it, stop it!

The farmer takes us back up to the farmhouse.

The sun is close to the horizon now, a gorgeous mellow light washing everything in syrupy orange. I try Detective Miller once more as Mum and I sit in our car before setting off home. Jagged nerves slash at me as she picks up.

'Hello?'

'Hello, is that Annie Miller?' I ask, putting the phone on speaker so we can both hear the conversation.

I explain who I am. The detective doesn't need a second prompt.

'Hello Emy, how's your mum? How's the research study at Beeswell Barracks? I've been keeping up to date on it all.'

'Oh, it's fine thanks.' I glance at Mum and offer a reassuring smile which she reciprocates. 'I'm actually ringing about something related to that. Is now a good time?'

It doesn't matter if it's a good time, a bad time or the last time. Detective Miller's not getting off this phone until I've explained exactly what's happened this afternoon. The need to unburden myself to someone who knows the case *and* can talk back is overwhelming – ready to burst out like a smoker's cough.

'Now's fine,' she says, patient and interested. 'Go on.'

So I tell her. Everything. I can feel my voice rising, my talking pace quickening as I whip through it all, desperate to convey how serious I am, but fearing more and more that the whole theory sounds bonkers.

'What do you think?' I end the explanation in a pant.

There's a silence down the line. Is she thinking? Is she still there?

'Hello? Annie?'

'Emy, this could be it. This could be exactly what it is. Obviously, we can't tell yet but we need to get this looked into as soon as possible.'

I turn to Mum and brandish a huge thumbs up; my mouth's dry as I try to formulate some kind of coherent reply.

The chief superintendent beats me to it. 'It's Saturday evening now, and we haven't got a hope in hell of getting anything going tomorrow. But I'll do some teeing up in the morning. We need the cadaver dogs at both sites first thing Monday. Are you and your mum OK to come back to the farms, point us in the right direction?'

'Yes! Yes, of course. Thank you! Thank you for taking it seriously,' I splutter, tears filling my eyes.

'We need to not get ahead of ourselves,' the detective says. 'So let's bottle it for now and I'll phone you tomorrow with details for Monday. But I can tell you, we haven't had a lead like this in years.'

* * *

Chief Superintendent Miller does call on Sunday. We are to be at Bill and Gladys' farm for 9 a.m. on Monday. We can take the dog squad down to the wall, forensics and crime scene photographers in tow. I get the sense DCS Miller is hopeful; I won't let myself be anything other than cynical and pessimistic. It says something about you when a hardened detective with decades of experience with killers and criminals and all manner of nastiness is the less sceptical one.

Mum doesn't write much down or type out many messages. Sunday is a day for reflection, for hope, for prayer. For waiting.

She doesn't sleep well either night – the huge black bags under her eyes are a giveaway. As is the fact I can hear her padding downstairs and putting the kettle on before 6 a.m. on Monday morning.

We set off well in advance and get to the courtyard on Bill and Gladys' farm at about 8.20 a.m. The police aren't here yet; we sit drinking endless tea with Gladys as we wait. She's got that same flowery apron on from Saturday. Does she sleep in that thing? She's got a cracking kitchen though, I'll give her that. Exactly what you'd expect in a farmhouse: slate floor, Aga, porcelain sink the size of a bathtub, huge window above it looking out onto rolling hills. She puts out a rack of toast, complete with huge ramakins of butter and jam. Neither Mum nor I touch any of it.

Bill's been up hours already, she explains. Irrigating potato fields after the dry days, I think she says. It's hard to hold on to any topic for long.

On the outside Mum looks calmer than I feel, sitting with both hands gripping a mug with her latest top-up of tea, making small slurping noises as she sips. She's not taking in Gladys' chatter much either though, I can tell. Exhaustion weighs her down – emotional more than physical.

DCS Miller arrives at about five to nine in an unmarked car. Mid-fifties, she's still dyeing her greying hair blonde. Her skin is weathered and brown from countless long breaks at her family's holiday home in Majorca. I've not seen her since my mid-twenties, but I remember oddly specific details from when she was around a lot in the months after Sam disappeared. She's stout, a neat flick of black liner over each eye. To look at, you could mistake her for a cantankerous Peggy Mitchell type. But her burst of excitement and effusive hug at seeing us reminds me what a sweetie she truly is.

Having not had time to say much more than hello, however, the dog squad arrives – bang on 9 a.m.

Gladys offers to lead the party in the one Land Rover still outside the farmhouse and we get in along with DCS Miller.

The detective does the lion's share of the talking as we bump over the courtyard and into the fields beyond.

'Cadaver dogs are one of our most valuable resources,' she explains. 'If there's a body, they'll sniff it out, doesn't matter if it's 10 ft underground or if it's been there for decades. Extraordinary talent.'

No response from us in the back seats. Too tense.

'They go through about 1,000 hours of training,' she goes on. 'Very labour-intensive course. But my goodness do they pay us back. German Shepherds usually. It's a common misconception that they bark and go crazy if they do sniff out any remains. Quite the opposite. They'll be all action normally. But if they do sniff out a body, they stop there and then, sit right down and stay totally silent.'

Part of me wants this trundle across the fields to last forever. I'm not ready for either outcome. Something or nothing. How could anyone be? It's like sitting your driving exam, waiting on a pregnancy test, speaking in front of a thousand people and losing your virginity all at once. The awareness of how mentally unprepared I am is mind-buckling.

I grab Mum's hand. If I'm a mess, how must she be feeling, locked up in her own head?

She glances over and squeezes my hand back. A small smile and then a look away is all she can muster.

We reach the spot, get out and wait for the dogs' van to park up too. A single middle-aged man gets out and opens the back doors to reveal a single German Shepherd. I don't know why, but I'd expected a whole team of dog handlers and half a dozen hounds to be unleashed.

I point out the string on the rock and the man thanks me. He leans forward, undoes the dog's lead but holds its collar.

'Good boy, good boy,' he says softly.

He gives a quick tap on the front of the dog's chest, lets the collar go and instantly the dog's nose drops to the floor, twitching and fidgeting over the dusty ground. Is that it, has it started?

No one makes a sound. I daren't even audibly breathe for fear of causing a distraction. The only noise is that of the dog's paws patting on the earth and its short, sharp sniffs.

The handler walks slowly alongside the wall, his hand out and tensed open at his hip. The dog follows, snaking back and forth between the edge of the crops and the base of the drystone wall, nose constantly millimetres above the ground.

Over to the crops, turn, across the path, get to the wall, turn, path, crops, turn, path, wall, turn...

No cloud in the sky but the sun's yet to warm up. I grab Mum's hand again, she's quivering.

We all watch as the dog and trainer nudge away from us towards the gate of the field. It takes about two minutes.

'Good boy, good boy,' the handler says as they reach the end of the field and turn around. Nothing. We need the dog to sit, not bark or dance or roll over. We need it to stop and sit. That's the sign, that's what DCS Miller said. But the dog doesn't stop. They're walking back towards us.

What if this isn't anything to do with Elkins? What if this is just string and stone and earth? It suddenly hits me that the hope I thought I'd been denying myself for the last thirty-six hours has infiltrated regardless. Deep down I didn't even contemplate that this wouldn't lead to a discovery. A body. Sam's body. But what if it isn't? What will that do to Mum? Another stab at her heart, another sapling of faith cruelly cleaved back to the root.

The handler and German Shepherd are back next to us now, still searching. The man looks at the detective and shakes his head; the gesture's small but I spot it.

He continues past and the dog follows. Still no one says a word. They head towards the other far corner of the wall.

Mum squeezes my hand tighter. How am I going to rally her after this? Yet another dead-end. DCS Miller literally said this was the best lead they'd had in years. Where do we go from here? We'll have to go to the other site too, first. Mum'll still believe he could be there. But when he isn't, then what?

The dog edges away, a plodding pendulum running out of wall. There can't be more than 15 ft left before the handler reaches the far end of the field –15 ft, 14 ft, 13 ft, 12, 11.

The dog sits.

32

Bones found at both sites. Three front teeth missing in both skulls. That's two bodies found, two still out there. Vinny Elkins, Damian McAree, Nathan Brockhurst, Sam Whirberth. It means a fifty-fifty chance we've found Sam.

DCS Miller says it could take more than a week to get DNA confirmation. Her actual words were: 'Could take ten days, could be any time before that.'

She might as well have got her iPhone out and said: 'Siri... concoct a sentence to guarantee insomnia.'

Monday was dog squad... then digging up the bodies. Tuesday was spent at home. According to my phone that was tracking my movements, I covered twelve miles, 25,000 steps – and I didn't leave the house. Just pacing around trying, and failing, to distract myself. I'd thought Mum would need me there, but she didn't need anyone: too numb, too shaken, too much to compute. I talked *at* her a lot, but I'm not sure she reacted once. Her life's been on pause ever since Sam disappeared, but now it seems her existence has ceased all together, not willing to do anything more than breathe until DCS Miller calls with the results.

I couldn't bear another day of watching her zombify, so on Wednesday I took my Olympic-grade pacing to the streets – twenty miles covered, 42,000 steps, and a growing family of blisters to now care for.

By Thursday, feet battered, Mum still unreachable, I forced myself into the office. So here I now am. My phone is set to 'loud', but it won't stop me tapping the screen every ten seconds to make sure I haven't missed a critical call from the forensics lab.

The phone does ring at one point and my skin almost tears from my body. But it's Harrington, reminding me that, despite the breakthrough, efforts must not drop in getting a confession out of Shenton. The one thing that stops me inflicting a telephonic evisceration there and then is the sure knowledge that one day soon Leon Courtney-Peltz will end this man's political career. My mouth salivates as I picture all the popcorn I'll eat as I watch Harrington's defenestration from Westminster.

To say I can't focus properly in the office is a heinous understatement. Robbie's full of questions about the bodies. I reinvent the discovery of the knots in the stones in my retelling of the tale, making it sound like it was a hunch I had, based on some old evidence – my *string theory*, I call it. Very drole. He is suitably in awe of my deduction, fabricated as it may be. But he simply can't know I was out there with Mum, searching, as Sam Whirberth's sister. No, I'm afraid the only option we have is for him to believe I'm a psychological genius, my hands are tied! I try to fob off all his other queries, however. I tell him I've got a migraine, which holds him at bay – for about five seconds. This is how Mum must have felt with my incessant babbling at home the past few days.

Eventually, he beats me into submission with his relentless inquisition and genuine concern for the victims' families. Bastard.

'So we're sure they're both Elkins' victims?' he checks.

'Forensic archaeologist said they were both men, from the shape of the pelvis. Sternal ribs gave them both an age of around 23,' I explain.

'But that's older than our victims.'

'When they were taken,' I correct him. 'Both had severe spinal curvature which, given what we know so far, suggests they were kept in a cage with no chance to stand up – for years.'

'Years?' Robbie baulks.

'Both skulls having their front teeth missing is the clincher, obviously.'

Robbie nods, processing everything. 'I know the skulls didn't have all the incisors, but they had the canines and molars too... isn't that enough to identify who each one was?'

'Both sets of teeth were severely decayed so couldn't be verified; suggests lack of dental care over a prolonged period since their last check-up.'

'This all seems worse than with the Ollie Vaughn remains. He was found within weeks of going missing, wasn't he?' Robbie continues.

'My theory is Elkins got better at keeping them alive as he went along,' I reply. 'He kills his brother, wants replacements to maltreat the same way, but knows the more you abduct the greater the chance of being caught. He went too far with the first one, didn't feed him etc. Then finessed the formula so he could keep them just about alive for longer... a lot longer.'

'What does this do to our accomplice theory?' he poses.

'Still stands. Who knows what he was doing with these men? Could have had other sick fucks, at least one, coming over to do *whatever* with them. Then they'd owe Elkins – it'd make them perfect accomplices. It'd be in their interest to hide the bodies and would explain why they've never come forward.'

Chi suggests we stop talking. She claims it's making her feel ill, but I know she's doing it for my sake. These two new bodies confirm just how long Elkins was willing to keep his victims locked up. Years and years of torture, neglect, dehumanised a little more every day. But strangely I don't mind talking to Robbie now I've started. It's all horror too abhorrent to attach to reality. And it's over. That's the crumb – you can't even call it a crumb – the *atom* of comfort I cling to: for Sam, it's over.

'They spotted osteomalacia in one of the skeletons,' I go on. 'Soft bones caused by lack of vitamin D. Apparently the disease takes several years to develop. So obviously…'

Neither of them says anything. Even in his own absence, Elkins' behaviour is bewildering people into silence. Classic.

I sit with my thoughts, picking apart a daisy in my mind – they've found Sam, they've found him not, they've found Sam, they've found him not.

After plucking one particularly pessimistic petal, I make a decision: I need to talk to Elkins. If we have found Sam, there's no need to speak to that man ever again, but if we haven't… then I need to carry on as usual.

It's the umbrella rule – you take one out with you, it inevitably won't rain; you leave it at home, you'll be caught in a storm. Better to keep probing when I don't need to, than risk sitting here in complacency thinking it's all done and dusted when it isn't.

I phone through to the security team. 'Elkins to the interview room, please. Don't take "no" for an answer. Use force if necessary.' I hang up.

Chi spins round, petrified. 'Em, we aren't allowed to force them into...'

'Today we are. He fell to pieces when we mentioned an accomplice,' I interrupt. 'What'll he give away now we have bodies? I want all four victims, Chi.'

She glares but doesn't speak.

'All four,' I murmur, just to her. 'Then there won't be any doubt.'

33

Ten days since I was last in a room with him. Ten days since he was being escorted back to his cell covered in his own vomit. Ten days that have been so chaotic, emotional and intense that they passed in a blink. And yet more has changed in that blink, than in the whole decade that preceded it.

The discovery of the remains garnered big licks on news bulletins and websites on Tuesday, with follow-up pieces making yesterday's and this morning's papers so we've not been allowing any publications in the common room. Chi's handled the PR explosion masterfully.

Not that Elkins himself would have stumbled across the headlines. He's not left his room since our last little chat. Done nothing but lie on his bed in despondent inertia. It took him three days to come to his door to collect a meal. But then it was straight back to the bed, straight back to nothing.

I enter the interview room and he is sitting up straighter than usual, ready for me.

'Feeling better?' I ask, taking my own perch and placing my phone face down on the table, ever-ready for that elusive call.

'Yep,' he says, gravelly but engaged.

I'm so used to interacting with him almost daily that ten days is a tangible gap. His hair is noticeably longer, there's a darkness under his eyes that wasn't there last time. Even his jaw cuts a millimetre tighter due to undernourishment.

Do I tell him about the bodies straight away? Let him talk? Return to asking him about an accomplice? I don't want to overwhelm him with developments too quickly, his stomach might chuck another wobbler. 'You've spent a lot of time in your room since we last spoke.'

He raises his eyebrows, turns his mouth down and tilts his head to the side as if giving the comment genuine consideration. Then he nods in agreement.

There's a whiff of confidence, an ease with the interactions that's so unlike him.

I take aim. 'You ready to talk about who helped you with the bodies?'

'It was me alone.'

'OK...'

'I killed Vinny alone. I killed Vaughn alone. I killed McAree alone. I killed Brockhurst alone. I killed...'

'What was with the technicolour yawn last time then?' I jump in. No way he's using Sam's name today. No way.

'Ask a doctor.'

He's regrouped, his guard sky-high; it feels like he's being a touch more assertive too, not content to let me control things. I was hoping he'd be teetering – he's rock steady. He doesn't know what I know though.

'No accomplice. OK,' I accept with my words only. 'So what happened with Ollie Vaughn? Why did you fail in hiding him?'

'"A thinker sees his own actions as experiments and questions – as attempts to find out something. Success and failure are for him answers above all."' he chimes.

'I don't want Nietzsche, I want *you*.'

He tuts and looks away.

'So, Ollie Vaughn. What happened?'

'Can't remember,' he offers.

He's lying and he doesn't care if I know it.

It's back to the bad old days, no insight, no answers, no progress. I still have my trump card about the two bodies but I want to save it.

'You never normally bring your phone in,' Elkins says, nodding at the device.

Shenton would be savvier than that, he'd piece together that I must be waiting on a call and that it must therefore be important to me, would probably work out it must be to do with Elkins, and would put that together with the lack of newspapers in the Hive the last three days and decipher everything that's going on. Elkins isn't so sharp, thank goodness. That's the difference between them. Shenton is a narcissist casting his nets constantly, picking up anything and everything to feed back in and use to his own ends – a social super-computer. Elkins is the opposite – a medieval fort, caring only that no one breaches the walls.

'Did your dad ever show remorse for beating you and your brother?' I pose, grasping desperately as is the usual custom at this point in our conversations.

He gives a trademark shrug. 'He was a tyrant. Tyrants don't apologise.'

'Your mum then, did she show any guilt at having to leave you both alone with him before she died?'

'She had *nothing* to be guilty about.' The affront in his voice is good, it's real.

'Do you remember your last conversation with her?'

Then it happens again. His voice snaps back into the spine-chilling tone of his mother, his head jittering around as he replays the line: *'Don't worry about me, Frankie. Mummy's just dandy. Look after Vinny. Look after little Vinny.'*

Then he's still and silent again.

'She asked you to look after Vinny? What the hell happened?' I blurt out.

I feel the crunch of a thousand eggshells shattering beneath my feet. He doesn't respond.

'Come on, you have to see this doesn't add up. Did your father kill Vinny? Do you feel guilty for that and that's why you said you killed him?' My own rambling pricks at an idea and I follow it. 'Did you and your dad bury your brother together? But then after your dad died you were alone, and burying the next one was a lot harder than you thought. Ollie Vaughn was a botch job. So for McAree, Brockhurst and Whirberth you got in extra help to make sure they'd never be found?'

He stares at the floor throughout my conjecture, face unmoved.

Answer me, damn you! Am I close, am I making headway?

No eye contact, no movement, just his lips nudging open a fraction for a moment: 'Have you heard of *amor fati*?'

As it happens, I have heard of *amor fati* in my extensive research on Friedrich Nietzsche. But I play dumb and tell him I haven't.

'*Amor fati*,' he strikes up, 'is not wanting for anything, either that was, or that could be, or that isn't. Simply existing in the world as it is right now. A love of one's own fate.'

'All just "accept everything exactly how it is", right? OK... so you're all zen about what we find out, yeah? If we find all the bodies, that will just be *amor fati*, will it? *Que sera sera*! Such is life! No! You care *way* more than that!' My finger jabs the air at him.

'*Amor fati* isn't just bearing what is necessary, but loving it,' he quotes gently with an actual smile spreading across his lips. 'You think answers will change things. I'm telling you – they won't.'

That arrogant, callous face is the spark, my words are the detonator.

'We've found remains that match your victims.'

His eyes explode as I stare into them, just as I'd hoped. Every last trace of a grin gone from his sunken, pockmarked face. He's trying to work out if I'm bluffing. My turn for a spiteful, provocative smirk.

'Been in all the papers we've been withholding from Beeswell this week. I'll bring one in for you to look at. *The Times*' coverage has been particularly impressive.'

Utterly still, the permutations rip through his mind like machine-gun bullets.

'Who?' he growls.

'Don't know yet, waiting on DNA.'

'Where did you find them?'

I hold my answer back. He's studying me, as if my body might give up the names without me even speaking; the usual indifference replaced with a blaze of impatience.

'Where did you find them?'

'Does it matter?' I tease, luxuriating in his annoyance.

'Where did you fucking find them?' he snarls between his gritted, yellow wolf teeth.

I give in: 'Farms around your old house in Bedale.'

'How did you find two at once?'

'The string you left on stones to mark the fields gave it away,'

I clarify, wanting to leave him in no doubt that this is real, the game is up.

His gaze darts around the floor again, hopping between hidden thoughts like lily pads.

'It's time to draw a line under all this,' I instruct him. 'Tell us where the other two are now. It's over.'

He blinks hard, eyes still lowered.

I've never spoken his own name to him. Never permitted him the dignity. But I hear myself saying, 'Frank.'

He looks up to see my eyes heavy with tears I prayed wouldn't come. 'Frank, will you take us to the last two sites?'

'You'll never find my brother, and I'll never lead you to him.'

My head swims in euphoric glee; my eyes flicking around the room as I assimilate the loose words. *We'll never find his brother* – that means Vinny Elkins isn't one of the two bodies found around Bedale. If he knows we've found two bodies there and he's still sure one isn't Vinny, there's now a two in three chance we've found Sam.

It's hard to recapture my composure. 'Please, Frank,' I whisper, leaning forward across the table, straining for the chance to pluck the words straight off his tongue. 'Then at least give me the location of the other grave that isn't your brother's.'

'You don't get Vin,' he reiterates with new-found conviction, sniffing up hard.

'I hear you, I hear you, but that still leaves one more boy unaccounted for,' I add, handling the words like the unstable core of a nuclear weapon. 'We can have him, right?'

He swallows hard. '*Amor fati.*'

'No, Frank. You don't want us finding your brother's body, I get that. But that's not *amor fati* either. That's you caring about something and wanting a certain outcome. Tell us where the other grave is, and we never go looking for Vin, yeah? He can rest in peace and all the other families can lay their sons to rest too.'

'I can't,' he says, shoulders slumped. 'I can't, I'm sorry, I just...'

A harsh, intense buzz makes us both jump. It's my phone – it's Detective Miller.

Really? Right now?

I snap to my feet, whip the phone off the desk and dart out of the interview room before answering.

'Hello, Emy,' Detective Miller starts. 'I won't beat around the bush. We've got the DNA results.'

34

Alone with the chessboard. That's a novelty. Joe has missed that over the last few years. He always plays better without outside noises and people distracting him, looking at him, judging him.

Actually, he plays at his *very* best one-on-one, up against a competitor. That really focuses the mind, knowing there is someone opposite, trying to trick you, counter-trick you, destroy you, counter-destroy you. But that's only fun when the competitor is good enough to fear.

He is yet to come across a single inmate in any prison who possesses both the skill required to play chess, and the fortitude to persevere when Joe is clearly winning.

At his previous lodgings, he'd sometimes tease unwitting inmates across the board. Make a deliberate mistake: hang a rook, leave a file open, engineer a discovered check against himself, ignore an opportunity for mate in three – just to see if they would capitalise on it.

No one ever did. And the fun of the contest would leak away like water in cupped hands.

There's no chance of finding such an opponent in this tiny lock-up. Maybe the next place will be better.

It is certainly a privilege of free men that they can seek out individuals of their choosing, others who think like them, act like them, play chess like them. Nothing compares to the electricity of battle. Locking horns, straining every sinew to outwit, outflank and outmanoeuvre your adversary. And then, finally, crushing them, crushing *the life* out of them, all on pure merit.

Is there any other sport where one can truly say that luck played no role at all? You can prepare all you want, you can play the best game of your life, but if the opponent is stronger, they will overpower you. And they will devour you. The straightforward justice is one of chess' many amazing qualities.

So no... no real friend to play against, but if that must be, then silence is golden. Frank's been ill in his room for over a week, and in Frank's absence, Tim Shenton has only ventured in occasionally to make his horrible jibes before slithering back under his rock. Joe is therefore blessed with space and time to invest in the board.

Why has Emy still asked Frank in when he's ill though? While Joe sits here, good as gold, waiting only for her. He thought after their last talk she'd been pleased. He's got it all planned what detail he'll give her next, once she's flirted it out of him. He's played the conversation out in his head a thousand times, exactly how he wants it to go. He can't wait!

And yet she humiliates him by leaving him alone in this rotten room, vulnerable to Tim Shenton's nasty anaconda-like attacks. Does she really care about him as much as he does her? His beautiful girlfriends do – they always will. He thought Emy was one of them, maybe the most special of all. But lately, starved of oxygen, white-hot inferno has cooled to crackling flame.

He fiddles about with a turgid middle game, the computer bot stubbornly defending on the matriarch's side while Joe struggles to see any alternative lines, having rashly traded his light-squared bishop for one of the computer's knights in the early skirmishes.

The main door to the common room opens; Frank lumbers back in.

'Feeling better?' Joe chirps, smiling. 'Was that seeing a doctor or Emy?'

'Obviously the latter, you imbecile,' comes the inevitable sneer from behind him as Tim uncoils himself and lurks at the door to his cell.

No need to turn round, Joe. Be cool.

Frank ignores them both and slams his cell door shut behind him, but to Joe's horror he can hear Tim's small deliberate footsteps tapping along the polished concrete floor towards him.

'Three guesses who she's going to call into her room next out of the two of us,' Tim lauds. 'I'll give you a clue, it ain't the chump playing checkers.' He pulls out one of the seats at Joe's table and spins it round. Putting one leg either side of the chair, he straddles it and leans his elbows on the back rest so close to Joe that he can smell his fellow inmate's egg breakfast.

Be cool, Joe. Be cool.

Tim looks down at the electric chessboard and then back at Joe. Joe's eyes haven't moved off the board, but his hands are down by his sides; he sits stock-still.

'You're not going to win just sitting there,' Tim mocks. He reaches out to touch the screen but Joe is too quick, his hand snapping out like a frog's tongue and sticking to Tim by the wrist.

'Please leave me alone,' Joe says between his teeth, eyes still on the board.

'All right, all right,' Tim concedes, patronising as if it's all an overreaction. 'Play your little games. I'll be dreaming about my next cosy chat with Miss Rose. The things we get up to all those extra times she calls me in and not you.'

Ha! Joe calls her Emy, not Miss Rose. How can Tim and her be that close if he still calls her by her last name? Joe doesn't correct his cellmate, however. He likes the fact no one else calls her by her pretty Christian name.

'Don't you want to know what me and Miss Rose get up to?' Tim tries again.

Nothing from Joe, eyes on the board, head bowed – hands back by his sides.

Tim starts in a high-pitched whisper that quickly grows louder: 'Uh... uhhh... uhhhhh... uhhhhhh.'

Maybe you should do it, Joe. That weak leg of the bedframe. You could snap that off in a second. You've thought about it before. Do it. Imagine that jagged edge. Sharp and sturdy.

'My hands aren't locked down in there, Joe. Unlike you,' Tim persists, leaning further forward so the chair is balancing on two legs. 'Free to roam.' His fingers tap along the table, walking towards Joe.

Tim lowers his voice again and moves his mouth closer. 'She's quite something, isn't she?' Each syllable slices through the small gap between them as his lips purse and open, enunciating with utter clarity. 'I'll let you into a secret... she tastes good,' he adds, even quieter. 'Tastes good as I pound her brains out.' And then, purring right into Joe's ear: 'Must be hard to imagine, Joe... you little fucking virgin.'

Joe bolts up, stealing an involuntary flinch from Tim. But Joe isn't looking for a fight. He walks back to his cell and closes the door softly.

Joe will leave Beeswell for good tonight, he has decided.

His adversary thinks he's got an advantage across the board. But Joe hasn't lost a game yet.

35

I'm not prone to carsickness. In fact, I've never experienced it before. But as I weave in and out of traffic now, slamming on the brakes, accelerating round corners like a rally driver, I feel nauseous. It's hard to tell whether that's the manic driving or the undiluted magnitude of the news I'm racing home to. To Mum. To Detective Miller. To Sam?

My mind oscillates around a singularity: why does the detective want to tell me in person – because they *have* found Sam, or because they haven't? I should have just insisted she tell me over the phone. But then I want to be with Mum when we find out, either way. For her sake. For my sake.

A bloke beeps as I cut him up on the inside lane of the dual carriageway. The audacity of a Mercedes moron complaining about anyone else's driving is contemptible. I swear back and leave him to shrink in the rear-view mirror.

Chi will need to know tonight, whoever the bodies are. We'll need the news out asap so it can make the morning press. Shit, and we'll need to tell the other families too. Whether it's their sons or not, they'll all want the update before the press release goes out. Or will DCS Miller be informing the other families? Yeah, she surely will. Maybe she already has. If Elkins was telling the truth about his own brother definitely not being buried around Bedale, then it's a two in three chance: us, the Brockhursts and the McArees. Time to draw – which family gets the bleakest, shortest straw of them all?

My phone rings. I fumble in my bag on the passenger seat, pluck it out and slide my finger across the screen to answer without seeing who's calling.

'Hello? Sorry, hang on...' I yell, careering across two lanes as I click onto speaker mode. 'Hello... hello? Sorry, I'm driving. Who is it?'

'It's Leon,' comes the tinny, shallow voice as I chuck the phone back on the passenger seat.

'Oh, hi!' I shout.

'Busy few days?' He's just loud enough for me to hear over the din of the road.

'Ridiculous, yeah. Up to my neck.'

'No, that's cool.' Even over the hum of traffic I can sense he doesn't quite mean it.

'You OK?' I check.

'Yeah, just wanted to see how you were,' he says.

Is this a guilt trip? I haven't texted him in like four days. The most emotionally turbulent, enormous four days imaginable. And he's acting all hurt. I have not got a millimetre of space or time for recriminations.

'Yeah?' I reply, since he's not bothered to elaborate on his alleged concern. 'No, I'm not OK, got about two hours' sleep the last three nights. Now's not a good time actually, Leon.'

'Sorry,' he replies, a little brighter. 'The Frank Elkins bodies! Been on the news they've found something. Another win for Beeswell!'

I'm about to rip into his prosaic praise when it clicks: he has no idea about Sam, I've never told him. As far as Leon is concerned, these skeletons are just two more success stories for the Hive.

'Urgh, look, this isn't ideal timing. But I need to let you know something.' Maybe I shouldn't tell him, but it seems mean to keep him in the dark now, and I haven't got the headspace to think of a cleverer way of dealing with his confusion. 'One of Elkins' victims was my brother, Sam. The last victim. Sam Whirberth. That's my real last name. So there's a good chance one of these two bodies we've located is his. I'm on my way home now to find out, one way or another. So this is just... I'm just...' My voice breaks. 'Sorry,' I try again, forcing the words up and out of my thickening throat. 'So it's just a bit of a mad day, y'know?'

'Oh, Em! I... Shit... I had no idea. Not that... I mean... that's not what I mean. I just... OK. I get it. Just call me or text me, whenever. I was just going to say I've got more Tim Shenton info, so just let me know when that's convenient. I...'

'No, don't worry. I should have said before,' I let a big sigh out as a bit of strength comes back to my voice. 'Please don't tell anyone at *The Times*. It's confidential, yeah? I'll message you.'

'No, of course, of course. Em, I'd never do that. You mean too much to me. Don't worry about messaging, I'll just see you at the brunch!'

'Brunch?'

'My birthday brunch, on Saturday. But actually, don't worry at all if it's...'

'Oh – no, no, yep. I remember. Definitely. Definitely!'

'Can't wait to see you.'

'Me too.'

We mutter goodbyes and hang up.

Urgh, that was awkward. It *was* nice to hear his voice though and the call was a small distraction at least. DCS Miller is sitting in her unmarked BMW, parked outside the house when I get there. She sees me pull on to the drive and gets out to meet me.

'Just arrived myself,' she explains. 'Shall we go in?' I study her face for clues but she must be a poker pro.

I unlock the front door, Mum is right by it. She'll have been looking out for us both from the lounge window ever since I texted her to explain why I was coming home early.

'I'd offer you a tea but I think we just need to know first,' I tell the detective.

I look into her eyes but she's not looking back. Mum and I sit on the sofa in the lounge, hand in hand; Mum gestures for the detective to sit in the chair opposite.

'OK,' DCS Miller begins. The bags under her eyes are stark and her hair looks like it hasn't been cleaned or brushed since we saw her on Monday morning. She pauses and puts her hands out in front of herself as if she's holding an imaginary crystal ball. She opens her mouth, says nothing. Then puts her hands back in her lap.

Say it's Sam. Say you've found Sam. Please. Just say it. Let it be real. Let it be over. We need this. We're so close. Let it be Sam. Say you've found Sam.

The detective has probably only stopped speaking for two seconds, but my carousel of pleading thoughts seems to have spun a million times.

'Look,' she tries again, coughing out a croak. 'I'm really sorry. But the DNA is positive for Damian McAree and Nathan Brockhurst. They're the two sets of remains. I wanted to tell you in person. But it's still a massive development and I'm more confident than ever now that we will eventually find Sam before...'

The words fade out. I turn to Mum, hug her, my tears

bleeding out on to her cardigan. She's patting my back and holding me as tight as she can one-armed, rocking me as my shoulders shudder and heave with the force of the crying.

'No, no, no,' I say over and over again.

The detective's still talking but I can't make out any of it. I'm done. I put my head in my hands and sob harder, letting the moans flow out freely in a way I never have before, too exhausted to fight. Mum must be crumbling too, but I have nothing left to give. The cruelty of glimpsing an end to all this and having it snatched away yet again – it's all-consuming. I keep my eyes closed tight, wishing myself away from this room, from this day, from this whole life. No one should have to go through agony this unrelenting and deep.

I think Mum shows the detective out because the next time I look up she's back sitting next to me on the sofa, handing me a cup of tea and a fistful of tissue and DCS Miller is nowhere to be seen.

'I'm sorry,' I wail, still not in control. 'You must be feeling...'

Mum shushes me and shakes her head. Slipping her bad arm out of its sling, she cups my cheeks with her cold, shaky hands. Her eyes are not full of pain, or hurt, or anger. They are not eyes for Sam, they are eyes for me.

I love you, she signs.

'I love you too,' I say back, snivelling loudly before blowing my nose.

Listen to the detective, she signs. *We are getting closer. And the wait is over for the other two families.*

'But I wanted to do this for *you*, and I thought we had...' I melt into a puddle again as more tears pour down my cheeks. 'I've let you down.' The words come out as a teetering squeak.

Mum shakes her head again and smiles, calm and assured. *I am so proud of you*, she signs.

'Do you ever want me to stop crying?' I demand, feeling a tiny bit more human.

She gives me another hug. I know the emotion will hit her later. Maybe she's trying to be strong while I'm here – to make up for my abject disintegration. But I feel afresh just why it's so important I find Sam for this woman. Because if anyone in the whole world deserves their one wish to come true, it is her.

I text Chi, explaining what's happened and asking her to look after the press release and field any queries for the night. She says that's fine.

Mum and I get into our pyjamas and turn the TV on. Usually she'll sit on the chair and I'll take the sofa, but tonight we cuddle up together. I know she was putting on a brave face for me, but we're both going to be fragile for weeks or even months after a roller coaster of a few days like that.

The evening speeds by. We watch the soaps, a quiz show on BBC4, some documentary about the royal family and a daft sitcom that doesn't make either of us laugh once. It doesn't much matter. I don't think I could tell you any details about any of the programmes anyway. It's all just noise as we hold each other.

I've never cried like that before. It's an unusual afterglow to be sitting in. There was something cathartic about it. A vague memory flits by of a research paper I read once, about how heavy crying releases oxytocin and should therefore be encouraged in patients suffering prolonged low mood. The pain and frustration of coming so close is still raw and hard to focus on directly. But there's an element of release too. I hope Mum gets that over the next few days, she's usually the crier out of the two of us.

The sitcom ends and I go to pick up the remote before the ten o'clock news comes on. I doubt the confirmation of the two men's identities will have made the bulletin this soon, but I don't want to risk accidentally seeing it.

I unfurl my arm from around Mum and realise she's drifted off to sleep. It's nice. She looks so at peace, so content. I get up as softly as I can and switch the channel. I think I'll stay down here until she wakes up. Don't want her coming-to in the cold, dark lounge alone.

I push my hands in the air to stretch then pick my phone off the table. It's been face down on silent all evening. I open the screen: four missed calls from Beeswell, all in the last fifteen minutes. I should leave it, it's probably just security wanting to know how to deal with journalists turning up now the Elkins news has broken.

I pad into the kitchen for some water. The phone screen flashes bright again, they're ringing a fifth time! I huff and pick up. 'Yeah?'

'Emy, that you?' It's Arthur, head of security.

'Yeah, what?' I snap.

'It's bad, Emy. It's Joe. He might've killed Tim.'

36

Today has been one of the worst of my whole life. Top five for sure. And I'm nowhere near done.

It's also my second stint breaking the speed limit on this one stretch of dual carriageway in less than six hours.

Light from the street lamps flashes by quickly, the dashboard flickering in and out of darkness.

I've never heard Arthur sound so upset. Actually, I've never seen him flustered by anything before that phone call.

Tim Shenton's been rushed to hospital, a deep wound in his neck. Arthur doesn't know if he was still conscious by the time the paramedics left.

Joe Okorie is locked and shackled in the interview room. Docile but weeping. I'm told he surrendered as soon as the guards burst in.

Frank Elkins is safe in his cell, I'm reassured.

How did Joe even do it? Should I have seen this coming? Robbie had been warning me Joe wasn't happy, but no one predicted *this*, did they?

The thing I hate most is having to leave Mum. This was

supposed to be an evening together. We deserved tonight – of all nights. And now she's alone, because one of these vile, useless men has thrown the mother of all hissy fits.

I want to annihilate him.

And what about the fallout? If Tim's dead, we're finished. What if he isn't but the press gets wind of it? Or worse... Harrington!

Urgh, too much.

'How do you eat an elephant? One bite at a time.' That's what Dad used to say.

So what's the next bite? Joe. Even if we do save the Hive, he's got to go. I know the inmates get a couple of extra privileges on my watch, but I draw the line at murderous violence.

The one clear-minded thing I did before leaving was call Robbie. He can help with Joe. Leave Chi with the press queries over Elkins' bodies. I've called her too, but only to let her know what's happened and tell her she doesn't need to deal with it.

I get to the barracks and pull up outside our building. Robbie's car rolls up about a minute later while I'm still in the driver's seat, in denial about everything.

'We're fucked,' I tell him as we walk towards the first entry doors.

'Don't say that,' he chirps back. '"Any success in life is made by going into areas with a blind, furious optimism".'

'Churchill again?'

'Sly Stallone,' he corrects.

A character renowned for being punched to a pulp – I can relate.

There are several police cars outside the precinct and two officers on the door. We explain who we are and they let us past. The clock on the wall of our office says 10.50 p.m. when we enter. No one should have to work at 10.50 p.m.

Arthur comes in, tracing-paper pale. He tells us what happened and shows us the CCTV footage.

Joe has apparently just been sitting on his bed for hours before this clip. But all of a sudden, he gets up. Over the course of about half a minute, he wrenches and pulls at one of his bedframe's legs, snaps it off, walks up behind Tim in the common room and drives the metal stake into Tim's neck, one hand on the weapon, the other wrapped around the side of his victim's head to keep it steady. It's so natural, so certain. The act of a man using muscle memory – a chilling vignette of how he slaughtered those women. Shenton grasps at the wound with both hands, the first large splats of blood hitting the floor before he does. The guards burst in a couple of seconds later and taser Joe.

'Had they talked earlier in the evening?' I probe, struggling to compute the graphic violence.

'In their last conversation before Joe went back to his room, Tim had been winding him up. Saying he'd been kissing you. And, y'know, other stuff about you, Miss.' Arthur looks very awkward, doesn't elaborate further.

We watch that conversation back too. Shenton in control – cruel, bullying, arrogant. Joe shrinking by the second. The two scenes could not be more contradictory.

'He's going to have to leave, isn't he?' Robbie mutters, even his well of positivity running dry as he realises what his leading man has done.

It's not quite the same, but I imagine how inconsolable I'd be if we had to let Elkins go. I'd probably just leave the project there and then.

'He is, yeah,' I say gently. 'I'm sorry. I know how much time you've invested—'

'How long before we technically have to let him go?' Robbie interrupts.

I shrug. 'Regardless of what happens to Tim, the police will take Joe.' We spin round to look at the CCTV screens recording other parts of the building. Uniformed invaders stand in the common room, others in full, zipped-up body suits are taking pictures with large cameras. There are two women in plain clothes in the interview room, one sitting in my seat, the other standing next to her, Joe sitting opposite with his head bowed.

'We need to give Joe one last chance to confess,' Robbie declares. 'Don't let them take him without giving you one last shot, Em.'

I glance at Arthur. 'Reckon they'll let me? We can promise to record it all and pass it on to them.'

Arthur shrugs, his tight, buttoned-up blue shirt lifting and untucking slightly around his waist as his shoulders rise, pulling the fabric up over his prodigious belly. 'Dunno, ask them, not me.'

The senior detective is a memorably tall, willowy woman who is far too chipper and alert for someone who's been called out to a late-night skirmish between two heinous humans. I don't know where the words come from, but I argue with impressive cogency that Joe is in a high state of emotion, making him uniquely susceptible to finally giving up the whereabout: of his victims before he leaves Beeswell forever. Detective Long shanks acquiesces. Officers will continue photographing ar working in the common room, the detective will come a formally arrest Joe first thing in the morning. My final chat w Joe – his 'exit interview', as she puts it with a smirk – mus' recorded and passed on, as I had already offered. She m clear she's doing me a favour. This is very unorthodox, bt the sake of the families she is prepared to allow it. B desperate to prove she's a moral philanthropist for my liking, but we have a final window.

They haven't got anything useful out of him about the attack anyway, she explains. He just keeps demanding to speak to me.

Back in the office, the news sees Robbie rediscover his verve. He bops in his seat like a pneumatic pogo stick.

'OK,' I say. 'How do we handle this?'

'We should play on the fact he'll never see you again,' Robbie suggests. 'Like, this is his last chance to finally give you what you want, and if you two really do have a special connection, as he sees it, then wouldn't he want to prove that to you by making you happy?'

I nod, contemplating what I could say and do. It's hard to see it working. We have tried this kind of thing in the past, all that's different now is the finality of it, but the dynamic feels predictable.

I want to collapse, I'm so weary. But this attack on Shenton is ing to be terrible for the Hive, possibly fatal; a confession Joe could hold back that tide. *Tomorrow could be the day.* only if we still have Elkins, only if we still have Beeswell.

u need to make it clear he won't see you again, this is the e. But he'll ask why you can't visit him in future, so just rrington, or your government contract, or anything.'

oint, I suppose.

ld guilt trip him as well. He's having to leave you g your relationship, because of *his* behaviour,' n, speaking faster with every passing thought. A s has appeared out of absolutely nowhere. He's to his mouth one by one with the tip of his off him without asking, before all the other to the jaws of death. He just laughs, hyper

'Made you a strong coffee,' he says, dragging a steaming mug to the front of his desk. 'I'll watch in here and take down the transcript in real time.'

'I'm nervous,' I admit. It sounds pathetic, weak, inarticulate, but I still feel the need to say it.

Robbie doesn't make me feel silly though. 'Diamonds are made under pressure, Em.'

'Thanks,' I reply. 'This is going to have to be quite the performance to convince him.'

'Oscar worthy,' Robbie agrees.

37

'What have you done, Joe?' I say as I open the door to the interview room, jaded more than judgmental.

'Emy. Oh Emy, I knew you'd come.' He tries to stand but makes no progress as all four locked-down limbs struggle against their shackles.

I put my coffee down, take my seat, and say nothing. The unimpressed, overspent malaise in my expression is no performance.

'How's Tim Shenton?' Joe enquires, a puppy desperate for a pat on the head. His cheeks are salt-encrusted from the drying of real tears. Loathsome, cheap, self-pitying tears.

'You don't care about him.'

'I do, Emy. I never meant...'

'If you're about to say you never meant to hurt him, I will leave right now,' I snap. 'You wanted to kill him.'

'I just wanted him to stop. The nastiness... He's horrible,' Joe pleads.

'I've seen what happened. There is nothing he could have said or done to justify *that*.'

'He said disgusting lies about you, Emy. My love...'

'DON'T!' I shout, then take a breath. Robbie is going to analyse this interview like no other. I can't explode. However close the heat is to the tip of my tongue. 'Don't "my love" me after what you've done. You've ruined this...' I gesture at him and then back at myself.

Joe's bottom lip wobbles and he shakes his head. 'I just couldn't take him any more. But that doesn't need to affect us. We'll still carry on being *us*, won't we?'

'You must know there's no way you can stay at Beeswell now.'

He nods, unable to take his intense, yearning eyes off me. 'Yeah, but I'll write. And you can still come and see me.'

Robbie predicted this to a tee. Impressive.

'Why would I do that? You have known since day one that I want to know what you did with those women, and yet you've toyed with me. You've refused to tell me. You act like we're special, and yet you can't be honest with me. Boyfriends and girlfriends don't keep secrets from each other.'

I cringe twice. Once for using a cliché like 'boyfriends and girlfriends'. And secondly for pretending this eight-time woman murderer is somehow enmeshed in my affections. But both choices are calculated; I need to tap into that adolescent rejection that's driven Joe's whole adulthood.

Disintegrating, he takes a sharp breath in and then emits a drawn-out, high-pitched mewl.

A fresh gust of anger hits me. This scumbag has put the Hive's whole future in jeopardy. All my work, all the hope Mum has invested in it, all the access to Elkins, gone in an instant because Joe Okorie can't regulate his emotions. How dare this random man have any impact on whether we find Sam or not? And he has the audacity to sit here crying and yet still hold out on me as to where his own victims are. My blood, already simmering, nears the boiling point.

'Stop crying,' I grunt.

He doesn't, his cheeks glistening with fresh tears.

I remind myself again that Robbie is watching. I'm not in here for me – I'm in here for those families, I'm here for Mum, I'm here for the survival of Beeswell.

I get up, pull a tissue out of my bag and move closer to Joe. He stares at me, unblinking, as I wipe the tears away from his plump, dark cheeks.

'How long have you been here, Joe? Eight months?'

'Yes, exactly,' he whispers as I move away again.

'That's longer than any of your other girlfriends... before you'd go out and find a new one, isn't it?' *Girlfriends*, it's such a disservice to call them that. They were not consensual partners of this man, they were innocent women, butchered and kept as sexual ornaments to buttress feeble machismo.

He looks off to the side, counting, remembering, considering. 'Yeah, you're right, Emy. You're always right.'

The façade is unpalatable, but I need to reach him if I'm ever going to reach those women. 'You cared about them, you looked after them,' I tell him. 'You shared your thoughts and your dreams with them. Yes?'

He nods but looks bemused, unsure whether I'm encouraging him to reminisce or attempting to scold him.

'You've known me longer and we've had far more conversations. I've shown you far more attention than any of them.' *No shit, they were corpses.*

'You're the best of all. Definitely, Emy. Definitely.' He couldn't be more impassioned.

'I don't believe you. I want to know where those women are

Joe, and you are holding out on me. That doesn't feel like the action of someone who cares about me.'

He stares down at his navel and weeps yet again.

I can feel Robbie's desperate, bitter disappointment as we fail for the last time to make Joe Okorie confess. For all the people and reasons I need this to happen, I feel hope pissing into the gutter.

A dark patch is forming on his blue sweater as the tears slide off his chin and splat on to his front. A man on the outside, a quivering toddler on the inside, so desperate for companionship he'd kill and kill and kill for a hollow mirage of the real thing, never comprehending the consequences. Then fall in love with his psychologist in pursuit of the same. What lengths would he not go to in chasing this eternal, elusive connection?

How else can I possibly package this? I take a big sip from my coffee mug. It's lukewarm and horrible but the caffeine is a must. Eyelids heavy, cogs clanking in my brain at about a quarter-speed.

'We've played a sort of game in here, haven't we?' I gear back up, not sure where I'm going with it. 'You'd let me guess at things and if I got them right you'd admit it or reward me with another detail.'

'That was our thing,' he smiles, as if remembering our wedding day.

'Well, I don't think we've got time left for me to guess at everything. But if you don't want to tell me where they are, maybe we hit fast-forward and you just tell me all the details you were prepared to tell me, if I'd guessed them. Because this time tomorrow you'll be in a jail a long way from here, and you can either sit in your new, cold cell, reminiscing about this last special night we shared. Or you can tell me nothing, and deprive yourself of a final happy memory here. If you ask me... I think you'll need all the good memories you can get. It can be pretty bleak in a new place on your own.'

It's not going to work, he's going to see I'm painting a tale, that I don't actually feel or believe what I'm saying. I take a horrid sip of coffee.

'I love you,' he says, suddenly solemn.

My skin freezes, a mixture of revulsion and elation. Is he going to talk?

And then... he does. Methodical, candid, calm, specific, articulate. The modus operandi of one of Britain's most prolific killers, laid out for the very first time, for me and me alone. The Ghost Killer's confession.

Joe would flag down female drivers at the side of the road late at night. He'd pick quiet lanes with minimal through traffic. If the woman wasn't alone, or was too old, he'd just wave them off again. If they *were* alone, he'd get them out of their car with an excuse that his own car had broken down, walk behind them back to his own vehicle, then do the deed as soon as they reached it. Carotid artery slashed, body lifted into his boot lined with tarpaulin, his own blood-spattered clothing thrown in with them, a change into fresh attire at the side of the road, part one of the job done. Next, the chess player kicked in. Five steps ahead: if the victim's car was found at the scene, police would start by checking CCTV in that vicinity, and Joe would have been spotted. Instead, he'd get into the victim's car and drive off with the engine still warm so it would appear there'd been no delay in the journey at all. And he wouldn't just drive anywhere – he'd use any means possible to find out the victim's actual address. He offers examples too, this was decades ago so the clues were different and often numerous: a personalised cheque book in their handbag, the paper copy of their driver's licence, opened post on the passenger seat, a local A-Z atlas with pencilled in routes all leading to the same destination, an address book with an entry under 'home'. The victim's car could then be deposited back outside their own house. It left detectives searching the wrong area every time.

It takes a unique mind to think up such a clever sleight of hand. The grandmaster outsmarting the opposition in thought and deed. He's the only inmate here who handed himself in. Terrifying to think how long he could have got away with it otherwise. Police were chasing their tails, unsure if they were looking for a mass murderer, or were simply contending with a spate of young women running away from home. They had all vanished but there was no sign of a struggle at their home or in their car. No CCTV of them leaving home in the middle of the night. No message to friends or family. It made no sense – they were just gone, vanished into thin air. The 'Ghost Killer'. Joe's forward planning was so fastidious, he even made sure not to adjust the victims' car seats when he got in, despite them all being far shorter than him – no clue must give away that he had driven their cars back to their homes rather than them. This was the beginning of the nineties so DNA testing wasn't in play just yet – much to his advantage. He would then return to his own car the next afternoon, drive it home and wash the body in his bathtub.

He judders to a halt, ashamed to admit what he did next, which was almost certainly something sexual. That's not a part of the story I or the families need to hear about.

I give him permission to skip the full depths of his depravity. 'How many days before you'd put them in a chest freezer?'

'A week, give or take,' he answers, matter-of-fact.

I haven't been able to take all this in, there must be things I could have pushed to further understand how he avoided detection so successfully for so long. But the avalanche of information is disorienting.

'Joe, you've been so good, that must feel like a weight lifted, admitting all that to me. Thank you,' I say calmly.

He glances at me for the first time since telling his story, relieved that his shameful secrets haven't brought me out in pure disgust. I'm hiding it well.

There's one question left. The first question, the last question, the only question. And he knows it.

'Where are they, Joe?' I demand bluntly.

'Emy, I can't. I can't!'

'You're doing so well, you're so brave.' I lean forward, all tiredness dissolved, the holy grail so close it's within clawing distance. But close means nothing; you could be one wire away from defusing an atomic bomb – but make the wrong choice and all anyone will remember is the bang. Softly, I add: 'It's time to set yourself free, Joe.'

His mood regresses to despondency. The disciplined, precise storytelling adopted to explain his crimes gone, one chapter short of its ending. 'The minute I tell you, then it's over between us. It binds us, my love. Don't take it away, don't make me,' he pleads. 'I can't do it, my love, I can't do it!'

That's always been the fundamental issue in letting Joe grow attached to me: it kept him at the Hive, it kept him amenable, but it gave him no incentive whatsoever to divulge the critical fact. Even now, he's quite easily given up any other detail I want, but all the time knowing the one I really want is still safe, still mooring me to him.

'Please, Joe,' I try one last time, knowing what he's going to say. 'Please tell me where they are. It's time to give them up.'

He shakes his head, his stare troubled and earnest. 'I care about you too much to do that.'

That's it then. Joe will leave the Hive, the press will label the prison a lawless playground for killers, Harrington will soil himself and shut us down, Elkins will be transferred away, I'll lose my chance to find Sam and Mum will see her last flicker of real hope extinguished and never recover. It all plays out in my head like a disaster movie on fast-forward.

I feel Robbie's defeated eyes on me through the camera in the corner. *I tried, mate. We were close. If only it wasn't...*

I stop.

The idea strikes like a gunshot. A burst of heat swells around my collar. Of course! How could I not have seen it? The whole time he's been here, this was the only way it could end. How it *has* to end. My pulse rushes, prickly dynamite detonating in my chest. This is it. This is it!

My mouth's bone dry but I force the words out: 'Joe, do you trust me?'

38

Dad used to say: 'If an opportunity stares you in the face, don't wait for it to blink.'

As I leave the interview room, my body shakes with the imagined fear of what would have happened if I'd *not* just done what I did. The reality of the achievement too big to comprehend, my mind fixates on the luck, the jeopardy, how close I came to missing it, the sliding doors, the alternate timeline where Joe had taken his biggest secret with him. I don't feel elated, not yet. Instead heavy, sickly relief cooks my insides.

Robbie's jaw is bruised against the floor as I open the door to the office. Neither of us can speak. I pull up my seat and we face each other, me blowing my cheeks out, him not even that animated.

Full confession on tape. We sit in silence.

The lightning bolt had struck as Joe admitted he could never tell me where they were, because it would mean Beeswell, and therefore I, was done with him.

We'd always feared he'd feel that way, but it was when he said it out loud that the path became flood-lit. He thought the only way to keep me interested in him was to hold back the gold, but what if I flipped it? What if I told him the only way to keep me interested was to tell me everything? It wouldn't have worked if he was still in the Hive: he'd know he'd still be seeing me. But now he was leaving, it was the single, perfect moment to issue the ultimatum.

If an opportunity stares you in the face, don't wait for it to blink.

'Joe, do you trust me? You tell me where they are, and I promise I'll keep in touch, I'll visit you. You don't have to lose me, but only if you tell me everything.'

Joe took the women one at a time, over the course of several nights, to abandoned docklands in Sunderland near to a shipyard where he used to work. Critically, he threw them into the water at a spot where he'd observed the tide never dropped below four meters. Entombed in sealed bags weighed down with breezeblocks. He's given precise details of the location.

'Did you mean it?' Robbie asks in a shaky, quiet tone as he fishes a pack of family pack of Dairy Milk Buttons out of his portable tuck shop. First Rolos, now Buttons – he's a walking diabetes advert.

'About still seeing him?'

'Yeah.' Robbie studies me with forensic intensity.

I stare back, holding his gaze. 'I meant it. Not for him, for the families. Who knows what other questions there'll be if we do find all these women.'

Robbie lolls back to look at the ceiling. 'Nothing since Petty and now ten bodies in a week,' he says before shaking a palmful of the chocolates into his hand then slamming them at his gob.

I sit, stony faced. Of all the original victims we were searching for when the Hive opened, only two remain hidden, and Sam is one of them. How is that fair? It's the sickest, cruellest of jokes.

'This is incredible Emy. You must be buzzing,' Robbie carries on, his own elation pouring out now.

'I'm all over the place,' I admit, not meaning to be so candid.

'Napoleon once said, "The battlefield is a scene of constant chaos. The winner will be the one who controls that chaos, both his own and the enemies." You did that, *you,* Emy!'

'Never trust the French,' I mumble. 'You tired?'

'Not at all!' he cries. I believe him. He looks like he's downed a vat of espresso, jittering and bouncing in his seat as the full scale of what's happened lands much quicker for him than for me.

I look at him. He'd have every right to feel bereft: we've done it, his muse is a puzzle solved. But he's sporting an incredulous grin, no words necessary. *Don't cry because it's over, smile because it happened*: that's the kind of limp quote he'd come out with himself if he wasn't so overwhelmed.

'If you want...' I begin. Should I do this, is it wrong? I can't really see why it would be. Maybe it's the growing glee that I don't have to go home to Mum and mentally prepare her for the Hive to be shut down, but a wave of delight sweeps through me. 'You could get that game of chess in with him before the police come and arrest him. I think the detective will be back about 8 a.m.'

Robbie's eyes bulge.

I chuckle as I slip towards the door. 'But get some sleep too. And be back in for midday if you can, tomorrow's going to be hectic.' I turn back to face him. 'You've done well, Robbie. We got him.'

Robbie's mouth gawps open and shut voicelessly like a land-locked fish.

It's brisk but peaceful outside, light beginning to creep over the horizon. Shivering in the car, I pull out my phone. Adrenalin is coursing, a heady mix of shock and invincibility makes the next decision for me. Mum doesn't need to know how close we've come to losing the Hive this evening. No, tonight, we got the *Ghost Killer* and I still want to talk about it; I want to brag, I want to revel.

I message Leon.

> You up?

His reply comes back in less than ten seconds:

> Can be

I'm outside his flat 25 minutes later. An unexpected end to the most unexpected of days.

He opens the front door, eyes nine-tenths shut and we shuffle upstairs. His dark green dressing gown is nice to snuggle against as we get into his still-warm bed and I nuzzle my head into his chest. I could just stay here forever, his arms around me, the calm of this room, the comfiness of these sheets, the mellow, dull light from his lamp. No demands, nowhere to go, to be, to reach. Like time has stopped and I can just hide. I shouldn't lead him on, he deserves someone who can give back what he'd put in to a relationship, someone straightforward and loving and innocent the same way he is; but at the same time, I miss him when he's not there, he's the only man who makes me feel like a woman, not just a sister or daughter.

'What's happened?' he asks quite reasonably. His voice soft and croaky from sleep.

I just say it. All of it. I'd already admitted in the car that Sam Whirberth was my brother, but I explain it all properly. The whole reason the Beeswell project started, the buried bodies, the bodies identified today, the fight, Joe's confession. I just talk... and talk, and talk, and talk, and talk. The only movement is to occasionally look up from my comfy vantage point to check Leon hasn't fallen asleep. He never has, but he lets me speak, listening and holding me. I don't miss a detail, even adding that I've let Robbie play chess against Joe before he leaves the Hive.

Unburdening myself is as physical as it is emotional. Shoulders loosen, tense jaw relaxes, my eyes finally grow heavy. The light's strong around the edge of the curtains when Leon suggests I get some sleep. He switches off the lamp and kisses me on the cheek; all thoughts falling away as my head leans into the pillow.

* * *

He wakes me up with a cup of coffee because any other way would be intolerable. It's just gone 10 a.m. It feels bizarre that I wound up here last night. I wasn't thinking straight, like I was drunk or something. I suppose I sort of was – intoxicated with mental exhaustion and relief.

Locking myself in Leon's bathroom, I assess the cosmetic damage. I look woeful: a carcass drained of blood and punched in both eyes, hair mangled, breath so pungent you could almost chew on it. I run the tap, drag wet fingers through my hair and try to brush my teeth with Leon's toothbrush without him hearing.

Pauper's primp complete, I attempt to make a quick getaway and fail miserably. I could never ever be a burglar.

'You're going to burn out, Em,' Leon says, encouraging me to stay longer.

When he sees I'm intent on leaving he reminds me again about tomorrow morning – his birthday brunch with his friends. I promise I'll still be there, I owe him that after my impromptu trip here last night. Urgh, why can't I kill this relationship? For *his* sake, at least! I could never ever be an assassin either.

Harrington phones while I'm speeding back to the Hive.

His bark comes the split-second I accept the call. 'I'm on my way up to Beeswell.'

'We haven't got a spare cell, sorry,' I fire back, pleased to sound so sharp.

'You don't know, do you?' He bays.

'Know what?'

'Shenton's dead.'

39

No acknowledgment of my arrival from Chi as I enter the office. She's chuntering to herself between huffs of exasperation at her computer screen.

'Shenton's dead,' I say, flat with shock.

'I know,' she replies without looking up. 'The hospital leaked it to *The Guardian*. They phoned me asking for a comment.'

'Harrington's on his way up...'

'I know that too,' she interrupts. 'He told me.'

'Of course he did.' I force out a half-laugh. 'Is he staying at yours?'

She snaps round for the first time. No words but a look of pure fury. Then she's back to her computer, typing and tutting.

I wander over and put my hand on her back but she flinches. 'What's wrong?' I ask, clear and loud to guarantee a response.

She doesn't look up from the screen as she gabbles. 'Media is going mad for the two Elkins bodies...'

'McAree and Brockhurst,' I make clear.

'...and then the fight as well, it's *too* much, and that's before they all get wind that Shenton's dead.'

I head over to the kettle. 'Robbie and I were here—'

'*Guardian* are going live with it in the next hour. Harrington will be here about two.'

'Am I in trouble?'

'Dunno, ask him when he gets here,' she responds.

'I don't mean with Numb-nuts, I mean with you.'

Chi grunts, her fingers flicking back and forth across her keyboard like a concert pianist.

I stir boiling water into my mug of instant and chew the nail off my thumb. The incessant tapping and impatient groaning of my best friend are the only noises in the air.

All that hope and relief last night after Joe's confession dissolves. If a murder has been committed in the jail, we'll surely be closed. There's no amount of good PR or genuine results that can justify keeping an unsafe precinct open. That's what the press will say.

And how on earth do we even break the news about Joe giving up his victims? I'm going to have to handle all that on my own if Chi's this stressed. Robbie's been amazing but it might still be a tad soon to start sticking him on media calls – what if he panics and reverts to clichés and crisp recommendations? It's not fair to throw him under the bus like that.

Taking my seat, I look back down at the stump of my thumbnail and start nibbling at the skin around it. 'Chi. Robbie and I were here late last night and…'

Spinning back round, her eye contact is cold. 'I was up all evening taking calls on Joe and Tim as well as the Elkins bodies and it's worse this morning. I *cannot* stop.'

'Yeah?' I launch back, a struck match in a gas leak. 'And I had to sit next to Mum yesterday as a detective told her neither of those two bodies were her son's.'

Chi goes to retaliate but stops.

'Then, me and Robbie were back here sorting Joe out until four in the morning. No one's winning here.'

She looks to the floor, her chin and bottom lip shaking. 'I'm sorry,' she whispers.

I go back over and the hand on her back is more welcome this time.

'This is too much, Em. I can't keep going like this. It's making me...' she sighs, her shoulders slumping as she physically shrinks in her chair. 'I don't know, it's making me not *me*, y'know?'

I look down at her neat ponytail falling over her shoulder, the top vertebra sticking out of her petite neck as she leans forward, staring at the ground. One hand rubs her back as I continue to inspect my quickly diminishing thumb.

I can tell she's not right; she's wearing the same cream cardie and black YSL jeans as yesterday. I've never seen her wear the same outfit two days in a row before.

'Tell me honestly, Em,' she sighs. 'Why were you meeting up with Shenton after hours?'

'I...'

'Don't try to deny it,' she butts in. 'I asked Arthur. He told me you were calling Shenton into the interview room. But when I checked the tapes there were no interviews logged.'

I've hidden this from her for too long, she deserves better. 'He was helping me with Elkins.'

'How?'

'I dunno. He just kind of brought a different angle, fresh ideas. Elkins talked to him. He came up with the accomplice stuff, he came up with...'

'In return for what?'

This is the reason I didn't tell her. She's too savvy to think Shenton would help anyone out of the goodness of his heart.

I pause. 'Said I'd go easy on him, and if we found Sam I'd testify for the defence at his trial.'

Chi shrugs my hand off her again. 'You'd have testified for a child-killing rapist to get Sam back?' The words are delivered with genuine horror.

She gets to her feet, so close I can smell her rose-scented perfume. I have to look away, those blue eyes seeing me in a whole new light.

'We don't know if he was guilty or...'

'YOU DO KNOW!' she screams, not moving an inch, tiny drops of spittle hitting my cheeks. 'YOU'VE ALWAYS KNOWN, EM!'

She takes a deep breath and waits for me to reply. I can't.

She sits down and returns to face her computer.

'I had Leon looking into Shenton,' I begin shakily. 'He was finding stuff out. I hadn't given up on nailing him, I was just using Leon to dig rather than us here.'

'What would Andrew Stride's mum say if she found out you would've helped Shenton go free to get Sam?'

'I... I'm sorry.'

Her intention to leave my apology dripping in silence is ruined by Robbie bursting in, bright as a button. 'Have you told her?' he spurts.

Chi looks at him, then at me. 'Told me what?'

'Robbie, it's not a good time,' I caution.

'What d'you mean?' he checks, perplexed.

'Shenton's dead.'

The news stops him in his tracks, stranded halfway between the door and his chair, eyes wide. There's nothing more for anyone to say and he eventually remembers where he is and shuffles over to sit down.

Chi's return to sledgehammer typing is joined by the rustle

of Robbie opening a Toffee Crisp. 'We still need to get the news out today though, right?' he clarifies.

I glare at him. *Don't tell Chi yet*, my eyes plead.

'What?' he calls out, a foreigner to subtlety.

'What are you two talking about?' Chi demands, her chest rising and falling with impatience as she turns around again.

'Joe confessed,' Robbie says, nonplussed. 'Told us where all eight women's bodies are.'

Chi looks at me for confirmation.

I give a little nod. 'Seeing how stressed you were, I wasn't going to say anything until we'd sorted the backlog.' I thump Robbie with a fresh look of frustration.

'Then Em let me go and play him at chess. He won obviously but it was fascinating, Ruy Lopez opening with...'

'Robbie, we've got a hell of a lot on today,' I rebuke. 'It'll be me putting out the news of Joe's bodies. Chi's snowed under...'

'Let's wait until Monday,' she suggests, engaged and more civil with Robbie in the room. 'We don't tell Harrington, we clear the decks, get out the press releases about the two Elkins bodies and Shenton's death and sort out the queries and calls. Then deal with the Joe confession news on Monday.'

'I don't think we can hold out on the police that long,' I point out.

'They've got Joe now, they can interview him as much as they like. We give them our file when it's ready,' she insists.

'Yeah, but also, Harrington is going to be shitting bricks about the Hive now Shenton's dead,' I say. 'We need the Joe bodies as a counter.'

'You tell Harrington and he'll have an MOJ press release out within half an hour. He won't tell the families first, he won't tell the police. It'll be carnage, and I'll have to pick up the pieces on what's already our busiest ever day.'

'That's why I'll cover the Joe stuff.'

'OK, so who's our contact at the *Express*, or the BBC, or Northumbria Police? Who's the first contact for the families of each of Joe's victims? Do we call them, do we message them, do we email them the news? You don't know because it's *my* role. You need me when this breaks. And today is not that day.' Chi looks at me, anger replaced by desperation. 'Please. Tell Harrington on Monday. It's too much all at once.'

I don't want to, but if this helps Chi get out of her funk then I'll sit on the breakthrough over the weekend. One other small crumb of comfort has come to me as we've been talking: Harrington might hate the bad publicity, but with Shenton dead, there's no chance of a trial and therefore no chance his pervert son's name gets released. He might be elated when he arrives.

40

Harrington is not elated when he arrives.

'What the fuck happened?' he demands, as diplomatic as he is attractive.

'Okorie snapped one of the legs off his bed and stabbed Shenton in the throat with it,' I state.

Has Harrington put on weight? I usually see him standing, or sitting behind a desk, but in person, perched on an office wheely-chair, his gut looks enormous. He must have crushed little Chi. Gross.

She's sitting by in demure silence, reinforcing every horrendous habit perpetuated down history of how women should act in the company of important men. I bet he loves that about her.

I've sent Robbie off so he doesn't have to endure this. Goodness knows what he'll find to do with himself for an hour, although he took a bag laden with sugary comestibles out with him, so I'm sure he'll survive – even if his teeth don't.

'It's a disgrace. How didn't you see it coming?' Harrington blathers on in theatrical despair.

'How didn't I foresee an impulsive attack by a prisoner

who'd shown no sign of violence since he's been here? The guards were on Okorie within seconds. There's no more they could've...'

'If the press pile in on this, you're finished, I'll shut the place down like *that*.' He clicks his chubby red fingers.

'Yes, you are very powerful,' I reply with crushing apathy.

He shuffles around in the chair, looking down at it as if the cushioning is at fault for his lack of comfort, rather than his thick, lumpy arse.

He grits his teeth. 'Should never have given this place the green light.'

'You've travelled an awful long way for a bollocking in person. I feel very spoiled.' I peer at Chi, hoping for some backup against this gargantuan, gormless goblin. But her eyes are still placed firmly on the floor. Coward.

'Shenton could've sued. You're bloody lucky he's dead,' Harrington growls.

'Not as lucky as you,' I hit back.

Thankfully he misses my kneejerk response, so enraptured by his own temper. 'You'd have never got him to confess; he had you in the palm of his hand.'

Chi lets out a shrill laugh at my expense. My indignant eyes meet hers, and she returns to zen-like neutrality.

'We've identified two more of Elkins' victims *this week*! Beeswell works when we are given inmates that fit the study parameters.'

'Great.' He shrugs. 'I don't think you understand. The two Elkins bodies have just been obliterated by the fact you let one third of your inmates murder another third of them. It's going to take a sodding miracle to find a story bigger than that.'

Joe's confession is a huge belch waiting to roar out of me. I really, really want to tell him – that'd clamp his jowly chops shut good and proper.

Turning to Chi, his whole demeanour changes. 'You've done a good job with the comms, doll. But you're not a magician.'

She sucks in air like it's poisonous before apologising and asking with no passion whatsoever whether it wouldn't be at all possible to have a bit longer to work on the other inmates rather than shutting the project down now.

I pick up the baton, desperate to inject some energy back into our side of the argument. 'You wanted to avoid a trial with Shenton. You got what you wanted. You need to brief every media baron and his designer dog that Beeswell is still a viable, groundbreaking...'

'The optics are broken, you silly bitch,' he snaps. 'I needed Shenton admitting it, not snuffing it. My reputation's buried in this place.'

I ponder whether to point out that I've had bowel movements I cared more about than Barnaby C. Harrington's reputation. I choose not to, but this isn't working.

If an opportunity stares you in the face, don't let it blink.

'Can I speak to you alone?'

Chi gives me daggers that I evade as I walk towards the door and motion for Harrington to join me. If she doesn't want to go in to bat for the team then it's time to change the game.

Unsure of what's going on, Harrington follows me down the corridor and into the interview room. I hit the switch inside the door to ensure our private conversation won't be recorded for Chi to hear back in the office.

Neither of us sit, lucky for him – his green tweed check suit fitting a little better over his belly now he's on his feet.

'Joseph Okorie has told us where his victims' bodies are. All eight, OK? This place is getting results. Just buy us time. Eight new bodies, that beats the Shenton stuff, right?'

'All eight found?' Harrington checks, rearranging the area below his belt with a characteristic lack of common decency.

'Not found, but he's given us a location. We're going to put the news out on Monday.'

'Monday? It goes out today! Has to – to mitigate Shenton blowback. Even that won't save you though.' He moves a step closer – his breath smells like chicken left in the fridge too long. 'On my way up here, I hadn't made up my mind whether this place needed to close immediately. But now I have. Decisiveness is a popular trait with voters. I gave your little experiment a chance, we've dug up most of the bones, but now it's done.' He walks towards the door still talking. 'I'll draft a statement; playtime's over. The world doesn't revolve around your little brother I'm afraid.'

I want to hurt him, torture him, make him beg for his life then take it anyway.

Say it. Say it! This is why you really brought him in here, away from Chi. Say it! Before you bottle it. Sam first, think later.

'I know about your son.'

Harrington turns; his initial lack of expression is impressive. Not a twitch of red nose or flick of bushy eyebrow. But the lack of words is admission enough.

'I know he downloaded that video of Andrew Stride, I know it's under injunction, I know there was a damn good chance that injunction was going to get lifted if Shenton's case had gone to trial. So I think it's in your best interests to let me keep this place open.' I stop talking before my voice shakes and I refuse to lose the staring contest.

Something's shifted. Strong annoyance upgrades to lava-like fury in his heartless, narrow eyes.

'You don't know what you're talking about,' he growls.

'Try me.'

'Even if there were such an injunction, no paper would break it, that's the whole point. And if there was one, it now won't be jeopardised by a trial, so don't you dare try to blackmail me. You are nothing, I am the sun.' He speaks deliberately and keeps the volume low, fighting not to explode.

'OK, but what's not under injunction is you trying to fix a trial, you trying to undermine a police investigation, you not caring a jot for the families, you forcing Shenton on us despite him not fitting the study brief at all.'

The volcano erupts.

'IF YOU CROSS ME...' His face flushes scarlet. He strides over – so close I have to lean back to avoid our heads touching – and drops his voice to a whisper. 'You cross me and Frank Elkins will be out of here in a second. Then next week? Maybe he's found hanged and poor Mummy never finds her boy. You stupid little cunt.'

I swallow hard and maintain eye contact. 'The Hive stays open.'

His nostrils flare like a bull's. A glance to the side, and then: 'You're on life-support.' He stalks back to the door; it bangs shut behind him.

41

Chi is back to committing grievous bodily harm on her keyboard as I tiptoe into the office. I think I just out Harrington-ed Harrington. There's a euphoric swell in my bones at not only surviving his onslaught but fighting back. Not that Chi's going to see it that way.

'I had to tell him about Joe's bodies.'

She stops bashing for a moment but doesn't look round, then begins tapping again, less hard. 'You promised.' Her voice is steely sober, cold too.

'He's threatening to shut us down.'

No reply – she's got her selective-hearing aid in.

I stay facing her, waiting for her to turn. 'I'm sorry.' Still she doesn't move. 'Don't put it out tonight. The press release on Joe's bodies, I mean. You've got enough to do. Let's pretend it hasn't happened until Monday. We go again after the weekend, give ourselves a break for...'

'Can't do that,' she states without elaborating.

'I'm telling you we can.'

'The families need to hear it from us, not Sky News.'

'OK, you're right, but it's my fault. So finish up and get anything else forwarded to me. Put an out-of-hours on with my number and email address. I'll sort all the replies on Joe, on the Elkins bodies, on Shenton.'

'I'll draft a statement for the eight families now. We'll need to give it to them at the same time we inform police to start searching,' she explains. Still no glance in my direction, her tone clearly, intentionally, pissed off.

'No, Chi... honestly.'

No reply. Just more typing. Clicking. And typing.

'Chi...'

Tap. Tap. Tap. Tap. Tap. Tap. Big slap of the enter key. Tap. Tap. Tap. Big exhale. Tap. Tap. Mouse-click. Tap. Tap. Tap.

'If you're going to ignore me, don't blame me for being overworked. I'm literally telling you...'

She swings round, every bit as livid as Harrington had been in the interview room. 'Robbie had been warning you for weeks that Joe wasn't coping. But you let Shenton keep bullying him. Now I understand why.'

'Robbie never predicted this, Chi.'

'No, of course, you aren't to blame for anything,' she spits.

'Look, go home, take a week off, whatever, just...'

'I can't!' she cries. 'If I don't do it *right now,* he'll leak it. The families deserve better.'

'Fine, let me do it then!' I repeat.

'In the time it'd take to show you, it's quicker for me to...' she grunts in frustration. 'You promised you wouldn't tell him.'

How is she not understanding this? 'He was about to shut us down!'

'You put Sam before Andrew Stride's family, you put Sam before patient safety, you definitely put Sam before me.'

'Oh, don't be such a martyr.'

She nods, but she's not agreeing. Looking away, she bites her lip and lets out a sharp snort of incredulous laughter. 'A martyr? Yeah, that's it, isn't it? If you'd really wanted to help, you'd have learnt all this stuff months ago. You'd have kept your mouth shut to Harrington, like I asked. You preach to Harrington about the families but I bet you can't name a single victim's relative outside the Elkins case. Can you?'

'OK, so you're much better with the families! That's why you do that stuff. You're good at it. If you're that bothered about them you should be wanting to get this information out to them. Not a second to waste!'

'What d'you think I was doing?' she yells.

'And I'm trying to help!'

'Not because you care. You just want me to be OK with what you did, so you can move on, carry on living in Emy World. Not have to think about anyone or anything else.'

'This isn't for me, it's for Mum!'

'Yeah, and screw anyone else whose whole life doesn't revolve around the same exact priorities,' she says, at her absolute cattiest.

'No one made you be part of this!' I bark, so angry I can barely form words. 'You've never complained before, and now we're getting somewhere you're whinging about a couple of late nights.'

'I would do anything for these families, including your mum. What I am not here for, is you to ride roughshod over me. You'll justify absolutely anything if you think it'll help find Sam. You made a deal with one of the *inmates*. Can you not see how messed up that is? Screw everyone else. Screw me. I've done more to get you this far than anyone.'

'Go then, you obviously resent being here. Just go. I'll deal with the families. You make it sound impossible, but I bet it's not that hard. After all... I am one of those families!' The last words are shouted so loud the whole barracks can probably hear. 'Or if you really want to help keep this place open – go fuck Harrington again. You always did work best on your back.' I'm panting as I stop.

Chi looks at me. That one struck deep. Should I take it back? No. She's lost all perspective, leaving me to fight for the Hive on my own – let her stew.

Robbie comes in from his enforced break not looking at all like a man who has been in this building for about twenty of the last twenty-four hours. You don't see *him* throwing his toys around.

I turn away, my cheeks hot enough to fry steak. I place the cooling flats of my hands on my face to ease the blaze and wander towards the kettle.

'This is awkward,' he quips, the sudden silence louder than a jet engine. 'Talking about me, were you? Well, carry on...' He puts on his Churchill voice: '"Criticism may not be agreeable, but it is necessary."'

He left with snacks, he's come back with lead balloons.

'I'm going to do the rest at home.' Chi packs up her things. 'The families and the police will know by 6 p.m. about Joe's bodies. It'll be out to the media before eight.'

I don't reply.

'See you Monday,' Robbie calls after her as the door slams.

'She's a bit strung out with the press and all this coming at once,' I tell Robbie, without him asking. He accepts the explanation, untroubled by the tension he just witnessed. Ignorance is bliss, and that's why men breeze through life.

'Do you think there's any chance Joe lied about those bodies?' he asks instead. Of course that's who he's still thinking about!

'You've seen his tapes, he always gets weird – even more weird – when he lies. Can't do it. He didn't get weird when he described that dockyard in Sunderland. I'm confident.'

'It's just...' Robbie's mouth twitches. 'When we were playing chess he was saying how he can't wait to see you again. Which is very *Joe*, obviously. But he was kind of framing it as if you were still going to be trying to tease details out of him. Just made me nervous he might have been lying to keep the game going, y'know.'

'Well that's the way he sees our relationship, although I hate using that word. He's always seen that dynamic like we're playing a game. I'm not surprised he's already looking forward to the next time and imagining it that way. And maybe he *has* got more details. There are definitely more questions *I* want to ask. But in terms of where the bodies actually are – he was telling the truth.'

He smiles and gives me a thumbs up.

'Head home, Robbie,' I say. 'I know I said today was going to be busy, but you've worked your socks off. I'll field any late calls. Whatever Chi puts out, she'll put out, but let's try and lie low as much as possible until after the weekend.'

'Thanks, boss,' he says, picking up his backpack. 'Oh, we should go through that latest Elkins interview you did on Monday too, if we get a chance.'

I agree, recalling it. 'Oh yeah, he starts talking about *amor fati*, doesn't he?'

Robbie walks towards the exit. 'Yeah, that one.'

'I suppose he did kind of admit his brother isn't buried where the others were,' I check, trying to remember what we even talked about. Usually I can recite every last murmur from my times with Elkins but the last twenty-four hours – that is literally all it's been – have been a hurricane in a bomb blast.

'It's more that he lets slip that Sam Whirberth isn't buried around Bedale either,' he says, throwing the line away like one of his empty crisp packets.

An icy blast of adrenalin grips me – all the drama and failure and success and fear dropping away. It leaves a single straight track between me and Robbie: his words hurtling towards me.

'What?' I force out.

'Elkins – I think he accidentally admits Sam Whirberth isn't buried where we thought.'

42

I rescind Robbie's early finish and tell him to print out the transcripts from my interview with Elkins immediately.

He does a better job of hiding his frustration than I would and logs back on, instinctively unzipping his bag and plucking out a family-size pack of Haribo Tangfastics.

But this candy man is dangling something far more alluring than sweets. Elkins let slip that Sam isn't buried near the other bodies – that's what Robbie said.

My intern's made a mistake, misunderstood something. Has to have. I know I was somewhat distracted during that session with Elkins, waiting for the call from DCS Miller, but I'd have spotted a clue that whopping. Obviously, we can't leave without me verifying I'm right, though.

Transcripts printed, I scan my copy while Robbie sets up the video and speakers. I don't see Sam's name anywhere. Robbie's messed right up. All those empty carbs and sugary snacks and hours of missed sleep have turned his grey matter shit-brown. At least it's taken my mind off Chi for five minutes. Sort of.

The playback starts and we concentrate in silence. Robbie's

hyperactive hands plunge in and out of the sweet packet, twitchily. I shut my eyes and try to detect any hint of emotion or tell in Elkins voice. But all I can hear is my colleague's Haribo bag crinkling.

Would have been nice if Chi hadn't stormed off early too. Her insight may have helped if there *is* anything of note. But noooo, she's too...

Urgh. Stop it, Em. Get over it. Focus!

I take a deep breath, open my eyes and hone back into the paper transcript as the conversation plays out on the screen too.

> Emy Rose: We've found remains that match your victims.
> [Frank breathing heavily]
> Emy Rose: Been in all the papers we've been withholding from Beeswell this week. I'll bring one in for you to look at. *The Times'* coverage has been particularly impressive.
> Frank Elkins: Who?
> Emy Rose: Don't know yet, waiting on DNA.
> Frank Elkins: Where did you find them?
> [Emy doesn't answer]
> Frank Elkins: Where did you find them?
> Emy Rose: Does it matter?
> Frank Elkins: Where did you fucking find them?
> Emy Rose: Farms around your old house in Bedale.
> Frank Elkins: How did you find two at once?
> Emy Rose: The string you left on stones...

'There!' Robbie cries.

The sudden jolt back out of the transcript makes me jump. 'The string on the stones?' I check, completely lost.

'No, the...' Robbie turns around and pauses the tape. 'The "two at once" line.'

I stare at him, fearing I was right – this isn't a thing.

'He knew there were two bodies,' Robbie says, excitable like a labrador bounding after a ball.

'We all knew there were two bodies.'

'Noooo,' he chuckles. 'You hadn't said how many bodies there were, you'd just said we'd found remains. And then, when he heard *where* they were he said, "How did you find *two* at once?"'

'But I'd never said there were two,' I concur, starting to grasp the thread of the idea.

'Exactly!' Robbie roars in jubilation. 'Which means, he knew there were only ever two bodies to find near his home. Elkins' own brother Vinny and the last victim, Sam Whirberth can't have been buried there.'

No, the bodies *have* to be around Bedale. Elkins can't drive. He could just about scrape his van around locally without a licence but no way he was going further afield. He doesn't know anywhere else. Even if he did have an accomplice, they had a system that was working. It's inconceivable Elkins would change it with Sam. The Bedale burials match up with statistical models, they fit psychological trends. Why would he bury the first and last victims somewhere alien to him or switch to a different method of body disposal? That is not how the mind works. And yet Robbie's right – Elkins does seem to genuinely let slip there are only two bodies near Bedale. So what on Earth happened to his brother and Sam?

'Wait!'

An idea bursts inside me. Elkins' molecular mistake spreads out into a map that could lead us all the way out of this hell. 'What if his *brother* was the accomplice!'

Robbie looks at me, his mouth slightly ajar.

I stand up and begin to pace. Every thought is coming out in capital letters. 'What if Elkins never killed his brother, just said he did to hide the fact Vinny was the accomplice all along? What if this brother is still alive somehow, somewhere?'

I begin to tumble down logical steps, thumping into them hard, one after another, struggling to keep up with a whole new world of possibilities rolling out ahead of me.

'So he's been protecting his brother all this time?' Robbie checks, trying to keep up with the trail.

'Yes! That would be a good reason to keep the secrets: so his brother can stay free!'

'But why?' Robbie asks, not knowing how strong this theory is. He probably knows about 1 per cent of what I do about the Elkins murders. But my brain is firing tester shots in all directions at every different detail and piece of evidence I know about these crimes, and this new theory is a direct hit on nearly every single one. It fits better than Elkins' official story. It fits better than anything Mum or I have ever come up with. It's a struggle keeping my head in the room as it runs off down tangents and rabbit holes looking deeper and deeper into an alternate reality that feels more and more believable.

'How about this?' I rattle off. 'The brothers get sick of the beatings from their dad so Vinny kills him. Elkins helps cover it up because... Yeah, Elkins covers it up because he'd promised his dying mum he'd look after Vinny. Then they decide it's better if Vinny goes into hiding.'

'But why would the two of them then just start abducting other men?' Robbie ponders. 'Wouldn't that draw more attention to them?'

'I don't know, the abuse they'd both suffered as kids will have left them horrifically confused and unable to process conflicting emotions. Cruelty is as cruelty does. But the key is, they did it together.'

'Why would Elkins be found with all their teeth – including the brother's?'

'Maybe he kept them for exactly the reason that transpired. So that if anyone was ever going to be linked back to the murders from that household, he could let them find the teeth in his van and say, "Look, it was me, my brother's dead,"' I posit. 'Shenton always said it was almost as if that evidence was planted, too good to be true.'

'Shenton?' Robbie asks, completely thrown.

'Never mind.'

He moves on. 'OK but where is this brother now?'

'I don't know,' I admit.

'And where's Sam Whirberth buried if, as Elkins suggests, he's not in Bedale?'

'Maybe Elkins doesn't know. Maybe the brother was still holding Sam, err, Mr Whirberth, elsewhere when Elkins was arrested,' I shrug, trying to ignore the fact that such a non-answer will be of no comfort whatsoever to Mum.

'And why have there been no more victims since Elkins was caught? The abductions stopped as soon as he was arrested.'

'Maybe the last one died and the brother hasn't dared try to abduct anyone without his big brother Elkins around since,' I propose.

'Yeah, but if Elkins was the mastermind when it came to burying them, then you'd think we might have maybe found the body of the last one, Sam Whirberth, if the brother had to hide him alone.'

I huff. 'Maybe the last victim never died then. Maybe Vinny has kept him alive. Then there'd be no grave to find and also that'd be an explanation for why there haven't been any more kidnaps.'

The words come out icy cold and cerebral. But as they thaw,

tremors start up in my soul, tectonic plates grinding as the whole fabric of my world shifts.

Maybe the last victim never died.

I'm beyond any feeling I've ever experienced before. Frightened, bewildered, disbelieving. The realisation billows outwards, like a mushroom cloud destroying every thought, every memory, everything I ever knew.

Sam could still be alive.

43

Mum stares up at me from the sofa, bemused by my clumsy, bungling attempt to bundle in through the front door.

The TV news is blaring out its headlines. Joe Okorie's face flashes up on the screen. I pick up the remote and turn the set off.

She raises her finger to point back at the screen, thinking I've missed what's being reported.

'Mum,' I assert, loud and officious. 'What if Sam's still alive?'

Her eyes shrink, confusion replaced with haunted sorrow. It's not like the idea of Sam walking right back in here hasn't occurred to Mum a million times. That's one of the main reasons we need his body. The mind never truly finishes one chapter unless you give it a new one to read.

But another, major discipline of the bereaved is to actively seek to move on. To tell yourself day in, day out that the facts are the facts. And the person you've lost truly is lost. If I wasn't confident we were closer to unravelling the mystery now than we ever have been before, it'd be the most cruel thing I could do: filling Mum anew with baseless hope about her dead son.

'I know, I know,' I say. 'Elkins had Sam's teeth. He admitted the murder. But he's slipped up – gave away that there were only two bodies buried around Bedale... we think.'

Mum raises a hand, not ready for the onslaught. She picks up the whiteboard off the table and scribbles:

How did you get him to admit that?

'He let on, by accident. I've brought the recording home with me, you need to listen. But he definitely hints there aren't any more bodies around there.'

She rubs out her first message with the cuff of her same hand, her other wrist still out of action in its sling.

Maybe he buried Sam somewhere else.

'But we've always known they must have been buried somewhere local to him, if he buried them at all. We were sure of it! I think Elkins' brother Vinny was his accomplice. And Elkins has covered for him. He lied about killing Vinny so police would never go looking for him.'

Where is he then? Why have we never seen him?

'I don't know, he could be miles away, counties away.'

Maybe the brother buried Sam alone.

'But then why no more abductions since? Sam still being alive would explain that. And also, it seems like Elkins is the one who was good at hiding bodies. The string round the rocks in the walls, that was Elkins. If anything, I'd bet Ollie Vaughn was buried by the brother, that's why his body was found. Then Elkins buried the next two and did a much better job. When you hear the way Elkins slips, it all adds up.' I pull my laptop out and prepare to load the offending interview.

Mum's good hand shoots up again; I don't need her to write down why. She doesn't want to hear Elkins' voice. Never has. She turns it off or walks out every time it's ever come up on the TV.

'Mum, you need to hear it, to understand what I'm saying. Please!'

She isn't looking at me, she's looking across the lounge at a picture: her, Dad, Sam and me. Just like I do in the interview room, but with an actual photograph in an actual frame. She could be thinking one of a dozen things, or more likely all twelve things at once. Sam must be about nine in that snap. He's wearing glasses – so is Mum. She never needed them, but he was so self-conscious about wearing his own set at school that she got a pair too, to make him feel less silly. A mother utterly committed to her son.

She points at the ceiling, by which I understand her to mean that if we are to watch the video back at all, it must be in the room where she keeps all her evidence. Keep the voice contained, seal the evil in.

'Good idea,' I tell her, rubbing a hand down her shoulder. Paltry comfort compared to what she's just agreed to.

Tea? she signs as we stand up.

'Coffee, strong one please,' I request.

We scale the stairs, me holding both our hot drinks, Mum holding my arm, planting both feet on each step before attempting the next one. The anticipation and impatience are agonising. Seriously, I've had sexual encounters that didn't last as long as this short walk.

Finally, on to the landing and into the office room with its usual chaotic milieu of splayed wads of paper, photos on the floor, half-scribbled thoughts on ripped sheets pinned against the wall. The map with Elkins' property at the centre has been updated. Two conspicuous red circles precisely drawn on in permanent marker – the spots Damian McAree and Nathan Brockhurst were found. On the desk, atop the mountains of notepads, is the copy of Robbie's transcript from Elkins' previous interview last week that Mum has evidently been scrutinising. It is complete with Robbie's abrupt final line:

[Interview terminated as the sound of vomiting is heard.]

'It's freezing in here.' I rub my hands together.

Mum leans down and switches on the little, old bar heater she likes to use. I heave a cardboard box stacked with loose news cuttings off the spare chair and switch on the lamp, with its softer orange glow. Mum shuts the door and takes her normal seat, the salmon-coloured cover on the padding is frayed and worn away from the frame along the edges. There's a dank smell in the masses of paper, years and years of absorbed damp.

'I'll play it – listen out for when I start talking about the bodies we've found, and everything we both say after that,' I say softly, shuffling my seat closer to hers.

She looks into nowhere, brings her tea up to her mouth, takes a tiny sip, then gives a single nod.

She's not actively sat and *listened* to Frank Elkins since the day of his sentencing more than ten years ago.

It hits me afresh. That whole time – if this theory is true – ever since Elkins pleaded guilty, since we were told Sam was definitely dead, my brother has in fact been living, existing, thinking, maybe even waiting. It's so horrifying a reality to grasp that part of me wonders whether it'd be better to simply find his body like the others'.

Mum sticks her index finger out and rolls it over a couple of times: *Get on with it.*

I open my laptop and lean it on one of the less precarious piles of notes, angling the screen towards Mum, and press 'play'.

Her eyes are shut however, lips pursed tight, good hand gripping her own knee.

I wish I could leave her to it, or at least march around distracting myself while it plays out. But Mum will be calmer if I stay, and I don't want to distract her by making any noise. I pluck out that CCTV image the day Sam was taken, of Elkins in his van. It looks like Elkins, but what if it's not, what if it's his brother? The clarity is poor; it could be. What if the brother was the getaway driver? That loose line from Elkins has literally redefined every last image attached to this case.

The key bit of the conversation comes, passes and goes. Mum is unmoved, eyes still fastened shut. In fact, the whole recording ends and Mum still doesn't open her eyes. If it weren't for her fidgeting fingers, I'd think she was asleep. Then a tear escapes, sliding down her cheek, it's shape appearing to change as the curvature of it catches the soft light of the lamp. Then a second one leaks out. She takes a deep, wobbly breath and opens her glistening eyes.

I encase her cold hand in both of mine, but she shakes the arm free.

Listen again, she signs.

We watch the interview four more times back-to-back. On the fifth playback, I know it'll be the last. Not because Mum tells me, but because she spends the whole time warming her right hand by the heater – she's getting ready to write.

The tape ends once again. She picks a biro that's lost its lid out of a cup of pens on the desk, finds a blank sheet among the disarray, and starts scribbling.

I try to work out what she's writing from her expression. She doesn't look like someone who's just realised her long-dead son is actually alive, but she is concentrating very hard, which suggests she is taking Elkins' words and my interpretation of them seriously. Her mouth moves as she writes some of the words, a fascinating habit for a mute person.

She hands me the paper and I read it aloud:

> *'I agree Elkins messed up. But he may have still buried Sam and his own brother and just guessed that we'd found the other two. But I am 100 per cent sure Bedale is the only place he buried bodies. That hasn't changed. And yet his own words now hint Sam and Vinny aren't there. Very odd the brother was never seen after the first murder. He must have never left their home. Maybe Elkins abducted the men as friends for the brother. But then where is Vinny now?'*

'That's got to be the focus now, surely,' I tell Mum, looking up. She gives me the same rolling index finger sign from earlier, urging me to carry on reading.

> *'Vinny surviving would also explain why Ollie Vaughn was buried so badly – if it was done by this odd, reclusive brother, and then Elkins buried the next two much better.'*

I break off from her message again, still not finished. 'Exactly. Maybe the brother was never keen on killing and burying them, maybe that came from Elkins. But that would mean the brother might have decided to keep Sam alive once Elkins was arrested.' I read on...

'If Elkins has just admitted there were only the two bodies hidden around Bedale, it gives us permission to think from scratch. Rewrite everything else we know.'

'OK,' I say, relieved Mum is persuaded so quickly but also a little overawed at now having to plot next steps rather than simply spend the rest of the night trying to convince her.

She scribbles a much shorter note:

So what next?

I raise my eyebrows. 'More coffee.'

44

We turn in at about 4 a.m. We haven't got much further with the new theory, but we have gone over scores of potential flaws the same way I did in the office but much more thoroughly: looking for paradoxes, testing the strength of the argument, and have *still* come back up finding it robust and convincing.

Mum continues to think it's more likely Sam has died, given that none of the other men survived anywhere near as long as the ten years he's been missing. I am more optimistic – no body found and no more victims since suggests Sam is still serving a purpose.

How Vinny could have remained incognito for literal decades is a detail still eluding us. But if we make that one leap, everything else falls into place.

It's almost dawn as I shuffle across the landing, my body screaming for bed and no morning alarm.

I don't even bother undressing, crawling under the duvet fully clothed and curling up in the foetal position. The cool pillow feels good.

* * *

Waking up warm, cocooned, still in the same position, is immaculate. I roll on to my back and let my eyes acclimatise to my room naturally. The day is being courageously held at bay by the curtains, the same ones I had growing up. A little light leaches through the garish criss-cross of tangerine and hot pink squiggles, draping the walls in coral-coloured shadows.

My jeans cling to me, constrictive and annoying. There's a reason no one's invented denim pyjamas. It's 1.05 p.m. I don't think I've slept in this long since uni.

Sam could be alive. That's the next thought that lands. Sam could be out there. What would he look like now? Would I recognise him? Does he miss us? Has he given up hope?

Don't be so morbid! If he's alive, that is only good news.

If.

With a huge yawn, I pick the sleep out of my eyes then stretch my arms and legs out like a Catholic on the rack. Out of yesterday's clothes, into an old tracksuit and my dressing gown, I potter downstairs and find Mum watching the news channel.

A bright yellow banner across the bottom of the TV screen reads: *Bodies found in search for Ghost Killer's victims.*

'Wow!' I shout. 'Wow wow wow!'

Mum's looking at me, shaking her head with a heart-warming mixture of disbelief and pride.

The news anchor explains that police are reporting multiple bodies found in refuse bags, six so far, with searches ongoing. Detectives say the tip-off came from the Beeswell centre in Northumberland. I play the coffee table like a conga drum.

'They'll find eight bags down there,' I assert. 'It's all exactly as Joe said. I *knew* Robbie was fretting over nothing with Joe's confession. Oh no! I'll actually have to visit him. Needy bastard.'

Mum makes a light-hearted grimace.

Tea? She signs, getting to her feet with her own empty mug.

'Please. Could you stick some toast in? Two slices.'

I curl up on the sofa to follow the full bulletin. Joe's mugshot flashes up, a lot younger with none of the little grey curls with which I've become so familiar around his ears. Then a generic shot of Beeswell. A thrill whizzes through me.

Of course, the black dog then bites – what are you celebrating? That same man killed another of your inmates just yesterday, the project's on the rocks... and you still don't have Sam!

But the sunny me is winning today, for a change.

Harrington had better see all this positive coverage the Hive's getting. The media isn't leading on Shenton's death, they're leading on our breakthrough, *my* breakthrough. Bet I've got more missed calls than a runaway bride.

Urgh, I left my phone in the spare room before heading to bed. I heave myself up and plod back upstairs. I can hear the phone buzzing before I reach the door.

Speak of the devil. It's Harrington. Probably just a begrudging 'well done' regarding the bodies on the news. Can I ignore him? Hmm... no, get it out of the way.

'Hi.'

'Finally!' He wails. 'Has *The Times* called you?'

'What?'

'*The Times*! The newspaper! *The Times*! Have you spoken to them?'

'No,' I stutter. 'Why?'

'They're publishing tomorrow. Beeswell's dead. I'm shutting it down. Should have done it yesterday.'

'What are you on about?'

'They're sinking us both. They know everything. Full exposé. They can't mention my boy's link to the Shenton case but they're going to say I leant on the police and you and the CPS. "Ulterior motives",' he squeals in panic.

'No! But what's there to say about Beeswell? We have nothing to hide.'

'Hogwash! They have enough shit to drown you ten times over. They *must* have called you. They wanted a response from the MOJ an hour ago.'

'Response to what?' I cry.

'Okorie attacking Shenton. The way you talk to the inmates. The rules, the lack of rules. Did you let the intern play chess against Okorie... as a *treat*? It sounds like a fucking circus.'

My blood freezes. 'We're literally all over the news for finding Joe's bodies. We get results!' I struggle to breathe as panic descends.

'Don't be so stupid. They're vultures. I'm telling you now, you'd better have a great response to all of their questions or you'll never work again. But Beeswell's done. Finished. That's it.'

'Don't scare so easily. It's *one* story,' I plead. 'Is this you? Did you leak all this?'

'Preposterous! I come out almost as badly. Apparently, they have a source with a direct link to your project. If anyone's blabbed it's you! Who do you know at *The Times*?'

'I haven't blabbed to anyone!'

'That article with Leon Courtney-Peltz. What else did you tell him?'

'I...' Words won't form. The walls close in. I can't see or move.

'What?'

'I've been seeing him a bit,' I mumble, shock paralysing my ability to lie.

'Ha! You've been played, dear. And now you're radioactive. I can't be within a thousand miles of your stupidity.'

'He wouldn't betray me,' I mutter, trying to recall the big flashing warning signs I've so evidently missed.

The maniacal cackle down the phone is cruel. 'You really are a stupid bitch. Beeswell's over. Elkins is being transferred tomorrow morning. You will not hear from me again.'

The call goes dead.

Leon couldn't have screwed me over. Why would he? I literally slept at his house the night before last.

My stomach lurches like I'm on a plane plummeting to earth. I have to grip my phone hard to quell the quivering that's taken hold of my arms. There are half a dozen missed calls from Leon on my phone too. And a string of WhatsApps. I read through them.

The realisation is a fresh knife to the heart. Birthday brunch with his friends! That was today. I forgot. The texts start this morning, cheery at first: he can't wait to see me, he's arrived at the restaurant, asking how long I'll be, resending me the address. But then excitement morphs into impatience: checking if I'm nearly there, offering to come and pick me up, asking me to call him, telling me they are going to start without me.

I blink in stunned disbelief. There's a gap of over an hour between the flurry of messages and the final one. But it's there at the bottom of my screen, waiting for me like the showstopping crescendo to a stone-cold nightmare. It simply reads: *Fuck you.*

45

I could have stared at the screen for ten seconds or ten minutes. I have no answers, only blind panic and pitch-black dread.

The screen lights up again. I don't recognise the number but answer, torpidly.

'Hello. Is that Emy Rose?' comes the woman's voice, playing dumb but fooling no one.

'Yeah.'

'Hello, Dr Rose. This is Jess Barker from *The Times*. We have some questions to ask you regarding the Beeswell detention centre.'

I don't respond.

'We've been given some information about the centre.' She's cocky, shameless. If I was trying to tear someone's life apart, I'd at least have the good grace to sound apologetic. Who hurt you as a child, woman?

On she goes: 'Many of the claims relate to you personally. So we really do need to put these allegations to you.'

'Yeah?' I brace for impact.

'Our source says you are emotionally manipulative towards your inmates. That your claim that the project is a scientific study is fundamentally compromised by a conflict of interests, namely that you are the sister of Sam Whirberth, Frank Elkins' final victim. That you allowed Tim Shenton to goad Joseph Okorie continuously because you were in league with Tim Shenton to try and get a confession out of Frank Elkins. That this constant goading eventually led to Okorie's attack that killed Tim Shenton. That you pretended to be Okorie's girlfriend in order to make him confess to the whereabouts of his victims. That justice secretary, Barnaby Harrington, foisted Tim Shenton on you in desperation to avoid a trial that would have implicated his son. That you let a colleague play chess against Joseph Okorie as, and I quote, "a treat".'

'It's Joe Okorie, not Joseph,' I correct.

'Is that your only comment on the accusations?'

'It's all a cracking yarn, I'll give you that. When's the movie out?'

'Is it a yarn based in reality?' she fires back.

'Who is your source? Leon Courtney-Peltz?'

'I can't reveal that, I'm afraid,' the reporter smarms.

'That's a yes.'

'What do you say to these allegations?'

'I refuse to corroborate anything you've just said,' I state.

'Do you deny it?'

I pause. I could deny it. That would buy time. Can they prove any of it? Was Leon recording me at any point when I discussed the case with him? Who knows? How can I trust anything he may or may not have done any more? It must be him if they know about Harrington's son. I didn't even tell Chi about that.

'We have broken no laws in our relentless pursuit of closure for the victims' families,' I declare, the reporter's aggression helping me focus out of pure indignation. 'Any story that attempts to overshadow the highly successful work we have done is not on the side of these poor families. That's my whole statement. It must be printed in *full*.'

I hang up. Clarity cools like condensation on glass. I must make Leon retract the claims. If I can convince him to take the story back, we smother it at birth.

I make the call, still rooted to the same spot as when Harrington phoned.

No answer from Leon.

Fear spirals again. Will this wreck everything with Elkins? With no Beeswell, will he ever speak to me again? He'll know I'm Sam's sister. Will Harrington get a restraining order like he threatened to, so that I can't see Elkins? What if he uses his contacts to get him killed, too, like he said he would if this all came out? What if Elkins' brother sees the story, sees that I'm hunting for Sam and decides to flee, leaving my brother locked up somewhere to die? What if Sam *is* already dead but we still lose our best chance at getting his body back?

I'm in the car, racing to Leon's. How could he do this? Who would be that vicious and vindictive? The spite is incomprehensible. Journalists, they're all cut from the same shit-stained cloth. Vermin!

Time accelerates away from me. I'm at Leon's flat, bashing his door like a mariner trapped below deck on a sinking ship.

Finally, footsteps grow louder from the inside, plodding downstairs, then a clink of a lock releasing.

Leon looks at me and tries to shut the door again but all of a sudden I'm a rugby player, shoulder-barging it open and pinning him against the wall behind.

'Take it back,' I order. I could claw his throat out if I didn't need it so badly, so he can call *The Times*.

He looks startled in the extreme, feral eyes wide and fixed on mine. 'What?' He makes no attempt to escape my face two inches away from his.

'How long have you been planning this? Or is it just punishment for missing today?' I take half a step back and exhale. 'This is what you rats do, isn't it? Nothing's real. Everything's just there to be ripped apart, right?'

He's glancing down at my lips, watching the words tumble out, then back at my savage eyes. He opens his mouth but can only conjure a choking noise before shaking his head and putting his lips back together.

'Phone them, tell them you got it wrong. Beeswell is thriving. You got your info wrong,' I instruct, like he's a child being taught how to apologise after trampling the neighbour's daffodils.

The shaking head becomes more exaggerated. Then he coughs. 'What're you on about?' He's groggy but calm. 'You need to leave.'

'I can't lose Beeswell, Leon. Drop the massive overreaction, it's just a birthday. Get some therapy, get a cat. I don't care. Just don't kill my chances with Elkins over a stupid fling.'

'A fling? Nice. I don't know what you're on about with all this. But it was humiliating earlier,' he grunts, not looking sorry at all. 'I told you how much it meant, and you couldn't even be arsed to tell me you weren't coming.'

'I forgot! I'm having the longest, busiest, worst week of my life! And even if it *was* just that I couldn't be arsed, that's no reason to blow up Beeswell. I trusted you!' I scream the final words, anger at his self-pitying obsession burning hotter with every additional second he persists with acting like he's the injured party.

Exasperation soars in his voice. 'Trusted me with what?'

'*The Times*! Harrington's been on to me too. He's closing the Hive. *The Times* know everything. They know about Harrington's son, about me and Sam. They even brought up Robbie playing chess with Joe. Stuff I haven't told *anyone* except you! They're flaying me alive.'

His eyes are wide and understanding. 'Em, I haven't told anyone anything. I know what that place means to you. Why would I try to bring it...'

'Cut the bollocks. Why would *your* paper be running a big exposé on Beeswell, at the exact same time you're looking into Shenton and Harrington, and not keep you in the loop?'

'I hadn't told them yet! The fewer people who know, the better, for your sake mostly,' he says, before looking off to the side. 'If what you're saying is true, I've just *lost* my exclusive.'

'Whatever. The game's up. Call them back. Get it out of the paper. You must know the best way to kill a story, yes?'

'Em.' He stands taller and puts his hands on my shoulders. 'I have nothing to do with this.' The words are delivered with assurance and security – the kind of tone that you couldn't pull off if you were lying, unless you were one of the Tim Shentons or Barnaby Harringtons of this world.

Leon didn't leak it.

I look into those yearning eyes and plummet into the void. 'But then how do they know everything?' I crumble into his warm, strong chest. 'Who would take us down?'

He wraps those impressive arms around me and squeezes me into him as I howl over and over, 'Who? Who?'

'Who knows all the details *The Times* knows?' he whispers.

'You, me and Harrington. I didn't tell anyone but you.'

'That can't be right,' he suggests, coaxing the logic out of me with sensitive and gentle precision. 'Who else could know all this information? What about your intern?'

'Robbie? No, he doesn't even know Sam's my brother.'

'Chi?'

'I made sure not to tell her about Harrington's son,' I clarify, thoughts tearing through me like tornados as I seek and fail to land on any plausible explanation. 'I took him into the interview room to speak to him about it, so she wouldn't hear.'

'And she definitely didn't listen in?'

'There's a relay between the rooms, but I switched it off. I made sure I did.'

He blows out his cheeks – defeated.

'Unless...' I brood.

'What?'

'I think the relay switch stops all sound and video from the interview room to the office.'

'*Think*?' Leon repeats.

I pull out my phone, instinctively knowing how I can find an answer to this, the millionth question to pound my mind so far today.

Robbie picks up quickly.

'Robbie, the switch in the interview room, does that cut the live feed to the office or just stop it automatically being recorded onto the system?'

'The latter,' he states, sounding muffled between loud crunching noises. 'Sorry... having some chips. But yeah, if you plug in your headphones and switch your computer's input feed to the interview room you can still see and hear everything from in there even if you turn off the feed, it just means it isn't committed to the hard drive with all the other security footage.'

I end the call.

Leon's worked out from my face what's happened. He grasps

both my forearms, nudges me a step backwards again, restoring eye contact, his expression one of patience and pity.

I look away as the humiliating depth of her deception poisons every cell of my being.

Frothing waves of fury and heartbreak crash against the rocks of callous betrayal.

Chi did this.

46

I'm sitting on Leon's sofa. He pours me a whiskey to still the shaking. The first sip makes me wince, burning from the tip of my tongue to the pit of my stomach. I see the rest off.

He says he knows the reporter who called me. He's going to ring her, see what more he can learn.

Words won't form to respond. The eye of the storm in which I find myself is so unfathomable, so crushing, that outward expression is impossible.

The press is going to devour me. Beeswell is finished. I've lost my best friend. We will never find Sam.

Is this how Mum feels? Locked in, so buried under the weight of emotional calamity that speaking is simply an inadequate and pointless form of expression?

Leon's talking in his bedroom. The door's shut but you can tell he's livid.

Still trapped in a silent stupor, I find myself calling Chi. No plan. No message to relay. No venom to spit. I don't know why I bother. Maybe in the redundant hope she'll convince me she's not guilty. An automated voice tells me the number has not been recognised. Changing her number? She truly is gone. How did I not see she was this unhappy? How did I not spot a level of pain and hatred that could have built up to such a spiteful extent? I replay our last conversation over and over again. All the mean things I said, the lack of gratitude, shouting at her, shaming her, asking her to screw Harrington. I picked her apart using a story she told me in confidence. Was that the moment our friendship shattered? If so, sinking the Hive would have turned from a fantasy to a formality – a release, a relief with the only family left out of pocket being the one undermining her.

Thoughts and emotions are tumbling over each other like freight in a truck as it plunges over the cliff edge.

I will never forgive her. I might deserve this. But Mum doesn't. And if Sam is alive, he doesn't deserve it either. I will never forgive her.

Leon comes back out of the bedroom, twitchy and agitated, hand brushing through his hair. 'It's bad,' he states. 'They're going ahead. Gist is that Beeswell was anarchy. I told Jess that's bollocks, that it's got so many results for families, that it was run almost identically to any other prison. But she's not listening. It'll be on the website this evening and the front page in the morning. They're even going for an emergency court order to remove the injunction so they can report on Harrington's son, but I think he'll get that delayed at least. Oh, and he's now confirmed to them the centre will be shutting tomorrow.'

I sit unmoved. The words barely compute. They just hit me and bounce off – fists pounding castle walls.

Next thing he's sitting beside me, holding my hands, telling me how cold they are.

'It's your birthday.' They're the only words I can manage as I turn to look into his eyes.

'Don't worry about that,' he insists.

'I'm sorry.' I say it in a monotone but he reads the honesty beneath the malaise and kisses me on the cheek.

'Probably for the best,' he adds. 'I think I was falling in love with you.'

I give a small, mousy snort. 'Maybe that's your present. Bullet dodged.'

Quiet falls. The eye of the storm has moved on now. The ruins stretch in all directions, but the blind panic and powerlessness has passed. I could spend forever picking up the wreckage or I could sit here and do nothing, and neither option would be right or wrong.

'I'm not sure if it makes any difference to anything now, given he's dead. But I finally found Shenton's friend, the one people kept telling me to track down. He told me he was too scared to speak because of what Shenton might do, but he phoned me back after the news broke that he'd died yesterday. Said Shenton used to get him to put a plastic bag on his head while Shenton raped him. Exactly the same as Andrew Stride. Shenton killed Andrew; any jury would have sent him down if they'd known his past.'

'And I sided with him to try to get to Elkins,' I murmur, disgusted with myself.

Leon rests his head on my shoulder.

'Make sure it gets out how guilty Shenton was,' I tell him. 'You deserve the kudos for doing the job the police should have done. And Andrew's mum needs to know his killer was caught.'

'I will,' he replies.

A silence draws out.

'I don't know what to do,' I confess after a long, long time.

He doesn't respond straight away, his thumb brushing up and down mine as he sits up straighter to look out of the window.

'I don't know either,' he eventually says, calm and solemn. 'But what I do know is that the only way to guarantee not finding Sam, is to stop trying.'

* * *

I had forever to crack Elkins. Then I had months. Then I had weeks. And now I have hours. But while I still have those hours, I will not stop trying.

I return to Beeswell. Back into the eye of the storm.

47

The sun's still high in the sky as I reach the base. Waiting for clearance at the first perimeter of security, a spotty boy in a white shirt and cheap grey suit trousers scampers over and knocks on the passenger side window.

'Dr Emy Rose?' he calls at me, the sound muffled by the glass. He looks about eleven.

'Yeah?' I open the window enough to let his words pass through but not his hands.

'Oh, I'm Terry Junes from the *Daily Mirror*. Was wondering if you could...'

'The *Mirror*?' I check. 'Don't you have to go through puberty first?'

'I'm twenty-one, I'm on work experience,' he splutters without confidence, his head leaning to the side as he bends forward awkwardly and tries to aim his voice through the gap. 'Any comment on the discovery of all of Joe Okorie's victims and the death of Tim Shenton?'

'How did you know I'd be here?' I demand, more amused than anything else. The gates, which had opened to allow me in, are shutting again, but I have so many more questions for this yappy, prepubescent terrier.

'I didn't. News editor told me to come to Beeswell and see if I could get anything.' There's a hint of West Country accent if I'm not mistaken. It's an extra layer of absurdity to the already-peculiar scene. A sweaty sheen is painted across his forehead by the beating heat of the day.

'I hardly ever come here on Saturdays. How long would you have stayed if I'd never showed up? How long have you already been here?'

'Been here a couple of hours. Would've probably stayed here until seven-ish. Whenever they call up to say I can go. Any comment on Joe Okorie's victims or Tim Shenton?'

He's a persistent pup, I'll give him that. Plus, he's not here to stir up trouble; the rest of the media are a day behind *The Times*' story.

'You poor thing. Did you drive here? No of course not, you're not allowed to drive until you get to sixth form, are you?'

He gives an awkward chuckle, letting me walk all over him. 'Erm, I did drive yeah. Tried to park outside but a guy came out and made me move the car half a mile down the road, so I left it there and walked back up. If you want, I can get in your car and we can go inside for a proper chat.'

I belt out a laugh. Wow, it's good to have a moment's relief. 'You can't get me done for child abduction that easily, Terry Junes.'

'What are you here to do today?' he enquires. He's brandishing his phone in his right hand like a gunman holding up a supermarket. At first I wonder if he's filming me, but then it becomes obvious he's just recording us, Dictaphone-style.

'None of your business.'

His shoulders slump and his mouth flaps as he tries and fails to keep the conversation going. I look at that skinny face, those spotty cheeks. Sam had acne, suffered a lot of bullying at school because of it.

'So you want a line, Master Junes?'

'Erm, err yeah!'

'OK, I can tell you exclusively that Beeswell micro-prison is closing tomorrow because one of my colleagues has leaked highly delicate and private information to *The Times*. She's also been sleeping with the justice secretary, Barnaby C. Harrington. Get that detail in. Her name's Chiyoko Aoki, make sure to use her full name. And just to give your story a bit of spice, Terry Junes, I can also tell you that Harrington is a spineless, callous charlatan who would rebury all the bodies we've found if he thought it'd get him a promotion in government.'

Right on cue, the gates to the base reopen. I leave Terry Junes' mind to scramble in my rear-view mirror.

The Times, Harrington and Chi all kneecapped in one serendipitous blast. Somehow the exchange is a tonic, reminding me of who I am and what I am and, maybe most importantly, what I refuse to be – a victim.

I park up and enter the Hive. Arthur is at the security desk as usual. It's a Saturday afternoon, does he never leave?

I tell him to get Elkins into the interview room, but not to shackle him to the chair.

This can't be like any other interview. This is the Hail Mary pass, the ejector seat before impact, the defibrillator after cardiac arrest. This is it.

* * *

'I envy the police,' I tell Elkins upon entry to the interview room, a cage of my own making I can't wait to never see again.

He gives a sharp shift in his chair, caught out by the lack of warning. His hands are knitted in his lap. They're the one part of him I've never really studied, given they're usually pinned to his sides. They're less weathered than his facial features, less red. Smaller than one might expect.

I take my seat opposite. He's yet to look up, as predicted; the hunched shoulders and head lolling forward very much on brand.

'Do you know why I envy the police?' I ask in the sort of tone that suggests I'm not waiting for a response.

Elkins obliges by continuing to ignore me.

'It's because they get to follow a standard formula when interrogating suspects.'

He's determined to keep studying the ground.

I get up, take a deep breath and begin pacing. 'Pleasant. Pressure. Panic.' I spell out. 'That's all they have to do. Be *pleasant* to the suspect – win your trust, get your guard down. You start oversharing as you build a rapport with the cop. Ah, there's the rub. The detective then turns – uses those loose-lipped remarks against you, makes clear you're not as clever as you thought you were, that you've basically just given yourself away, so you might as well confess. That's the *pressure*. Then my favourite, the *panic*. The wily officer highlights how badly you've ruined everything for everyone, that no one is there for you any more. You are alone. This makes confessing seem less scary. Things have already hit rock bottom. In fact, maybe it's the only way left to mitigate what you've done – y'know, at least it'll make the copper happy, she's the only person you have left in the world to please. And... poof... confessions you swore you'd never ever make come spewing out.

'Pleasant. Pressure. Panic. A little contrived making it triple

Ps, I'll grant you. But the technique is peer-reviewed, psychologically proven to produce results.'

I glance down at him. He's still slouching forward, uninterested.

'But I can't do that,' I go on, recommencing my walk around the room. 'That's why I envy the police. I don't have that luxury. "And what luxury is that, Miss Rose?" I hear you ask!' I point a finger in the air like a preacher reaching the crux of their sermon. 'The luxury of novelty. These detectives aren't spending days and weeks and months with these people. They investigate them, they get them in for interview, they either charge or release them. A suspect doesn't get the chance to learn how the detective ticks, whether they're being genuinely pleasant or faking it, whether they're exaggerating the pressure or being real. The suspect doesn't know whether to listen to their own panic signals or not. That is a massive advantage for any detective. But here, at Beeswell, I interact far too much with you to pretend. You'd see right through it. And I'd lose any rapport or progress we'd made. So the dance then becomes more complicated, as you can imagine.'

I am walking in tight circles around the table and chairs, eyes stuck on the specimen in front of me. His thumbs tapping, everything else is frozen.

'I decided when I first opened Beeswell that there was no point pretending, trying to make you all like me, then using it against you. I'd just be doing myself a disservice and undermining my own efforts. So I was myself: rude, disparaging, impatient, cynical, dry. I'm sure you could think of some more robust words, couldn't you, Frank?'

No movement.

'And with the other inmates, that helped. I was myself, and in their own ways, they found an authenticity in that, I think.

Something real they could latch onto as opposed to the never-ending conveyor belt of detectives, psychologists, lawyers, warders and chaplains patronising them, oversimplifying them, not listening to them. And in time I genuinely feel I got to know them, that I got to decipher them a little, and that helped me to unpick them, get to the secrets, y'know?'

The thumbs have stopped tapping again now.

'I never felt like that with you. And for the longest time I thought it was you, and your walls and your silence and your stubbornness. But I've changed my mind. Because I haven't been treating you like the others, Frank. I've been myself with them, I've let them have it, warts and all, take it or leave it. Real. But with you, I've still been playing a role. Faking it. D'you know why, Frank?'

No movement.

I arrive at my seat, fingers pressed against the table as I lean forward to loom over him.

'Do you know why, Frank?' Every syllable is stuffed with admonishing heat.

Those sunken eye sockets, that gaunt jaw, it all finally tilts upwards until he can see me above him. A small shake of the head; his eye contact holds.

'Because for you, I've been faking something. Forget Emy Rose, Frank. I'm Emy Whirberth.'

48

His first words of the conversation are croaked from beneath wide eyes, suddenly vulnerable. 'Sam's... sister?'

I remain standing. My turn not to reply as I examine his reaction. He's surveying my whole face, trying to locate traces of memories. Maybe he remembers me sitting next to my Dad as he made his televised plea for Sam's return right after he disappeared. Maybe it's the sentencing hearing when he stared in cold indifference at all the families up in the viewing gallery, as his jail term was handed down. Maybe he doesn't recognise me at all.

But he remembers the name.

He croaks again: 'Why didn't you tell—'

'And what? Give you an extra reason to keep it all secret? Sit opposite you, watching you revel in my misery? You could have toyed with me, twisted the knife. You'd have broken my spirit, and laughed as you did it.'

He widens his field of vision, looking around the room, only half hearing me as his mind whirs at its own secret pace.

'Is that what I should have done? Told you… appealed to your sense of *heart*?' I demand in mock understanding. 'Have I got you all wrong? Go on then, Frank. Where's my Sam?'

'I've got nothing to say.'

'Nothing to say,' I repeat with disdain. 'You'd get on with my mum. Well, there's one thing I *do* want to say. I think Sam's alive. And you know how to find him, as well as your own brother!'

He relocks his focus on me and shakes his head with calm control. 'I can't.'

'WHY?' My voice breaks, legs buckling, strong upright stance perishing into the chair.

Face-to-face now, it's clear he's fighting it all back, pushing it down, battling himself not me.

'I've been back through every conversation we've ever had, every piece of evidence the police have on you, and I cannot see a single clue as to where your brother might be. But you must know. You must!'

'*Amor fati*,' he mutters.

'Fuck *amor fati*! I will never be content until we find him. Even if he is dead. You can't hold us to ransom. You don't get to choose whether we find Sam or not!'

'Yes, I do,' he says in a soft tone.

'Are they alive? Tell me that.'

'I've been inside so long, how would I…'

'But you know your brother, Vinny. What do you *feel*? It was him who buried Ollie Vaughn. But he messed it up, didn't he? So you buried McAree and Brockhurst. But if that's the case, and we can't find Sam, either Vinny suddenly got a lot better at hiding bodies, or there hasn't been another body to hide.'

'How do you know all this?' he barks, his own flash of anger shocking him back into silence.

'I'm not putting out if you don't.'

His eyes narrow; his lips remain pursed.

'At least tell me *why* you won't tell me,' I beg. 'Please! I need to understand.'

'I promised Mum, I've told you that.'

'Told me what?' I demand, trying to recall which strand of which tortured conversation in the last eight months could possibly relate to this cryptic admission. A beam of light illuminates one specific exchange. 'You promised her you'd always look after Vinny just before she died?' I question gently, head nodding, holding eye contact, mimicking his clasped hands: any social cue that could make him drop his guard.

'I deserve this,' he whispers, having to look away as he repels another wave of emotion. 'I deserve it.'

'Deserve what?' I push, leaning forward and grasping his cold, slim hands. I've never touched this man before. The skin on his hands is soft, but aged and shrivelled like those of a much older man's. The initial frisson of fear at making contact swells into anger as I think about how little he deserves any sort of human interaction compared to his victims and their families. But I keep hold of those bony hands – matter over mind. I push again. 'Frank, you deserve what?'

'All of it!'

'I don't understand.'

He doesn't react. I snap back to my feet in frustration and face away from him. 'You're being transferred in the morning. Shenton's dead. Harrington's shutting us down.'

There's no response, verbal or otherwise, from behind me.

'They're going to tear me to shreds because of who I am, being Sam's sister. Using this place to get to you. All that. I'll never work in psychology again.'

I turn back to face him. The sympathy behind his eyes is

deeper and more authentic than any look ever exchanged in this room before.

'They're going to get a restraining order so I can't speak to you any more, too,' I continue. 'Harrington even threatened to have you killed, make it look like an accident, so I can't get to you.'

I move away again, walk to the wall and rest my head against it, shutting my eyes. I don't know what to do. I've failed Mum, I've failed Sam. I'm not strong enough to cope with what's coming in the days and weeks ahead. I screw my eyes up as tight as I can, trying to offset the need to scream.

The words from behind me are quiet, but clear. 'He was just a boy.'

I turn slowly but don't interrupt. Elkins is looking down, lost in a memory. 'He was begging me, and I just watched. And I could tell, in his eyes, he was thinking...' His words drown in his throat.

'Who was thinking? Your brother?'

There's a moment's silence, the gap between the lightning bolt and the clap of thunder. Then it happens; Elkins' chest shudders and pulses as sobs gush out in violent bursts. 'He trusted me! I let it happen!'

'Let what happen?'

'About a month after Mum died, Dad had been on a binge for something like three days – locked us in the house. Vin'd be a teenager. We were starving, Vin's screaming for food. Dad finally comes back steaming, hears Vin and says he'll kill us both if Vin doesn't shut up. Dad was terrified someone might hear, call social services or something.' Frank's eyes are closed, trapped in the past. His mouth shudders as he summons the ghosts back into being. 'But Vin's delirious, we're so hungry. Dad'd never hit Vin before, Mum wouldn't let him, it was always me. But she's dead now. He starts laying into him, fists like bricks. I try to pull him away. And... and...' another huge breath in and a fortifying pause. 'And he tells me he's teaching Vin a lesson. If I leave him to it, he won't beat him too bad but if I try to stop him he'll keep going until Vinny stops crying for good.'

His mouth bobs open and shut as he grapples with the final line, before it explodes out of him, from what seems like the deepest, rawest cave of his soul: 'So I let him do it!'

He pulls his hands up to his mouth, rocking back and forth, eyes still shut. 'Dad takes his belt off. Vin goes quiet, just meat on a hook. Dad's coming down so hard he's panting. I know how much that belt hurt, but Vin just lies there on his front, face to the side, looking at *me*. I could see he was thinking, "Why aren't you stopping him? Why?" He trusted me!'

I sit opposite, my own hands now propping the sides of my head up on the table. 'He would have understood,' I reply pathetically. 'If not at first, once he was older. He'd know you loved him.'

'I couldn't cope,' he grunts back, clearing his throat to wrestle back some composure. 'I went out, left Vin alone with him...' he tails off again, teetering. But another deep breath and a burst of anger brings his voice back stronger 'Who *does* that? Leaves their little brother to get chucked about, broken bones, busted nose, fearing for his life? A coward. A coward!'

'Frank, you were a victim too!' I insist, surprised by my own concern.

Elkins bats the observation away with a strong shake of his head. 'It's unforgiveable.' He's much more matter-of-fact all of a sudden, as if detaching completely from the event. 'That's the only night I ever drank – sat in a pub until closing, then came home and Vin's in the lounge, unconscious with blood...' he waves a hand around his own head with lazy imprecision '...

everywhere. I thought Dad'd killed him. But he was still breathing. Dad had knocked his front teeth out.'

A nasty chill of realisation shoots through me. 'Knocked his teeth out? Was it front two at the top and one underneath?'

Elkins nods at the floor.

'You took the other boys' incisors out so they'd look more like Vinny,' I deduce out loud. 'Wait. You accidentally told Tim Shenton you didn't know how to pull teeth out... It was Vinny who did it to them, wasn't it? So that he wasn't the only one who looked like that.'

He ignores my line of questioning, still trapped in his own story. 'I patch Vin up but he doesn't say a word to me,' he explains. 'I don't blame him. Anyway, I'm working with Dad on farms by this point, we had a van each, same plates on both so we didn't have to pay tax twice. I get up in the morning and Vin's gone, taken one of the van's too. Dad goes apeshit but what can we do? He doesn't want to report a stolen van because then he'd get in trouble over the copied plates.'

'Why didn't you report Vin being missing?' I probe.

'Authorities didn't even know he existed. Dad'd kept him out of schools and off any social service radars his whole life. He'd have been taken away if anyone found him and I didn't want that. I wanted him to come back to *me* so I could look after him like I'd promised Mum before she died.'

I sit, unable to think of anything to say. How can such a horror story be real?

'I killed Dad,' Elkins offers, the words rolling out as casually as if he's describing his lunch. 'About a week after Vin went. I thought he'd come back soon. I couldn't have Dad doing that to him again, and I thought if Vin came back and saw I'd got rid of Dad, maybe he'd trust me again.'

'How did you kill him?'

'We sat up, I got him drinking heavy. I'd be about – what – nineteen, twenty at this point? It's hard to tell as we never knew our birthdays.'

The detail is thrown away but strikes hard. The upbringing these sons endured was about as psychologically traumatic and cruel as it's possible to imagine.

Elkins continues: 'He's downing vodka, laughing and joking and slapping me about and making sick jokes about Mum and Vin and I sit there and take it, knowing all I have to do is keep him drinking. He passes out. I pull him on to the floor and force more of the booze down his throat, then take a cushion and hold it over his face for what felt like an hour. He was never touching Vin again, I owed Vin and Mum that at the very least.' There are tears sailing down his cheeks one after another. He wipes his eyes and face with his forearm but the flow doesn't stop. 'And I swore that day that I would protect Vin forever, no matter what.' The words are forced through his bared, canary-coloured teeth.

'Coroner's report said your dad died of cardiac arrest likely caused by alcohol poisoning,' I remember.

Elkins shrugs.

'Why not admit to killing him when you got picked up?'

'He deserved to die a drunk, not a victim.'

'Why had he kept Vinny under house arrest his whole life?'

'Dad'd got into trouble about me when I was younger. Services almost took me. Dad just didn't fancy the hassle again and Mum was too scared to stop him. She got to stay at home with her baby; that was enough for her.'

'Then what happened... after your dad died?' I prod, desperate to keep him talking as we stampede towards the murdered boys, towards Sam.

'I thought Vin would come back, but he didn't – not for

months. But I reasoned he must be OK because the spare van hadn't been found and brought back to me. If they'd found it abandoned somewhere the plates would have matched to my address, wouldn't they? If the van was safe and sound, surely Vin was too. But then...' He stops and tugs up both sleeves of his tracksuit.

It's coming.

'He comes back, in floods of tears. Van outside. It's pissing it down and he's standing at the door gabbling about something, real upset. I yank him inside, give him a hug but something's not right. I don't get it at first, but as he calms down, I realise – he's talking like Mum.'

'What d'you mean?' I demand, wrong-footed.

'High-pitched, sort of gentle... I can't explain it, but if you'd met Mum you'd understand. He was saying Vinny was dead in the van. I kept saying, "Vin, you're not dead, you're here, you're here mate, you're home. Dad's gone, you can stay! It's OK." But he kept saying it, "Vinny died, I couldn't help it, he's dead, he's dead."'

Elkins switches in and out of the impersonation with ease, it's the same voice he's descended into a dozen times in this room. The creep of it still crawls under my skin.

'He took me to the van. There was this bloke in a cage, slumped over dead. I lost it,' he confesses, speaking downwards. 'I'd been so happy to see Vin, but I couldn't deal with that. I sent him off, told him to get rid of the body.'

'Ollie Vaughn,' I interject.

Elkins nods. 'He came back afterwards, said it was done. I should have known he hadn't done it properly. He was only gone an hour. I hadn't seen him since Dad'd beat him, but he didn't seem, I dunno, fully there. No way he'd hidden the boy properly.'

'What reason did he give for doing it?'

'Doing what?'

'Killing Ollie,' I state.

'He didn't kill him,' Elkins contradicts, looking up, ruffled. 'The boy had starved.'

I roll my eyes – like the fact he'd starved to death made Vinny any less culpable.

Elkins reads my reaction right. 'He wasn't right in the head!' He snarls with indignation. 'He spent the rest of that night talking like Mum, pretending he *was* Mum. Dad must've done him brain damage or something when he'd laid him out because he was *not* my brother any more. I wanted him to stay, but he left with the van in the morning and was out of my life again.'

My own anger explodes. I'm incensed at how avoidable the rest of this sick story was. 'He'd come home with a body, was clearly deranged and you *still* let him leave?'

'AND I'D DO IT AGAIN!' Elkins shrieks. 'I WOULD DO IT AGAIN AND AGAIN AND AGAIN! It was *my* fault, I left him alone with Dad! I abandoned him once, I would never betray him like that again and I will die before I let him be judged by people who have never known what it means to live like we did.'

'You can't change what happened to him, but that doesn't absolve him! He is responsible for more deaths of innocent people than your father ever was. Maybe your father was abused as a child too. Where's your compassion for him?' I yell back, stare so intense it could crush steel.

'I am responsible for Vin, no one else.'

I bow my head in resignation. He will never betray his brother, just like I'd never betray mine; an impasse built on equal, opposite interests. And since he holds all the cards, he can just…

My heart stops. That's it: the key to it all. How have I been so stupid? It's so simple yet changes everything, an epiphanic flash bright enough to floodlight a black hole. This isn't about me loving my brother, it's about Frank Elkins loving his. And with that realisation comes the spark of an idea so terrifying and brilliant it takes my breath away.

49

ck the time: 9.30 p.m. Far too early yet. Plus, while I'm
ng my hands against the roaring fires of my idea, Elkins is
I need to encourage him towards the plan. I don't know
ly, but it won't happen if we stay silent.
n to pick up the story. Vinny told Elkins where he'd
g with the second van before he disappeared once
d with the address, Elkins made a trip to see his
ew lodgings – and was disgusted by what he

in a dilapidated static caravan on the site of
this farm was, Elkins won't say. It can't be
Mum would have come across it. He
d come by the living situation, but he
lave for this farmer. Elkins hasn't got
landowner. 'Dirty toad', he keeps
s the squalor Vinny was living in.
anded the dirty toad let Vinny
d Elkins to Vin's van, aban-
d up the back. There, in the

cage, was another young man – Damian McAree. The dirty toad said if Elkins dared take Vin away he'd go to the police and dob them both in for abduction. Elkins tried to talk Vin into letting the kid go, but Vinny was adamant he was 'looking after' the boy.

Bewildered and trapped by the farmer's threat, Elkins returned home, at a loss for what to do.

It was over a year later when Vinny showed up at his door again. Same floods of tears, same story: Damian McAree had died. Exposure this time, Elkins reckoned. 'Vinny didn't want to bury the body on the dirty toad's land for fear he'd find out and go to the police. So he brought them back for me to deal with.'

'What was with the string you put on those rocks at the burial sites?' I ask.

'I was petrified someone might find Vin and somehow link the deaths back to him. I reckoned if I marked where I'd buried the bodies, then if suspicion ever fell on Vin, I could take police straight to the bodies without risking misremembering where I'd put them, ensure it looked like it must be me rather than him who'd done it all along. How could I know exactly where the bodies were if I wasn't behind the abductions? I didn't think anyone else would ever notice the string or use it to find the bodies without me.'

You clearly don't know my mother.

'What hurts most,' Elkins explains – candid in a way that couldn't be less characteristic, 'is that this dirty toad was treating Vin just like Dad did, like a slave, and yet Vin'd rather drop the body off with me and then go back to him. That's how little trust Vin had left in me.'

'It's Stockholm Syndrome,' I clarify. 'But by proxy. He's trying to recreate his home life before your mum died. The farmer, like your dad, is in charge, Vin's the stay-at-home mum looking after the little-un. It's a coping mechanism, Frank. That's not your fault. It doesn't mean he didn't still love you. When the victims died, when he really needed help, he still came to you.'

Elkins looks to the side, pondering the explanation. He needs to know all is not lost with his brother, that there's still a living, breathing relationship between them – one that he can still rekindle if someone were to give him the chance.

The third victim – Nathan Brockhurst lasted even longer. Apparently by this point, Vinny had moved the cage into his caravan to keep the young man warmer, easier to check on. He was getting better at keeping them alive. But Elkins reckons Brockhurst committed suicide, and from the injuries he describes on the body when Vinny brought it to him, I'd agree. He buried Brockhurst, begged Vinny to stop abducting boys, to move back in with him, but it was no use – Vinny wanted to get back to his twisted horror of a household fantasy. Sam went missing the same day.

'Why were the teeth and the DNA of the victims found in your van rather than Vinny's, if he was using the other one?' I ask.

'Pure luck,' Elkins admits, an increasing ease about him the more he unloads. 'Vin had worked out how to drive better than me but he was still no expert. Think he'd burned something out in his van. He swapped them overnight after picking up the last one. Erm, I mean...' He realises he's dismissed Sam as 'the last one'. I affirm I know who he means. He's trusting me with more and more, even worrying how I'll react to things he's saying. Another good sign.

'He'd ruined his van, so jumped into mine with Sam and left me with the dodgy one,' he goes on. 'The engine screamed, there was a smell of burnt rubber whenever you accelerated, but both vans still had the same plates, so I figured it was fine. The fact the teeth Vin had collected were all still in there when police searched the van was helpful when I confessed, but it wasn't planned, as I say.'

'The CCTV frame they found near where Sam went missing, the one that finally got police on to your trail. Right plates, guy in the picture looked like you, but it was Vin, wasn't it?' I process.

He nods.

It's gone 11 p.m. next time I check the clock. It'll be dark outside.

'Frank, I don't think Vin hates you or resents you. I think he misses you. He made sure to keep the boys away from you until he needed your help. Then he came home every single time. I think he'd been protecting you: he knew you didn't approve so he kept it away as much as he could. And you've now spent almost a decade in prison for him. Imagine how much that must mean to him.'

The opinion is unsolicited but I'm relieved to see it accepted without suspicion. He nods, shoulders slumped forward again, eyes on the floor, back to factory settings. 'You're probably wondering why I've said all this tonight,' he grunts without looking up. 'Why not before?'

'A little,' I admit.

'I've never met anyone who cared about the case as much as you.' He rocks back again to take me in. 'Obviously, now I know why. But if this is the last time we are to see each other, then there's no one else who'd be more likely to give me answers.'

'Give *you* answers?'

'Why Vin did it, what his motivations were. I always thought it was some loneliness thing, but then that didn't fit because if he'd just been lonely, he could've stayed with me. It had to be deeper. And why choose that dirty toad over me? But it's clearer now. Thank you Emy.'

He just said my name. The residual hate I harbour from years and years of thinking he was my brother's killer sees me recoil on instinct. But there's a vulnerability present that's so alien to every other interaction we've had before. I need to use it.

'What would you say to Vinny right now, if you could?'

'Not worth thinking about,' he replies, desolate. 'Even if he was caught, I'd never be allowed to see him again. And it's no use writing, he can't read.'

'But if you could... Come on, humour me. What would you tell him?'

He pauses, the corners of his jaw twitching as he tenses. 'I'm sorry, Vin...' He squeezes the words out as his eyes fill once more, his mind returning to that room growing up, his dad beating Vinny, him walking away. The defining moment of his life. 'I'd give him a hug, tell him I love him.'

I get up and start walking around the small room. 'Y'know, George Petty, he was in here once and I asked him why he turned up at that family's house at three in the morning, the family he killed. Bit of a basic question really. But d'you know what he replied?'

Elkins shakes his head.

'He just shrugged and said *"carpe noctem"*.'

'Seize the night,' Elkins translates.

'Correct. And for the longest time, I hated it. He'd killed five people, I was asking questions about it, and he had the audacity to quote some poxy Latin at me, as if he was a scholar who'd got the world all worked out, far too clever for me. Completely ignoring what he'd done. No, not ignoring it, even worse... basking in it!'

I glance back at Elkins. His eyes follow me around the room. 'But now I can't get the phrase out of my head. 'Seize the night.' Petty was evil, but that concept of waiting for the perfect time, then taking an opportunity you may never have again, I don't know...'

I retake my seat. Elkins looks confused. Contemplating saying it out loud makes me feel woozy. My pulse is racing. 'What if you *could* say sorry to your brother? What if you *could* hug him?'

'What?'

'See him again. What if you could?'

'I'm not allowed visits or visitors, it'd never be sanctioned.'

'I'm not talking about the rules, Frank. I'm talking about tonight. You, me, let's go. I'm serious.'

Elkins pushes his eyebrows together, trying to comprehend what I'm offering.

'Either you'll be transferred in the morning and the chance will disappear forever. Or... we go now. Take me to him, Frank. You and your brother, together again.'

'Then you'll know where he is, he'll be arrested.'

'He needs psychological help badly, Frank. He'll be taken to a hospital but you could explain it to him, coax him towards the help he needs. And tell him all those things you've had locked inside you for the last ten years.'

He's still not convinced. 'You'd be arrested too. Why risk it?'

'When you've got nothing, you've got nothing to lose. Your brother needs help, but he needs someone who loves him, too. You can do that, Frank. Just take me to him.'

'*Amor fati*,' he tries, but it's a kneejerk answer, said without conviction.

I aim for the heart I've so recently discovered Frank Elkins possesses. 'What about your mum asking you to look after

Vinny when she'd gone? What if you've been using *amor fati* to protect him, but it's actually just left him trapped and suffering. Wouldn't your mum want him to get the help he needs?'

'He wants to stay on that farm. He doesn't want to go into hospital.'

'He'd struggle at first, I don't deny it. But soon he'd be healthier, happier, freer. All these years, you've been so hard on yourself about what happened to Vinny. But Vinny doesn't hate you, Frank, he needs you. You want to make amends for leaving him with your dad all those years ago? Don't abandon him now. He's in a cage of his own, you're the only person he'll trust to lead him out of it.'

'What if he's not at the site?'

'I'm willing to risk it if you are. How far away is it?'

'Hours,' he says.

'It's now or never,' I remind him. 'We won't get much of a head start before the guards realise you're gone. But it's easier to get you into the car at night and there are fewer people around full stop. *Carpe noctem!*'

There's still hesitance. I get it. He's been incarcerated for years with nothing more to contemplate daily than what syrup to have on his porridge. A decision this big would take me months to contemplate. But that doesn't stop the clock ticking.

'You could be with him before dawn. Or you get transferred in the morning and lose your last chance to ever see your brother again.'

Elkins looks at me, fear evolving into something braver. And then he says it. '*Carpe noctem.*'

50

Three taps of my keycard and we go from interview room to army base car park without challenge or compromise. It's that easy. Lights in the distance illuminate the gateway out of the barracks. The expanse between us and that gate, and the pitch-black starless sky above, feel like they're brimming with spies, telltales ready to snitch on me, to ruin everything. My head swims as I lead us both to my car. I'm suddenly agoraphobic, paranoid and painfully aware of our vulnerable, open position.

'You're going to have to get in the boot,' I tell Elkins.

He peers at the back of the car and shivers as a breeze sweeps between us.

'Were you expecting a royal coach?' The quip comes across confidently, which is good, because it could not be more at odds with the terror pulsing in my chest as I contemplate anyone seeing us. 'I'll let you out eventually, obviously. You'll need to navigate. But there are guards on that entry over there and there was a journalist hanging about outside earlier, so we need to get away from the site without raising suspicion.'

I pop the boot open; he clambers in without any more fuss.

I wave at the security detail on the main gate as I drive up, surprised they aren't suspicious of my pounding heart as it must surely register on the Richter scale. They wave me through, and we're out on the open road, no reporters, no one to stop me.

It's not until I reach the motorway that the next part of the plan comes to me. Now we're off base, a thrill is coursing through my veins, knowing the hunt for *us* is about to begin. Shortly they'll be checking for my car, the number plate will be clocked on every camera it passes, fed back to the police and then used to reach us quicker, stop us sooner. I have a different idea.

It's just gone midnight when I pull up outside Mum's house. We are going to swap to her car. That'll give us a head start on the hunting pack. There is one thorn in this particular game-plan, however. What to do with Mum?

I pull up on the pavement outside, leave Elkins in the boot and let myself in to the house. Mum is still up, as I feared she would be.

Stalking over to me as soon as my feet cross the threshold, she signs: *Where have you been?*

'No time, no time,' I speak in a stage whisper. Holding her by the shoulders I look deep into her eyes, just illuminated enough by the soft lounge lamp for me to see her panic and frustration melt into confusion at my impatience.

What? She signs, noticing the tension drenching my every micro-movement. No one can read me like Mum. Her mood has moved on again already to concern and intrigue.

'Elkins is in the car. He says his brother could still be alive and he'll take me to where he thinks he'll be. If the brother *is* there, Sam might be too!' I explain, still in the heavy whisper.

There's a pause. And then without further consultation, she

turns around and pulls two coats off the hook, handing one to me.

'Mum, you can't come!' I insist with as much force as I can muster under my breath. 'I'll be arrested for this. I don't want you...'

She puts her hand over my mouth, soft but firm. Then signs: *We should swap to my car.*

Great minds think alike.

'I don't know for sure that Sam is there. And even if he is, Elkins' brother might flip out if he sees us trying to get him out. I don't know what's going to happen.'

Quick, quick, she signs, ignoring my disclaimer. *Let's go.*

I knew she'd want to come, that she wouldn't take no for an answer. How could she not come? After all she's been through, after all she's sacrificed. I don't think she even heard my feeble attempt to stop her. She is a woman on a mission. Coat on, keys in hand, she beckons me back out of the house. I make sure to leave my phone behind so that can't be tracked either, and Mum locks the door.

Where is he? She signs. She means Elkins.

'In my boot.'

I let him out. The next moment defies adequate description. My mum – petite, short, wasting away, arm in a sling – next to the six foot, lump of a man she has spent so many years despising from afar. She allows herself a look at him, but not for long. And then she's getting in her car passenger seat. Ten times more ready for this journey than Elkins or I will ever be.

He stands in the street, his expression barely visible in the darkness, shadows draping across his face as he turns his back to a distant streetlight. But his lack of movement suggests an understandable level of confusion.

'That's my mum. We're going to swap to her car to make us

harder to trail. You get in the back and direct us. Where are we heading?'

'North. Go up the coast towards Edinburgh first,' he says, matching my hushed tone. 'I'll tell you from there. Five hours if you floor it.'

The journey is quiet. Tense. Overwhelming.

Just last night I was having to coax Mum into even listening to Elkins' voice on tape. Now she is sharing a confined space with him. And she has to contend with the idea that she may be about to see her son again, the person for whom her whole life has been on hold for over a decade. But still unsure if she's racing towards her boy or just his bones.

Elkins is equally taciturn. Butterflies at seeing his own brother and the novelty of being outside are surely holding his thoughts hostage.

My own nervous energy goads me into trying to drum up conversation at first. 'One thing I never understood. You were ordered to come to Beeswell, but I couldn't compel you to answer questions. Why did you come into the interview room day after day, rather than just refusing? You never showed any resistance whatsoever.'

There's no immediate response from the back of the car and I can feel Mum's discomfort at the fact I'd engage with this man unnecessarily. But it's been the biggest question bugging me ever since Tim Shenton started asking it. Why? Why on earth would a man so beholden to his secrets willingly and consistently come to an interview room where those secrets would face such scrutiny.

'Paratrepsis,' Elkins mutters.

'Sorry?'

'In the wild, if a mother wants to keep a predator away from her young, she'll make a big display to keep the predator's attention on her, as she slowly leads it away from the nest.' There's a pause before he adds under his breath, 'How wrong I was.'

For the sake of Mum, I don't ask any more questions and instead let my mind race along ahead of the car as I wait for the inevitable blue lights and sirens to appear from nowhere and ruin everything. The monotony of the road and flash of each overhead light as it passes provides a hypnotic beat for me to focus on.

I wonder what Chi's thinking, how she's feeling, whether she's sorry. The day has been such a slalom of emotions, it's taken until now to even partially comprehend her role in it. Everything we've done together, the memories we've made, the drinks we've shared – not just since the Hive, but at uni and between-times too – has that really all been poured down the drain over one row at the end of a stressful week? It's hard to grasp. In lieu of police cars accelerating up behind me, I wonder exactly where she is, and whether her decision to sink the Hive will haunt her half as much as I hope it will.

Another dose of reality zaps: I bet security will have spotted Elkins and I have gone missing by now. I imagine the night staff pulling their hair out, cadets prowling the base looking for runaways. Harrington woken in the night. A huge manhunt launched for both Elkins and me. Will it have made the news yet? I try to bury the fear, put it in that rear-view mirror. All tha‍ matters is those streetlights flicking past. Each one counting ᴜ closer to our destination and maybe to Sam.

'Mrs Whirberth,' Elkins says with a croak out of nowhe puncturing my solitude. 'I just want to apologise for everythi He pauses, waiting for Mum to respond which, of course, doesn't. 'I know I'll never be able to explain my decisions tc but I just want to say that I never, ever wanted any other f to be dragged into this.'

'Mum can't speak,' I tell him. 'Traumatic mutism.'

'Because of...?' He doesn't have it in him to finish the sentence. He doesn't need to.

'Since the day Sam disappeared, yeah.'

No one says any more.

I try to lose myself in the asphalt again, but a small scratchy noise builds in my ear. It takes a minute to locate exactly where it's coming from, and a moment more to discern what it is. Then I realise it's sniffling, quiet gasps of breath as tears fall – coming from the back seat. My suspicion is confirmed when Elkins next speaks up, to instruct us to turn off at the following junction. His voice betrays a blocked nose and swollen throat.

Five hours is a long time, even at 90 mph. Too long. Thoughts fluctuate. What would Sam look like? The others had severe curvature of the spine. Will those front three teeth be missing? What if he's not there? What if he is there but refuses to come with us? Is Tim Shenton really dead? That life-altering news has been lost in the events of the last two days. I definitely haven't processed it. Did I really need to side with him, to use [...] to get to Elkins? What good did it actually do? I suppose he [as]ked the question about the accomplice. He forced Elkins [s]lipping up over never having pulled teeth out. He was the [per]son to tell me about the string tied round Elkins' belong[ings. Wo]uld we be here without Shenton's input? I don't know. [There]in lies his importance: if we are about to find Sam, I [won't cha]nge a detail of it, nothing that could jeopardise this [...] Mum, Chi, Robbie, Leon, Shenton, even Harring[ton he]lped get me to the point where I could convince [him] to where he thinks his own brother is. It takes [a c]hild, it took the Hive to unravel Elkins.

[The more we d]rive, the more I get used to it. I begin to pray [it never end]s. Just me and Mum eternally travelling to find Sam, a world where he is still alive in our futures, where Beeswell is behind us, but without the consequences of tomorrow. I'm going to be arrested. That scares me, but not enough to take my foot off the accelerator.

Deeper and deeper north we go; the Scottish border is hours behind us now. Endless cat's eyes glare at me. The roads get narrower.

The sky ahead is still darkest blue, but the sunrise is beginning to flirt with the horizon to my right when a groggy Elkins tells us to turn off the main road. Another ten minutes, then in a stronger voice than before: 'Take the next left, then through the field gate straight after. Turn your headlights off.'

We're here.

51

I pull in through the five-bar gate, the faintest light from the coming dawn helping me to navigate the larger bumps as we make our way towards a Portacabin on the far side of the field.

'That's the owner's, the dirty toad I told you about,' Elkins whispers. 'Go slowly and head through the next gate on the right, Vin's place was at the other end of the next field.'

How on earth did Vinny end up here? Maybe we'll never know.

I put the car into second gear and creep along, both unable to assimilate how suddenly the destination has crept up on us and also hyper-aware that I cannot let this mission end in failure because of sloppy, noisy driving at the last.

We pass by a row of three static caravans but Elkins urges me to keep going. I can feel how still Mum is next to me, everything tapering down to this singular event. The hope she never dared dream could be true, or the terror that has haunted her every nightmare; an answer to it all, either way, is looming into view.

Elkins' hand raises between us as he points off to the left-hand side of the second field. 'The light in that window, that's his place. Go a little further but *crawl*.'

I slow the car down even more, every stray stone the tyres creak over, every heave of the suspension as we roll along the uneven ground, magnified one hundred-fold. I don't want to go any further for fear of raising the alarm. And yet I want nothing more than to tear towards that faint yellow square of light.

We're maybe sixty yards from the caravan when my cautious ears win out. I switch off the engine and strain to see what's inside that square window. Kitchen cabinets or a cupboard, is my first guess. Without warning, a face passes in front of whatever we're staring at inside the caravan and all three of us jump.

'That's him! That's Vin!' Elkins hisses, suddenly excitable but still managing to keep the words under his breath.

The confirmation brings me out in an instant, icy sweat. It feels like the dawn is swelling in the field and a pang of fear hits that our cover might blow.

I take my eyes off that tiny square in the distance for a second to look at Mum, her own stare transfixed by the caravan. She feels my gaze on her and it jolts her into action.

Let's go, she signs.

'Mum wants to go in,' I whisper over to Elkins, who has taken off his seatbelt and is crouching between our front seats.

'I'll go first. If he flips out and there is anyone else in there, he could lash out. He has a shotgun. I...' A fresh wave of emotion catches in his throat which he tries to grunt away. 'I'll make sure your brother is safe, if he is in there.'

'How will we know when to come in?' I breathe back. A nauseous build-up of dread makes my eyes sting as I contemplate the danger I might have put Mum in.

'You'll know,' he says, the light of growing day bright enough now for me to see his eyes glistening. 'Mrs Whirberth,' he adds, turning to Mum. 'I know you can't reply, but I am truly sorry. I finally get it. Maybe I can reunite a mother with her son at last.'

With a solemn nod to me, he slips out of the car, leaving the back door open so as not to make any noise.

We watch as he shrinks into the distance. He waits a second at the door to the caravan, then goes up the two steps and enters without knocking. The faint slam of the door behind him just about reaches us in the car.

Then nothing.

The lingering cold of the night floods in through the open back door of the car. I hold Mum and she holds me, both quivering for so many reasons.

Time turns on us, each millisecond lasting a lifetime. The fear is excruciating. I defy any physical pain to match the agony of waiting in such fraught, powerless purgatory.

Mum hears it first, and squeezes my hands tighter, dragging me back into the field.

Raised voices.

The one that sounds like Elkins is getting louder. A face flashes in front of the window. Then a second one.

A scream.

A face runs back past the window.

BANG.

Mum and I turn to each other in unison.

Petrified.

BANG.

Panic rips through me as Mum flies out of the car and charges towards the caravan.

She's so quick I can't catch up with her before she's reached it.

'MUM WAIT!' I screech. 'MUM!'

She's up the same two steps and at the doorway.

She stops.

I run into the back of her. A wall of heat and the stench of rotting meat almost knocks me back on to the grass.

We stare in at a huge, lifeless body lying face down on the floor. A scarlet stain grows and grows in the back of the man's white T-shirt.

Mum jolts into action again. Through the door, she grabs the head of the dead man and twists it over so she can see his face. The eyes roll into the back of his head, his mouth lolling open. It's clear he's missing his front teeth. But it's not Sam. Is that... Vinny?

Mum turns right into the caravan and gasps. There, slumped with his back against the base of the wall, eyes and mouth wide open, is Frank Elkins. There's a fleshy, bloody trap door roughly crafted in the top of his balding head, with a double-barrel shotgun carelessly cast across his lap. The wall behind him is spattered in red matter.

The scene takes us captive for a second as we struggle to make sense of the horror.

A muffled noise splinters the savagery, barely perceptible over the million-miles-an-hour pounding of my heart.

'Vin? Vin?' The voice is thin but definite.

I look at Mum but she's already moving, stepping over Elkins' corpse and following the noise further into the caravan.

She stops at the door of a tiny bedroom. The lights are on and the noise has stopped; there's no sign of anyone in there. We fall silent, waiting for one more sign. Then it comes – a shuffling sound. I stalk round the bed, hunting the noise, and rip the blanket off a box in the corner of the room.

It's not a box. It's a cage. A cage with a man in it, naked, huddled in the foetal position and staring up at us.

His long beard and matted hair swallow up most of his

features but I connect with those huge, blue fear-filled eyes and drop to my knees.

'Sam!' I howl. 'Sam! Sam! Sam!'

The eyes I know so well leave me and focus on Mum, kneeling too now. Out of her sling, she pushes both arms through the rusty wire of the cage, grasping at his head as if she means to yank him out through pure force of will.

'Mum...?' he says, disbelieving, weak.

Tears stream down her cheeks as she nods.

'Mum...!' he says again, his own eyes filling up as he begins to tighten his own grip on her hands.

She leans her head against the metal and he does too, so their foreheads are touching.

'You didn't give up,' he cries, howls erupting so forcefully they shake the whole caravan. 'You didn't give up!'

She looks deep into his eyes.

And then she speaks. 'My darling boy, of course we didn't.'

EPILOGUE

I'm scribbling in my notepad. The bump of the car ride sees me jut the pen against the page.

'Could you drive a bit slower, chauffeur. Can barely read my own writing as it is.'

'Yes, m'lady,' Leon says in what I *think* is his attempt at an impersonation of Parker from *Thunderbirds*. He reverts to normal. 'I thought you and Robbie came up with all your questions weeks ago.'

'I keep getting fresh thoughts. Genius thoughts, some might say,' I tell him.

'Doesn't sound like you,' he replies instantly.

I slap his thigh as he smirks, keeping his eyes on the road.

'What d'you want for tea?' he asks. 'I'll go and do a shop while you're in there.'

'Your chorizo pasta please. Oh, and get some prosecco. Finally done with the Hive. We must celebrate.'

'Screw prosecco, champers or bust!' He finally turns and grins at me. That gorgeous, comforting grin. I'll never get bored of it. I push a hand through his messy hair, if anything, making it neater somehow.

We reach the drop-off zone outside the prison. Leon leans over and kisses me on the cheek. 'You're going to smash it, OK? Love you.'

I blow out a short, determined breath and meet his beautiful brown eyes. 'Love you too.'

There's a stench about normal jails that the Hive never had. The air hangs heavy with the rich aroma of sweaty pits and over-boiled, farty vegetables. I don't like the fact it's not my own territory either. I'd been into dozens of prisons before Beeswell, and it never bothered me, but now I've had a taste of autonomy, the fact I'm being marched along a corridor – unaware of where I'm going or who is around me – is stressful.

Inmates' eyes trace me as I pass them, suspicious, cold. We turn a corner and the warders stop abruptly next to a closed door. 'Just in 'ere, Miss,' one of them mutters, pulling down the handle and pushing it open. In the room are two more guards, standing either side of a table. Between them, seated, is Joe Okorie.

He reacts to my arrival like a dog whose owner's just returned from war. Straining to stand, he's pinned back down by the cuffs chaining him to the table and the lightning-quick hands of the warders gripping his shoulders, aggressive and certain.

There are tears in his eyes. 'Emy!'

'Joe.' My hostility for this man has only grown in his absence. Those eight women he killed – their bodies now all found and returned to their loved ones – had been abused in such disgusting, dehumanising ways. This other persona, his *feelings*, they repulse me. But I gave him my word I'd visit. And I still have questions. Robbie and I sat down and came up with loads. Ever since their chess match, Robbie's never lost the feeling Joe has plenty more to tell me so he's come up with a lot of angles and ideas to probe, bless him.

It'll be a one-off trip though, there's no way I can endure being dragged back to memories of the Hive time and time again, I need to leave that place behind for good. I can't even bring myself to reply to Chi's messages trying to reconnect. It's too raw to let her back in, for now at least.

The guards all leave, assuring me that a camera in the corner of the room is being constantly monitored. It's like the old days.

'I've been looking forward to this *so much.*' Joe almost bursts as I take my seat. 'I followed you in the news. The arrest, the sentencing. So happy they suspended the sentence.'

We agree on that. The only charge the CPS could make stick was that I facilitated the escape of a prisoner. Fair enough – I pleaded guilty. The judge could still have sent me down for up to ten years. As it was, she laid the blame for almost everything that happened at Barnaby C. Harrington's door. Cast out by his party in disgrace, he's up on myriad contempt charges but contesting them all. The trial's slated for next year.

'How's your brother? How's your mum?' Joe interrogates. I hate that he knows such personal things about me; the invasion of my privacy by the media has been hard over the last few months – it feels all the more acute from someone who deludedly thinks we're dating.

'Sam's still adjusting but there's progress daily and Mum's... my mum again. We're very lucky.'

'I can't believe Frank killed himself and his own brother! Mental,' he jabbers on.

Ah, that night. That life-changing night. Elkins last words. *Maybe I can reunite a mother with her son at last.* At the time I took it literally, thought he meant Mum and Sam. But the more time that's passed the more I think his plan shifted on our car journey, seeing Mum, the depths of trauma his brother had caused. I think Frank Elkins went into that caravan believing the kindest way he could protect his brother, both from himself, and the backlash the world was about to unleash on him, was to reunite Vinny and his own mother, not in this life, but the next. And then Frank joined them.

'It wasn't a night for the faint-hearted,' I say bluntly. 'But Joe, as I said in my letter, this meeting is going to be about your victims, and getting more answers for their families.'

'Of course, of course,' he says. 'I'm just overjoyed to see you, my love.'

'Boundaries, Joe,' I tell him, the same way I have a hundred times before. His affection feels all the more icky, now I'm properly in a happy, loving relationship.

'Oh Emy,' he pines. 'I feel so strongly that I need to tell you absolutely everything in a way I never have to anyone before.'

'OK good.' Blimey! Robbie was right, Joe has got more to say. I take my small notepad and clicky pen out of my handbag. 'Where do you want to start?'

'With the other eight girls.'

I look up, a shiver of terror racing down my spine. My mouth opens but I cannot speak.

'I know, I know... I should have admitted to all of them when I handed myself in. That's the whole reason I stopped, for goodness' sake – I'd completed my chess team, a perfect 16. But it somehow felt like too much to confess it all at once so I only let on about the ones sunk off the docks.'

It's hard to concentrate, the news is too disturbing. 'Where are the other eight?' I force out.

'Oh Emy, we are going to have such fun working towards

that, aren't we! One new detail every visit. That's our thing, right?'

*　*　*

MORE FROM TAM BARNETT

Another book from Tam Barnett, *How to Get Away with Murder*, is available to order now here:
www.mybook.to/HowtoGetBackAD

ACKNOWLEDGEMENTS

First, I would like to thank God, who is with me everywhere I go.

Next, Hannah and Harlowe, my gorgeous family. I simply do not have the words to express how happy you both make me. You are so, so precious; I've never felt so blessed. Roll on this brand-new adventure together!

Mum, hopefully this book restores a little of your faith in my state of mind. I love you very much. Anyway, I'm at Victoria now so I'd better go...

Dad, thank you for backing this book the same way you always do, helping me with such enthusiasm and diligence. Your passion for my writing will never ever get old.

It's been a year like no other, and we've had incredible family and friends around us. Doug, Jo, Alice and Aaron – you have been brilliant. Your selfless love and sacrifice have been amazing.

Mrs Paula Belcher, the Campbells, the Pliskins (especially Savanna!), the Knights, the Burnetts, the Barnetts, my secretly rather lovely colleagues, Trouser Banta, and all our friends – your excitement about our little growing family has been beautiful to see.

To everyone at Croydon Vineyard Church, and specifically our Connect Group, thank you for being there and giving us a warm, reassuring community to plug into through many ups and downs. Also thank you so much to Croydon University Hospital and everyone involved in caring for Hannah and our baby girl. Harlowe has already revealed herself to be quite the rascal with four stays in hospital needed, rather than the customary one, to ensure she was ready for the world. We really appreciate the sensitive, round-the-clock care we all received along the way.

I am so fortunate to be working with the publishing team at Boldwood Books and my fantastic editor Francesca. Thank you for your belief in me, your indispensable wisdom and advice and your gusto in turning this all into a reality.

Thank you to Euan Thorneycroft and AM Heath for representing me as a writer.

I am immensely grateful, and somewhat dumbfounded, by the idea anyone would pick up something with my name on. I try to write what I'd want to read, so if you want to read it too, then I'm in great company. An enormous, intergalactic-sized thank you for finishing this book. Hopefully we can continue to enjoy each other's company in the days, weeks and millennia ahead...

ABOUT THE AUTHOR

Tam Barnett is a journalist, living in London. His debut with Boldwood was How To Get Away With Murder, a darkly comic thriller set in the Wirral.

Sign up to Tam Barnett's mailing list for news, competitions and updates on future books.

Follow Tam on social media here:

facebook.com/TamBarnettBooks
x.com/TamBarnettBooks
instagram.com/tambarnettbooks
tiktok.com/@TamBarnettBooks

ALSO BY TAM BARNETT

How to Get Away with Murder

How to Read a Killer's Mind

THE *Murder* LIST

THE MURDER LIST IS A NEWSLETTER DEDICATED TO SPINE-CHILLING FICTION AND GRIPPING PAGE-TURNERS!

SIGN UP TO MAKE SURE YOU'RE ON OUR HIT LIST FOR EXCLUSIVE DEALS, AUTHOR CONTENT, AND COMPETITIONS.

SIGN UP TO OUR NEWSLETTER

BIT.LY/THEMURDERLISTNEWS

Boldwood

Boldwood Books is an award-winning fiction publishing company seeking out the best stories from around the world.

Find out more at www.boldwoodbooks.com

Join our reader community for brilliant books, competitions and offers!

Follow us
@BoldwoodBooks
@TheBoldBookClub

Sign up to our weekly deals newsletter

https://bit.ly/BoldwoodBNewsletter

www.ingramcontent.com/pod-product-compliance
Ingram Content Group UK Ltd.
Pitfield, Milton Keynes, MK11 3LW, UK
UKHW022040010825
461446UK00001B/5